I0640657

L. M. Smith

The house-keeper's guide and everybody's hand-book:

Containing over five hundred new and valuable recipes together with departments

designed

L. M. Smith

The house-keeper's guide and everybody's hand-book:
Containing over five hundred new and valuable recipes together with departments designed

ISBN/EAN: 9783337872649

Printed in Europe, USA, Canada, Australia, Japan

Cover: Foto ©Andreas Hilbeck / pixelio.de

More available books at **www.hansebooks.com**

HOUSE-KEEPER'S GUIDE

AND EVERYBODY'S

HAND-BOOK:

CONTAINING HER

FIVE HUNDRED

NEW AND VALUABLE

RECIPES

FOR THE MANUFACTURE OF FAMILY AND TOILET SOAPS, WASHING FLUIDS,
OINTMENTS, LIQUID POLISHES FOR MEN IN TIN, IRON, AND STEEL, INKS,
DYES, DOMESTIC MEDICINES, WINES, CEMENTS, PAINTS, VINEGAR,
PICKLES, PRESERVES, ETC. INSTRUCTIONS ON THE ART OF
COOKING, AND ALMOST EVERY ART PERTAINING TO HOUSE-
KEEPING AND DOMESTIC ECONOMY; TOGETHER WITH
DEPARTMENTS DESIGNED ESPECIALLY FOR FARM-
ERS AND MECHANICS, GIVING VALUABLE
INFORMATION UPON VARIOUS POINTS
CONNECTED WITH THEIR RESPEC-
TIVE VOCATIONS.

BY SMITH & SWINNEY

A RECEIPT WORTH MORE THAN THE PRICE OF THE BOOK TO EVERY HOUSEWIFE IN THE COUNTRY.

How to make tomato preserves better than peach or any other fruit preserves extant. Try it and see. Take the small, round variety of tomato (either red or yellow, and from three-fourths to one inch in diameter), and wash them clean in cold water, taking care to not break the skin; to every ten pounds of tomatoes take ten pounds of good, clarified sugar; make your sugar into a sirup, by the addition of a little water, and gently boiling till the sugar is all dissolved, then pour over the tomatoes and let them stand over night; next day put them carefully into your preserving kettle, and gently boil them over a slow fire for several hours, or till the juice has formed a thick, rich sirup, which can be ascertained by cooling in a saucer. When about half done, add two ordinary sized lemons, sliced fine, and nearly or quite half an ounce of good white ginger root, bruised or cut up fine, and also one-fourth of a pound of good plump raisins, and boil till done. Some receipts say scald and peel the tomatoes, and boil twenty minutes, etc. Pay no attention to such instructions, but make according to the above directions, and you will have a preserve more delicious to the taste than the best peach or damson will make. We have preserves in the house made according to this receipt, (the tomatoes costing 25 cts a peck), and peach preserves made from the best flavored peaches (costing $5 per bushel) as well as those made from the damson plum, and all, without exception, pronounce the tomatoes the best. If every housewife knew how cheaply and easily she could make up a batch of these preserves, *preferable to any fruit preserves*, she would never be without them. Don't be afraid of making too many the first time, for if you make a less quantity than will last you the season, you will afterward regret it.

To can fruit and preserve the original flavor without the liability of spoiling.—This process is so little understood upon scientific principles, and consequently attended with so much risk, that the majority of people prefer to pay three or four prices for their canned fruit, sooner than take the responsibility of putting it up themselves. The process, however, if properly understood, is perfectly simple, and attended with no risk whatever. We put up this season 32 cans of peaches, which cost us 18 cts a can, and they turn out as fresh and nice as they were the day they were put up, and as good as the best Baltimore peach at 75 cts a can. At the same time a lady friend, not understanding the process, put up one bushel, and they are now (Nov. 15th) all soured and spoiled. If the following directions be complied with, we will guarantee to pay for all you may lose by reason of spoiling:

Peaches.—Take good, juicy freestones, neither too hard nor too soft, pare and quarter them; put them into a vessel, and to each peck (before pared) sprinkle in layers as you pare them, one pound of white sugar and let them stand over night, so as to make a sirup. The next day turn off the juice into your kettle, and when it is hot put in the peaches (without a drop of water, as their own sirup will be sufficient), and boil till the peaches are hot and well scalded all through, but no longer, as too much cooking destroys their fresh flavor. Have your cans or jars ready, and while your fruit is still over the stove, fill up as soon as possible and seal them up as fast as you fill them, taking care to have the cans full, and the sirup over the top of the fruit so that none of the pieces will project above. Cut pieces of white paper, just fitting the inside of the caps, and lay over first, then put on your caps and wipe the mouths of the jars or cans perfectly dry, and turn over the wax boiling hot so it will adhere to the jar and make it perfectly air-tight. When the jars are nearly cold, turn them down, and if there should be any airbubbles, or other indications of their not being air-tight, heat the blade of an old case-knife, very hot, and go over the wax, so as to be sure and shut up all the holes. All kinds of small fruits—blackberries, raspberries, plums, etc.—are put up by heating in the same way. Also tomatoes, but the latter must be scalded, peeled and *thoroughly cooked*, with the addition of a little salt and pepper.

To open fruit jars.—Hold the mouths of the jars in hot water for a few minutes, with a striped cloth or a string held over the caps to keep them from falling down, and the wax will soften enough to loosen from the jars without getting any inside. Stone or glass jars are better than tin cans for fruit or tomatoes, as the acid contained in either will dissolve the lead, which will give an unpleasant flavor to the fruit, besides being positively injurious.

How to Cook Tomatoes.—Put your tomatoes into boiling water and scald till the skin begins to shrink or shrivel; take them out, and, when cool, (if you are in a hurry, put them into cold water), peel off the skin and cut out the core at the but-end, where the stem joins, as it will neither cook soft nor digest when taken into the stomach. Having well dressed them, put them back into your pot or stew-pan, and cook for half or three quarters of an hour, or till they have pretty well stewed down. Do not add any water, as their own water will be sufficient. Season with butter, salt, pepper, and a little sugar, just enough to take off the rank, acid taste, but not so as to make them in the least degree sweet, as this destroys entirely the flavor peculiar to them. Some prefer the addition of a little bread, finely crumbed, just before they are done. Suit your own taste in this respect.

A nice way to cook green corn.—Take a sharp knife and cut down the outside of the kernels all around as thin as you can cut them, then cut down the second time in the same way; now turn the knife and scrape all off the cob as clean as you can, and put the corn into a skillet, with a little water, and cook till thoroughly done. Season with butter, pepper and salt, and you will have the most delicious dish you ever tasted in the way of green corn.

These receipts are entirely original, as now published, and are worth more than the price of the book to every house-keeper in the United States, "no matter," as the *Springfield Republican* says, "how many receipt or cook-books you may have."

THE
HOUSE-KEEPER'S GUIDE

AND EVERYBODY'S

HAND-BOOK:

CONTAINING OVER

FIVE HUNDRED

NEW AND VALUABLE

RECIPES

ON THE MANUFACTURE OF FAMILY AND TOILET SOAPS, WASHING FLUIDS,
CEMENTS, LIQUID SOLDERS FOR MENDING TIN, IRON, AND STEEL, INKS,
DYES, DOMESTIC MEDICINES, WINES, CIDER, CORDIALS, VINEGAR,
PICKLES, PRESERVES, JELLIES, AND JAMS; ON THE ART OF
COOKING, AND ALMOST EVERY ART PERTAINING TO HOUSE-
KEEPING AND DOMESTIC ECONOMY; TOGETHER WITH
DEPARTMENTS DESIGNED ESPECIALLY FOR FAR-
MERS AND MECHANICS, GIVING VALUABLE
INFORMATION UPON VARIOUS TOPICS
CONNECTED WITH THEIR RESPEC-
TIVE VOCATIONS.

BY SMITH & SWINNEY,

CHEMISTS, ETC.

CINCINNATI, OHIO:
FOURTH EDITION— THIRTY-FIFTH THOUSAND.
1868.

PREFACE TO THE FOURTH EDITION.

So RAPID has been the sale of this truly valuable little book, that the first edition of 3,000 copies was hardly out of press before a new one was called for to supply the increasing demands coming from every quarter, and a second edition of 12,000, and also a third, of 10,000, are now exhausted, and a fourth edition of 10,000 more is now demanded.

It has been thoroughly revised, improved, and considerably enlarged since its first appearance.

Although the Authors have spent several years in collecting its material from various sources, in experimenting upon and improving recipes, and arranging them for publication, it is now gotten up and designed especially for the benefit of Disabled Soldiers and Soldiers' Widows; through whose agency it is being sold, and to whom we give more than one-half the net profits.

Its novelty, of combining such a multiplicity of practical recipes, and so much varied and useful information upon nearly all matters pertaining to housekeeping and domestic economy, commends it to all classes and conditions in society.

In addition to several valuable ones of our own, we have added a large number of new ones, never before made public; for some of which we have paid sums ranging from $10 up to $50, expressly for our book—making it the most valuable collection of family receipts ever compiled in one volume. At least one hundred can be selected from the entire work, any one of which would be worth its price to any family; while some of them are worth ten times that amount.

The Medical Department contains information of the most vital importance to every family in the land, while no economical housewife would be without the knowledge embraced in the Culinary Department, after having once been in its possession, for twice the consideration demanded for the book.

Its price, compared with that of other publications, may seem high; but when viewed in the light of its intrinsic value, and particularly with reference to the fact that we have given to the public several very important recipes of our own, from which we were manufacturing and selling articles of great value, at large profits, it is not.

The pages are large and the type small; and being solidly set, the book contains as much reading matter as is ordinarily included in two or three hundred pages.

While the directions given in each receipt are sufficiently explicit for the comprehension of all, we have aimed at conciseness and brevity, in order to condense a large amount of information in as small a compass as is possible.

By this means we are enabled to put the book to the Soldier at such a price as will yield him a large profit, and remunerate him for his trouble; besides, in a measure, compensating him for his past services in behalf of his country.

THE AUTHORS.

Entered according to Act of Congress, in the year 1865, by SMITH & SWINNEY, in the Clerk's Office of the District Court of the United States, in and for the Southern District of Ohio.

SOAP AND WASHING RECEIPTS.

Chemical Soap.—Take 2 pounds sal soda and 1 pound good stone lime (or 2 pounds slacked lime) and boil in 10 quarts of soft water; let it settle; pour off the clear fluid and add 2 pounds of tallow (or its equivalent in soap-grease, ¼ pound borax and ½ pound of resin, and boil together till the grease is all taken up, then pour into a shallow box, and, when cool, cut into bars. Two hours' boiling will generally be sufficient.

If you wish to make soft soap, add water to make it of the desired consistency, which can be ascertained by cooling in a saucer while boiling. Owing to the present high price of resin, it may be omitted till it becomes cheaper.

Again: Common bar soap, cut fine, may be used in place of the tallow or grease, by using double the quantity of water, and omitting the resin. Those who have lye soap already made, can make it go as far again, and wash with half the labor, by adding to each gallon 2 large table spoonfuls of sal soda and 1 of borax, dissolved in a little warm water, then using same as chemical soap.

Washing Fluid.—Take 2 pounds of sal soda, 1 pound good stone lime, and 2½ gallons soft water, and bring to a boil, when settled, pour off the clear fluid into a stone jug, and add 1 ounce of hartshorn and 1 ounce of borax, and keep it tightly corked. After boiling the lime and soda, for either the soap or washing-fluid, pour on water the second time; let it settle, and again pour off for scrubbing, &c.

To Make Soft Soap.—Take 20 pounds of potash and dissolve, in an iron kettle, with 25 gallons of cold soft water, and let it stand three days, if the weather be warm, and five or six, if cool. When all is dissolved, take 20 pounds of clear grease, or its equivalent in rough grease, and cleanse it with white lye; then strain it through a tin colander or sieve in a soap-barrel, and add the potash lye, carefully drained from the sediment; then pour on a few gallons of water, so as to obtain all the strength from the potash, and pour off again, after it has settled, into the barrel. This makes a superior article of soap—of which any housewife may be proud.

Directions for Washing.—Soak your white clothes one half hour in the morning, (or, if very dirty, over night,) in a tub of lukewarm water, with 1 pint of the soap dissolved in it; suds them out, wring and soap wristbands, collars, and dirty or stained places. Now have your boiler half filled with soft water just beginning to boil, then put in 1 common teacup full of the washing fluid, stir it up and put in your clothes, and boil for thirty minutes; now suds them out, rubbing on your hand a little any place where there may be any dirt left; rinse, and all is done. This plan requires no wash-board for white clothes, saves one-half the soap, and more than one-half the labor, and does not injure the clothes, but saves the wear and tear of rubbing on the board. These receipts alone are worth ten dollars to any family.

Directions for Washing Calicoes.—Calico clothes, before they are put in water, should have the grease spots rubbed out, as they cannot be seen when the whole of the garment is wet. They should never be washed in very hot soap suds; that which is mildly warm will cleanse them quite as well, and will not extract the colors so much. Soft soap should never be used for calicoes, excepting for the various shades of yellow, which look the best washed with soft soap, and not rinsed in fair water. Other colors should be rinsed in fair water, and dried in the shade. When calicoes incline to fade, the colors can be set by washing them in lukewarm water, with beef's gall, in the proportion of a tea-cupful to four or five gallons water. Rinse them in fair water; no soap is necessary, unless the clothes are very dirty. If so, wash them in lukewarm suds, after they have been first rubbed out in beef's gall water. The beef's gall can be kept several months, by squeezing it out of the skin in which it is inclosed, adding salt to it, and bottled and corked tight. A little vinegar in the rinsing water of pink, red, and green calicoes, is good to brighten the colors, and keep them from mixing.

Directions for Washing Woolens.—If you do not wish to have white flannels shrink when washed, make a good suds of hard soap, and wash the flannels in it, without rubbing any soap on them; rub them out in another suds, then wring them out of it, and put them in a clean tub, and turn on sufficient boiling water to cover them, and let them remain till the water is cold. A little indigo in the boiling water makes the flannels look nicer. If you wish to have your white flannels shrink, so as to have them thick, wash them in soft soap suds, and rinse them in cold water. Colored woolens that incline to fade, should be washed with beef's gall and warm water, before they are put into soap-suds. Colored pantaloons look very well washed with beef's gall and fair warm water, and pressed on the wrong side while damp.

Directions for Washing White Cotton Cloth.—Table cloths, or any white clothes that have coffee or fruit stains on them, before being put into soap-suds, should have boiling water turned on them, and remain in it until the water is cold; the spots should be then rubbed out in it. If they are put into soap-suds with the stains in, they will be set by it, so that no subsequent washing will remove them. Table-cloths will be less likely to get stained up, if they are always rinsed in thin starch-water, as it tends to keep coffee and fruit from sinking into the texture of the cloth. White clothes that are very dirty, will come clean easily if put into strong cool suds, and hung on the fire the night previous to the day on which they are to be washed. If they get to boiling, it will not do them any harm, provided the suds is cool when they are put in; if it is hot at first, it will set the dirt in.

The following method of washing clothes is a saving of a great deal of labor: Soak the clothes in lukewarm soap suds; if they are quite dirty, soak them over night. To every three pails of water, put a pint of soft soap, and a table-spoonful of the salts of soda. Heat it till it mildly warm, then put in the clothes without any rubbing, and boil them an hour. Drain the suds out of them as much as possible, as it is bad for the hands; then add water until cool enough for the hands. The dirt will be loose, so that they will require but little rubbing. Rinse them thoroughly in clear water, then in indigo-water. The soda can be procured cheap, by purchasing it in large quantities. Soda is an excellent thing to soften hard water. The soda suds will not do to wash calicoes in. It is a good plan to save your suds, after washing, to water your garden, if you have one, or to harden cellars and yards when they are sandy.

Directions for Cleansing Silk Goods.—When silk cushions, or silk coverings to furniture, become dingy, rub dry bran on them gently with a woolen cloth till clean. Remove the grease spots and stains. Silk garments should have the spots extracted before being washed. Use hard soap for all colors but yellow, for which soft soap is the best. Put the soap into hot water, beat it till it is perfectly dissolved, then add sufficient cold water to make it just lukewarm. Put in the silks, and rub them in it till clean; take them out without wringing, and rinse them in fair lukewarm water. Rinse it in another water; and for bright yellows, crimsons and maroons, add sulphuric acid enough to the water to give it an acid taste before rinsing the garment in it. To restore the colors of the different shades of pink, put in the second rinsing water a little vinegar or lemon-juice; for scarlet, use a solution of tin; for blues, purples, and other shades, use pearlash; and for olive greens, dissolve verdigris in the rinsing water; fawns and browns should be rinsed in pure water. Dip the silks up and down in the rinsing water; take them out of it without wringing, and dry them in the shade. Fold them up while damp; let them remain to have the dampness strike through all parts of them alike, then put them in a mangler; if you have not one, iron them on the wrong side with an iron just hot enough to smooth them. A little isinglass or gum arabic dissolved in the rinsing water of gauze shawls and ribbons, is good to stiffen them. The water in which pared potatoes have been boiled, is an excellent thing to wash black silks in; it stiffens and makes them glossy and black. Beef's gall in lukewarm water is also a nice thing to restore rusty silk, and soap-suds answers very well. They look better not to be rinsed in clear water, but they should be washed in two different waters.

No person should ever wring or crush a piece of silk when it is wet, because the creases thus made will remain forever, if the silk is thick and hard. The way to wash silk is to spread it smoothly upon a clean board, rub white soap upon it, and brush it with a clean hard brush. The silk must be rubbed until all the grease is extracted, then the soap should be brushed off with clean cold water, and applied to both sides. The cleansing of silk is a very nice operation. Most of the colors are liable to be extracted with washing in hot suds, especially blue and green colors. A little alum dissolved in the last water that is brushed on the silk, tends to prevent the colors from running. Alcohol and camphene mixed together is used for removing grease from silk.

Franklin Soap.—1 pound common bar soap, 1 pint alcohol, 15 drops citron elles, or other perfume, ⅓ ounce spirits of hartshorn. Have your soap cut very fine, put all the materials in a clean iron kettle, and stir it slowly till all is dissolved. Let it just come to a boil, and then take it up in molds or bars.

White Bar Soap.—Take 8 quarts water, 4 pounds common bar soap, ½ pound sal soda, 2 ounces alcohol, 2 ounces saltpeter, 1 ounce borax. Put all into an iron kettle, stir till dissolved, then boil for ten minutes.

Almond Soap.—Take 1 pound of quick lime and pour on 3 quarts of boiling distilled water; add 1 pound of salt of tartar dissolved in 1 quart of water; cover the vessel, and when cold, filter through a cotton cloth; a pint should weigh exactly 16 ounces Troy; if more, add distilled water; if less, evaporate. Then add one-third of oil of almonds, simmer them together for some hours, or until the oil forms a jelly; when cool, which may be tried by a small quantity, add common salt, then continue boiling till the soap is solid; when cold, skim off the water, and then pour into molds.

Transparent Soap.—Transparent soap is made by dissolving hard soap in alcohol, then drying. Most all toilet soaps are made by dissolving common hard soap with the essential oils of lavender, bergamot, rosemary, &c.

Writing Fluid.—Take 1 pound nutgalls, bruised, half a pound of logwood chips, and boil in 12 quarts soft water till evaporated to 8 quarts. Let it settle, then strain through a hair sieve, and add half a pound of green sulphate of iron, and 2 ounces sulphate of copperas, dissolved in a little hot water, 1 ounce crystalized sugar, and 3 ounces powdered gum arabic, or half a pound of gum senegal dissolved in a little hot water. Let it stand exposed to the air for 24 hours, then bottle. This Ink can be depended upon for deeds and records.

A cheap Ink, easily made, and good enough for family purposes, is made as follows: Bring 1 gallon soft water to a boil, and put in three-fourth ounce extract logwood, and boil two or three minutes; then remove from the fire and stir in 48 grains powdered gum arabic, 8 grains prussiate of potash, and 48 grains bi-chromate of potash. This ink can be made at a cost of five or ten cents for a single gallon, and as it does not spoil by freezing, it is best for school children.

A lump of salt, size of a hazel-nut, dissolved in each quart of ink, will effectually keep it from molding; or 5 drops of kreosote added to each pint, will have the same effect.

Indelible Ink.—Nitrate of silver, 1 drachm; rain water, 5 fluid drachms; mucilage gum arabic (fresh) one drachm; dissolve the nitrate of silver in the rain water, then add the mucilage. For the preparation, add to each ounce of the mucilage five grains of baking soda. Paste a piece of dark paper all over the bottle, and keep in a dark place.

Red Ink.—Take a half ounce viol, and put in a tea-spoonful of aqua ammonia; gum arabic, size of two or three peas, and five grains of good carmine; fill up with soft water, and it is soon ready for use.

CEMENTS AND SOLDERS.

Cement for Glass, China, Wood, Leather, &c.—Take ¼ pound white glue, 1 ounce white lead, dry, and ¼ pint soft water; put these in a tin dish, inside an iron kettle filled with water, and boil, stirring with a stick till all is dissolved; then add ¼ pint alcohol, and boil again till well mixed. Put in a bottle, and keep tightly corked. When required for use, set the bottle in a dish of water on the stove, and gradually heat till the cement is dissolved and of the consistency of cream; then apply a thin coating to one edge, put the parts immediately together, pressing firmly for a few moments, and set the article away a day or so to dry. The cement must be quite warm and thin when used; and, in cold weather, slightly warm the article to be mended, enough to take off the chill; otherwise it will get cold before you can get the parts together, and form a thin coating like paper between the joints, in which case it will not stick. In mending wood, and articles that are porous, don't press hard too soon, or you will press all out, except what the pores of the wood will absorb, leaving none to unite the broken surfaces, but press slightly at first, then hard, after a few moments.

Liquid Solder for Mending Tin, Iron, and Steel.—Take ¼ pound muriatic acid and drop in as many strips of zinc as it will dissolve, and, while boiling, add ¼ ounce pulverized sal ammoniac. Wet the tin around the hole to be mended with a drop or two of this fluid—first having scraped off the rust, if any; then lay on a piece of soft solder or pewter, and hold a candle or lamp underneath till it is melted. If the hole be large, either cover it with a small piece of tin, then a piece of solder large enough to cover all when melted, or set the dish on a cloth to keep the solder from running through, and then use a hot iron to melt it.

For mending iron and steel, wet the broken edges to be joined with this fluid, and then dip them into some filings of soft solder, and hold in a spirit-lamp, firmly pressing till the solder melts and oozes out of the seam, when the light must be blown out, and the article held perfectly still, till cool.

Another.—An amalgam of chemically pure copper, with mercury at a temperature of 450 degrees, will unite broken metals, glass, china, porcelain, &c., as strongly as before broken. At the expiration of ten or twelve hours it becomes sufficiently hard to take on a polish like brass or silver.

BEVERAGES.

Spruce Beer.—Take 3 gallons soft water, 2½ pints molasses, 3 eggs, well-beaten, and 1 gill yeast. Mix together equal parts oil sassafras, spruce and wintergreen, and put 50 drops of this mixture into two quarts of the water, boiling hot, and then put all together and let stand two or three hours, then bottle. For ginger flavor, take 2 ounces of ginger root, bruised, and a small handful of hops, and boil for half an hour in 1 gallon of the water, then strain and mix altogether.

Good Ginger Beer.—Take 2½ ounces ginger, 3 pounds sugar, 1 ounce cream tartar, the juice and peel of two middling-sized lemons, ½ pint good brandy, ¼ pint yeast, and 3½ gallons water. Bruise the ginger, and put it and the sugar into the water, and boil for twenty or thirty minutes; slice the lemons, and put them and the cream tartar in a large pan, and pour the boiling liquor on; stir it well, and, when milk-warm, add the yeast; cover it over and let it remain two or three days to work, skimming it frequently; then strain it through a jelly-bag into a cask, add the brandy, bung it tight, and at the end of two or three weeks draw it off, bottle and cork tight. If it does not work well at first, add a little more yeast, but be careful and not get too much, as it will taste of it.

Lemon Beer.—Take 3 ounces ginger-root, bruised, 2 ounces cream tartar and boil for twenty or thirty minutes in 3 gallons of water. Strain and add 6 pounds coffee sugar on which you have put ½ ounce oil of lemon, or ¼ ounce and three lemons all mashed up together, and add 7 gallons more water nearly milk-warm, then put in ¾ pint of hop or brewer's yeast, made into a paste, with 3 ounces flour. Let it work one night, and then bottle for use.

Royal Diamond Sirup.—Take 1 gallon water, 6 pounds loaf-sugar, 6 ounces tartaric acid, and 1 ounce gum arabic in another vessel. Beat up four tea-spoonfuls of flour, and the whites of four eggs, and add ½ pint of water in another vessel: when that in the first vessel is blood-warm, put in the contents of the other vessel, and let it stand three minutes.

To Use It.—Take two or three table-spoonfuls of the sirup to a glass one-half or two-thirds full of water, and stir in ½ tea-spoonful of pulverized super-carbonate of soda. This is a cheap and delicious beverage, much better and healthier than soda water; easily made, and can be kept any length of time without deteriorating. Keep in a glass vessel, as metal of any kind would spoil it.

Portable Lemonade.—Tartaric acid, ½ ounce, loaf sugar, 3 ounces, essence of lemon, ¼ drachm. Powder the tartaric acid and the sugar very fine in a porcelain mortar, mix them together, and pour on the essence of lemon by a few drops at a time, stirring the mixture after each addition till the whole is added, then mix thoroughly and divide into twelve equal parts, wrapping each up separately in white paper. When wanted for use, dissolve in a tumbler of cold water, and you will have good lemonade. Convenient for persons traveling, where they cannot procure drinks suitable to taste.

WINES, CORDIALS, AND OTHER LIQUORS.

Red Currant Wine.—Take cold soft water, 11 gallons; red currants, 8 gallons; raspberries, from 1 to 3 quarts. Ferment and strain. Mix raw sugar, 20 pounds; beet root, sliced, 2 pounds; and red tartar, in fine powder, 3 ounces. Put in one nutmeg, in fine powder, and add 1 gallon brandy. This will make 18 gallons.

White Currant Wine.—Take cold soft water, 9 gallons; white currants, 9 gallons. Ferment and strain. Mix refined sugar, 25 pounds; white tartar, in powder, 1 ounce; clary seed, bruised, 2 ounces, or clary flowers, or sorrel flowers, 4 handfuls, then add white brandy, 1 gallon. This will make 18 gallons.

Black Currant Wine.—Cold soft water, 10 gallons; black currants, 6 gallons; strawberries, 3 gallons. Ferment and strain. Mix raw sugar, 25 pounds; red tartar, in fine powder, 6 ounces; orange thyme, 2 handsful; then add brandy 2 or 3 quarts. This will make 18 gallons.

Strawberry Wine.—Take of cold soft water, 7 gallons; cider, 6 gallons; strawberries, 6 gallons. Ferment and strain. Mix raw sugar, 16 pounds; red tartar, in fine powder, 3 ounces; the peel and juice of 2 lemons; then add brandy, 2 or 3 quarts.

Raspberry Wine.—Take of cold soft water, 6 gallons; cider, 4 gallons; raspberries, 6 gallons. Ferment and strain. Mix raw sugar, 18 or 20 pounds; red tartar, in fine powder, 3 ounces; orange and lemon peel, 2 ounces dry, or 4 ounces fresh. Then add 3 quarts brandy. This will make 18 gallons.

Elderberry Wine.—Take of cold soft water, 16 gallons; Malaga raisins, 50 pounds; elderberries, 4 gallons; red tartar, in fine powder, 4 ounces. Mix ginger, in powder, 5 ounces; cinnamon, cloves, and mace, of each 2 ounces; peel and juice of 3 oranges or lemons. Then add 1 gallon of brandy. This will make 18 gallons.

Gooseberry Wine.—Take of cold soft water, 3 gallons, gooseberries, 3½ gallons. Ferment and strain. Now mix raw sugar, 5 pounds; honey, 1½ pounds; tartar, in fine powder, 1 ounce. Afterward put in bitter almonds 2 ounces; sweetbriar, 1 small handful, and brandy 1 gallon or less.

Compound Wine.—An excellent family wine may be made of equal parts of red, white, and black currants, ripe cherries and raspberries, well bruised and mixed with soft water, in the proportion of 4 pounds of fruit to one gallon of water. When strained and pressed, 3 pounds of moist sugar are to be added to each gallon of the liquid. After straining, open for three days, during which it is to be stirred frequently; it is to be put in a barrel, and left for two weeks to work, when a ninth part of brandy is to be added, and the whole bunged down. In a few months it will be a most excellent wine, *inferior to none.*

Blackberry Wine.—Having procured berries that are fully ripe, put them into a large vessel of wood or stone, with a cock in it, and pour upon them as much boiling water as will cover them. As soon as tho heat will permit the hand to be put into the vessel, bruise them well till all the berries are broken. Then let them stand covered till the berries begin to rise toward the top, which they generally do in three or four days. Then draw off the clear into another vessel, and add to every ten quarts of this liquor 1 pound of sugar. Stir it well, and let it stand to work a week or ten days, in another vessel. Take 4 ounces of isinglass, and lay it to steep twelve hours in a pint of white wine. The next morning boil it upon a slow fire till it is all dissolved. Then take a gallon of blackberry juice, put in the dissolved isinglass, give them a boil together, and pour all into the vessel. Let it stand a few days to purge and settle, then draw it off, and keep in a cool place.

Another Method.—Take ripe blackberries, press the juice from them, let it stand thirty-six hours to ferment (lightly covered,) and skim off whatever rises to the top; then to every gallon of the juice add 1 quart of water and 3 pounds of sugar, (brown will do,) let it stand in an open vessel for twenty-four hours; skim and strain it, then barrel it. Let it stand eight or nine hours, when it should be racked off, bottled, and corked close. It improves by age.

Rhubarb Wine.—Peel and slice the stalk of the leaf, as for pies; put a very small quantity of water in the vessel, only just enough to cover the bottom; cover the vessel, and gradually bring to a very slight boil; then strain, passing all the liquid; to this liquid add an equal quantity of water; to each gallon (after mixed,) add 4 to 5 pounds of brown sugar; set aside, ferment and skim like currant wine; leave in the cask and in bulk as long as possible before using. All wine is best kept in casks.

Another.—Take of sliced rhubarb, 2½ ounces; lesser cardamon seeds, bruised and husked, ½ ounce; saffron, 2 drachms; spanish white wine, 2 pints; proof spirit, ½ pint. Digest for ten days, and strain. This is a warm cordial, laxative medicine, good in weakness of the stomach and bowels, and for regulating and strengthening the whole viscera.

Damson Wine.—Cold soft water, 11 gallons; damson plums, 8 gallons. Ferment. Mix raw sugar, 30 pounds; red tartar, in fine powder, 6 ounces; brandy, 1 gallon.

Cherry Wine.—Cold soft water, 10 gallons; cherries, 10 gallons. Ferment. Mix raw sugar, 30 pounds; red tartar, in fine powder, 3 ounces; brandy, two or three quarts. Two days after the cherries have been in the vat, take out about 3 quarts, break the stones and return them to the vat again.

Peach Wine.—Cold soft water, 18 gallons; refined sugar, 25 pounds; honey, 6 pounds; white tartar, in fine powder, 2 ounces; peaches, 60 or 80 in number. Ferment. Then add 2 gallons brandy. Put all together in the vat, except the peaches and brandy, and let remain one day; then break the peach-kernels and put them into the vat, and ferment; then add the brandy afterward.

Apricot Wine.—Boil together 3 pounds of sugar and 3 quarts of water, and skim it well. Put in 6 pounds of apricots, pared and stoned, and let them boil till they become tender. Then take them up, and when the liquor is cold, bottle it. After taking out the apricots, let the liquor be boiled with a sprig of flowered clary. The apricots will make marmalade, and be very good for present use.

Apple Wine.—To every gallon of apple juice, immediately as it comes from the press, add 2 pounds loaf sugar; boil it as long as any scum rises, then strain it through a sieve, and let it cool; let it work in the tub for two or three weeks, or till the head begins to flatten, then skim off the head, draw it clear off and turn it. When made a year, rack it off, and fine it with isinglass; then add ½ pint of the best rectified spirit of wine, or 1 pint of French brandy to every 8 gallons.

Grape Wine.—Cold soft water, 5 gallons; black or red grapes, 40 pounds. Ferment and strain. Mix cider, 9 gallons; raw sugar, 20 pounds; barberry leaves, 3 handfuls; beet root, sliced, 2 pounds; red tartar, in fine powder, 4 ounces. Add white elder flowers, 6 handfuls; or sassafras chips, 4 pounds; brandy, 1 gallon. This will make 18 gallons.

Another.—Cold soft water, 6 gallons; any kind of grapes, 30 pounds. Ferment and strain. Mix treacle, 10 pounds; beet root, sliced, 1½ pounds; red tartar, in powder, 2 ounces; rosemary leaves, 2 handfuls; brandy, ½ gallon. This will make 9 gallons.

Another.—Cold soft water, 8 gallons; grapes of any sort, 100 pounds. Ferment and strain. Mix raw sugar, 20 pounds; beet root, sliced, 4 pounds; barberry leaves, 4 handfuls; red tartar, in fine powder, 6 ounces. Add coriander seed, bruised, 2 ounces; brandy, 6 quarts. This will make 18 gallons.

Ginger Wine.—Put into a nice boiler 10 gallons water; 15 pounds of lump sugar, with the whites of 6 or 8 eggs, well beaten and strained; mix all well while cold. When the liquor boils, skim it well; put in ½ pound ginger root, bruised, and boil it twenty minutes. Have ready the rinds (cut very thin,) of 7 lemons, and pour the hot liquor on them. When cool, put it into your cask, with two spoonfuls of yeast; put a quart of the warm liquor to 2 ounces of isinglass shavings; whisk it well three or four times, and put all into the barrel, with 1 or 2 gallons good brandy, or pure spirits. Next day stop it up; in three weeks bottle it, and in three months it will be a delicious, safe beverage.

OBSERVATIONS ON CIDER AND WINES.

To make good cider, the following general, but important rules should be attended to. They demand a little more trouble than the ordinary mode of collecting and mashing apples of all sorts, rotten and sound, sweet and sour, dirty and clean, from the tree and the ground, and the rest of the slovenly process usually employed: 1. Always choose perfectly ripe and sound fruit. 2. Pick the apples by hand. An active boy, with a bag slung over his shoulders, will soon clear a tree. Apples that have laid any time on the soil contract an earthy taste, which will always be found in the cider. 3. After sweating, and before ground, wipe them dry, and if any are found bruised and rotten, put them in a heap by themselves, for an inferior cider to make vinegar. 4. Always use hair cloths, instead of straw, to place between the layers of pummage. The straw, when heated, gives a disagreeable taste to the cider. 5. As the cider runs from the press, let it pass through a hair sieve, into a large open vessel, that will hold as much juice as can be expressed in one day. In a day, or sometimes less, the pummice will rise to the top, and in a short time grow very thick; when little white bubbles break through it, draw off the liquor by a spiggot, placed about three inches from the bottom, so that the lees may be left quietly behind. 6. The cider must be drawn off into very clean, sweet casks, and closely watched. The moment the white bubbles before mentioned are perceived rising to the bunghole, rack it again. When the fermentation is completely at an end, fill up the cask with cider in all respects like that contained in it, and bung it up tight, previous to which a tumbler of sweet oil may be poured into the bung-hole.

When cider has fermented for about one week in a cask, add half a pound of white sugar to every gallon; then allow it to ferment further until it has acquired a brisk and pleasant taste. An ounce of the sulphite of lime is then added to every gallon of cider in the cask, and the whole agitated for a few minutes, and then left to settle. The sulphite of lime arrests the fermentation, and, in the course of a few days, the clear cider may be poured off and bottled, when it will retain the same taste that it had when the sulphite was added. About an ounce of the sulphite of lime added to a gallon of cider, in any stage of fermentation, will preserve it from further change. A sparkling cider wine is produced by the mode described.

The following is another method of making cider wine: Take pure cider, as it runs from the press, and add a pound of brown sugar to every quart, and put it into a clean cask, which should be filled to within about two gallons of the top. The cask is then placed in a moderately cool cellar or apartment, and the cider allowed to ferment slowly, by the bunghole being left open till it has acquired the proper taste and sparkles, when a small quantity is drawn. The cask is then bunged up tight.

Grape wine should be allowed to remain for a long period in oak casks, after it is made, before it is bottled, otherwise it will be comparatively sour to the taste. This is owing to the great quantity of the tartrate of potash in the juice of the grape. When standing in a wooden cask, the tartrate is deposited from the wine, and adheres to the interior surfaces of the vessel, and it forms a thick and hard stony crust called "argol." This is the substance of which our cream-of-tartar and tartaric acid are made. In its crude state it is employed by silk and woolen dyers in producing scarlet, purple, and claret colors, in conjunction with cochineal and logwood. This explains the cause of wines becoming sweeter the longer they stand in casks in a cool situation.

Wines may be made of the juice of the sorghum-cane, by permitting it to ferment for a short period in the same manner as has been described for cider, then closing up the cask tight, to prevent access of air. The fermentation of all saccharine juices is due to the combination, chemically, of the oxygen of the air with some of the carbon in the sugar of the juice. A small quantity of alcohol is thus generated and absorbed by the fermented juice. Carbonic acid gas is also generated; when absorbed by the liquid and retained under pressure, this gas imparts the sparkling property of wine. When the saccharine juices are undergoing fermentation they must be tasted frequently, for the purpose of arresting the fermentation at the proper stage, because there are two stages of fermentation, called the vinous and acetous. The first is that in which alcohol is produced; the second, vinegar. Many artificial wines have a slight vinegar taste, which is caused by allowing the fermentation to proceed too far.

These hints will be useful to those who prepare light domestic wines These are now made very generally, and are held to exert a favorable influence in many cases of dyspepsia.

Port Wine.—Good worked cider, 20 gallons; good port wine, 5 gallons; good foreign brandy, one and a half gallons; proof spirits, 3 gallons. When all are mixed, color with elderberries, aloes, or burnt sugar.

Peppermint Cordial.—Take 1 gallon proof spirits; 1 pound of loaf sugar; a little more than 1 pennyweight, Troy, of oil of peppermint, and one half gallon of water.

Blackberry Cordial.—To 1 quart of blackberry juice, add 1 pound of white sugar, 1 table-spoonful of cloves, 1 of allspice, 1 of cinnamon, and 1 of nutmeg. Boil all together fifteen minutes; add a wine-glass of whisky, brandy, or rum. Bottle while hot, cork tight and seal. This is almost a specific in diarrhea. One dose of a wine-glassful for an adult—half that quantity for a child—will often cure diarrhea. It can be taken three or four times a day, if the case is severe.

LIQUORS.

As nearly all the liquors now used, especially those of a cheap grade, are manufactured from whisky and poisonous compounds, those who deal in such articles, especially druggists, should make their own, according to the following recipes:

Brandy.—Take pure cologne spirits, 4 gallons; best of French brandy, 1 gallon; loaf sugar, half a pound: sweet spirits of niter, 2 ounces. Color with burnt sugar.

Gin.—Pure cologne spirits, 4 gallons: Holland gin, 1 gallon; oil of juniper, 8 scruples; oil of anise, 1-10 ounce.

Rum.—Pure cologne spirits, 4 gallons, good Jamaica or St. Croix rum, 1 gallon; oil of caraway, 1-16 ounce.

These liquors are pure, and much better than those you buy ready manufactured—nine-tenths of which are made from bad whisky and noxious drugs. Those who are able, had better buy the *pure* foreign article from responsible parties; but at the present prices (from $8 to $12 per gallon) few are able to obtain it even for medicinal purposes; besides, in most cases of sickness, that manufactured according to the above, answers every purpose. The coloring matter is made as follows: Take any quantity of white sugar and mix with water till about the consistency of a thin mush; now put in an iron kettle or spider, and burn over a hot stove till it becomes of a deep-red black color, quite thick, and smells strongly from the burning. Add a little warm water, to prevent its hardening, and use this to color all kinds of liquors requiring any.

Cherry Bounce.—Take 1 barrel pure spirits, and put in from one-half to one bushel black (wild) cherries, and 6 or 8 pounds loaf sugar. You can reduce the strength by adding pure well, rain, or distilled water.

Black Cherry Brandy.—Stone 8 pounds of black cherries and put on them 1 gallon of brandy; now bruise the stones in a mortar, and then add them to the brandy; cover them close, and let them stand from four to six weeks; then pour it clear from the sediment and bottle. Morella cherries, managed in this way, make a fine, rich cordial.

Raspberry Brandy.—Take 1 gallon brandy, and ½ gallon water, and put into a stone jug, jar, or demijohn, and then add 1 gallon raspberries, and 1 pound of loaf sugar, and let it remain for a week closely covered; then take a piece of flannel, with a piece of Holland over it, and let it run through gradually. It may be racked into other bottles in a week after, and then it will be fine. Blackberry brandy may be made in the same way.

Vinegar.—1 gallon alcohol, 8 gallons water, 1 quart molasses, and a dozen white beans, done up in a brown paper, to form the mother. Let it stand two or three weeks in a warm place. This is equal to cider vinegar.

Another.—To 3 gallons soft water, add 1 quart molasses, 1 pint of yeast, and 1 ounce of cream tartar; let it stand four weeks in a warm place; then add as much sweetened water each week as you use of the vinegar. Cold tea is excellent to replenish vinegar.

DYEING.

To Dye Black.—Allow a pound of logwood to each pound of goods that are to be dyed. Soak it over night in soft water, then boil it an hour, and strain the water in which it is boiled. For each pound of logwood, dissolve an ounce of blue vitriol in lukewarm water, sufficient to wet the goods. Dip the goods in; when saturated with it, turn the whole into the logwood dye. If the goods are cotton, set the vessel on the fire, and let the goods boil ten or fifteen minutes, stirring them constantly to prevent their spotting. Silk and woolen goods should not be boiled in the dye-stuff, but it should be kept at a scalding heat for twenty minutes. Drain the goods without wringing, and hang them in a dry, shady place, where they will have the air. When dry, set the color, by putting them into scalding hot water that has salt in it, in the proportion of a teacupful to three gallons of the water. Let the goods remain in till cold; then hang them in a place where they will dry (they should not be wrung) Boiling hot suds is the best thing to set the color of black silk; let it remain in it till cold. Soaking black-dyed goods in sour milk is also good to set the color.

Green and Blue Dye, for Silks and Woolens.—For green dye, take a pound of oil of vitriol, and turn it upon half an ounce of Spanish indigo, that has been reduced to a fine powder. Stir them well together, then add a lump of pearlash of the size of a pea; as soon as the fermentation ceases, bottle it; the dye will be fit for use the next day. Chemic blues are made in the same manner, only using half the quantity of vitriol. For woolen goods, the East indigo will answer as well as the Spanish, and comes much lower. This dye will not answer for cotton goods, as the vitriol rots the threads. Wash the articles that are to be dyed till perfectly clean, and free from color. If you can not extract the color by rubbing it in hot suds, boil it out; rinse it in soft water till entirely free from soap, as the soap will ruin the dye. To dye a pale color, put to each quart of soft warm water, that is to be used for the dye, ten drops of the above composition; if you wish a deep color, more will be necessary. Put in the articles without crowding, and let them remain in it till of a good color; the dye-stuff should be kept warm. Take the articles out without wringing; drain as much of the dye out of them as possible, then hang them to dry in a shady, airy place. They should be dyed when the weather is dry; if not dried quickly, they will not look well. When perfectly dry, wash them in lukewarm suds, to keep the vitriol from injuring the texture of the cloth. If you wish for a lively, bright green, mix a little of the above composition with yellow dye.

Yellow Dyes.—To dye a buff-color, boil equal parts of arnotto and common potash in soft clear water. When dissolved, take it from the fire; when cool, put in the goods, which should previously be washed free from spots and color; set them on a moderate fire, where they will keep hot, till the goods are of the shade you wish. To dye salmon and orange-color tie arnotto in a bag, and soak it in warm soft-soap suds till it becomes soft, so that you can squeeze enough of it through the bag to make the suds a deep yellow; put in the articles, which should be clean, and free from color; boil them till of the shade you wish. There should be enough of the dye to cover the goods; stir them while boiling, to keep them from spotting. This dye will make a salmon or orange color, according to the strength of it, and the time the goods remain in it. Drain them out of the dye, and dry them quickly in the shade; when dry, wash them in soft soap suds. Goods dyed in this manner should never be rinsed in clear water. Peach leaves, fustic, and saffron, all make a good straw or lemon color, according to the strength of the dye. They should be steeped in soft fair water, in an earthen or tin vessel, and then strained, and the dye set with alum, and a little gum Arabic dissolved in the dye, if you wish to stiffen the article. When the dye-stuff is strained, steep the articles in it.

Red Dyes.—Madder makes a good durable red, but not a brilliant color. To make a dye of it, allow, for half a pound of it, 3 ounces of alum, and 1 of cream-of-tartar, and 6 gallons of water. This proportion of ingredients will make sufficient dye for six or seven pounds of goods. Heat half of the water scalding hot, in a clean brass kettle; then put in the alum and cream-of-tartar, and let it dissolve. When the water boils, stir the alum and tartar up in it; put in the goods, and let them boil a couple of hours; then rinse them in fair water, empty the kettle, and put in three gallons of water and the madder; rub it fine in the water, then put in the goods, and set them where they will keep scalding hot for an hour without boiling: stir them constantly. When they have been scalding an hour, increase the fire till they boil. Let them boil five minutes; then drain them out of the dye, and rinse them, without wringing, in fair water, and hang them in the shade where they will dry.

Slate-colored Dye.—To make a good dark slate-color, boil sugar-leaf paper with vinegar, in an iron utensil; put in alum to set the color. Tea grounds, set with copperas, make a good slate-color. To produce a light slate-color, boil white maple bark in clear water, with a little alum; the bark should be boiled in a brass utensil. The dye for slate-color should be strained before the goods are put into it. They should be boiled in it, and then hung where they will drain and dry.

To Dye a Lively and Beautiful Drab.—Light-colored fabrics—cotton, silk, linen, or wool—such as gloves, stockings, &c., can be dyed a beautiful drab as follows: To a pint of rain water add six or eight grains of nitrate of silver; when it is dissolved, stir it well, and immerse the perfectly clean fabric. See that it is well and evenly saturated, for which use a stick, not a spoon, nor the hands. When thoroughly soaked, it may be quickly wrung out with the hands, they being instantly washed. In a pint of water dissolve one quarter of an ounce of sulphuret of potassium, place the goods in it, and saturate well; then wash in clear water, and it is finished. It is better that the first-named solution should be hot, and a little time taken for wool. Glass vessels must be used.

A Few Hints on Dyeing.—To those who wish to have certain fabrics dyed, the following information will be found useful as regards the colors they will take. Thus, if the material be black, it can only be dyed black; brown, dark green, dark crimson, dark claret, and dark olive. Brown can only be dyed black, dark brown, dark claret. Dark green: black, dark brown, dark green, dark claret, dark olive. Light green: dark green, black, dark brown, dark crimson, dark claret, dark olive. Dark crimson: black, brown, dark crimson, dark claret. Light crimson will take the same as dark crimson. Claret: black, brown, dark crimson, dark claret. Fawn will take dark crimson, dark green, black, brown, dark claret. Puce: black, brown, dark olive, dark crimson, dark claret. Dark blue: black, brown, dark crimson, dark green, dark claret, dark olive, dark blue. Pale blue: dark crimson, dark green, black, brown, claret, puce, dark blue, dark olive, lavender, orange, yellow. Olive will dye brown, black, dark green, dark crimson, dark claret. Lavender: black, brown, dark crimson, claret, lavender, olive. Pink: dark crimson, dark green, black, brown (as all tints will take a black and brown, these colors will not be repeated), pink, olive, dark blue, dark puce, dark fawn. Rose, same as pink, but also orange, scarlet, and giraffe. Straw, primrose, and yellow will dye almost any color required; as also will peach and giraffe. Gray will only dye, besides brown and black, dark green, dark claret, dark crimson, dark fawn, dark blue. White silk, cotton, and woolen goods, can be dyed any color. As cotton, silk, and wool all take dye differently, it is almost impossible to re-dye a fabric of mixed stuff any color except the dark ones named. It will be observed by the above list that pale blue will re-dye better than any other color.

MISCELLANEOUS.

Arnica Hair Wash.—When the hair is falling off and becoming thin from the frequent use of castor, macassar oils, &c., or when premature baldness arises from illness, the Arnica hair wash will be found of great service in arresting the mischief. It is thus prepared : Take elder water, half a pint; sherry wine, half a pint; tincture of arnica, half an ounce, alcoholic ammonia, one drachm—if this last named ingredient is old and has lost its strength, then two drachms instead of one may be employed. The whole of these are to be mixed in a lotion bottle, and applied to the head every night with a sponge. Wash the head with warm water twice a week. Soft brushes only must be used during the growth of the young hair.

Lotion for Restoring the Color of Gray Hair.—Take half an ounce of sulphur steeped in alcohol, and a quarter of an ounce of sugar of lead, mixed with ten ounces of rose water, in a phial. The phial should be shaken every time the liquid is applied, which should be every evening, with a sponge, for about a week at first, then twice a week after the color of the hair is restored. The head should be covered with a close glazed linen cap after this lotion is put on.

Pomatum for Growth of the Hair.—This pomatum, applied to the scalp, acts as a stimulant to the roots of the hair, and as a nourisher to the hair itself, by stimulating the capillary vessels. In the immediate neighborhood of hair-bulb, the blood particles are more numerous and active. The ammonia, containing, as it does, nitrogen, one of the principal constituents of hair, horn, and nail, affords one of its direct elements of formation, and hence its value as a nourisher. It is utterly impossible for the animal economy to create hair out of any oil, because oil is destitute of nitrogen, but if grease be combined with ammonia, which yields nitrogen, then great benefit will be derived from the pomade so made. All pomades and oils that are used for the hair only act as a polish, but afford no nourishment. The following is a simple form for making the ammoniacal pomatum: Take almond oil, a quarter of a pound; white wax, half an ounce; clarified lard, three ounces; liquid ammonia, a quarter fluid ounce; otto lavender and cloves, of each, one drachm. Place the oil, wax, and lard into a jar, which set into boiling water; when the wax is melted, allow the grease to cool till nearly ready to set, then stir in the ammonia and the perfume, and put into small jars for use. Never use a hard brush, nor comb the hair too much; apply the pomade at night only.

Another Coloring for the Hair.—The following method is probably more simple, and safer than any other: Take equal parts of vinegar, lemon juice, and powdered litharge; boil for half an hour on a slow fire ; wet the hair with this decoction, and in a short time it will turn black.

Milk of Almonds, for the Complexion.—This much admired and harmless cosmetic may be prepared thus : Procure a quarter of a pound of the best Jordan almonds, which blanch, by putting them into boiling water for three minutes, and afterward into cold water for the same time ;

the skin or pellicle will then slip off by pressure between the thumb and finger. The almonds are now to be crushed in a mortar, and rubbed with a quarter of an ounce of the best white or curd soap. Continue the rubbing for a quarter of an hour, during which period gradually add one quart of rose water. When the whole resembles milk, strain through fine muslin. It is then fit for use, and may be applied to the skin with the corner of a soft towel, after washing. Those who are without a mortar must grate the almonds on a bread grater, and rub the ingredients together with clean hands. Fresh rain water, or plain distilled water, will answer in lieu of rosewater, where economy is studied.

Powder for Chafed Skin.—This preparation is universally applied for drying the skin, after washing, especially at the joints, which, if left even damp at certain seasons, produces chaps and chafing, often followed, if neglected, by inflammation. Violet powder is best prepared by mixing three parts of the best wheat starch with one of finely-ground orris root: the latter adds to the drying power of the starch, and imparts at the same time an agreeable odor, like that of the violet; hence the name of the mixture. It is also prepared by perfuming starch with essential oils without the addition of orris root; but though the scent of the powder is stronger, and to some more tempting to use, it is far less beneficial in its application. The scent, acting as a stimulant to the skin, increases rather than abates any tendency to redness. Unperfumed powder is therefore best to use, dusted over the part with a little swan's down, commonly called a puff.

For Whitening the Skin, and Removing Freckles and Tan.—Take one ounce of borax, two ounces of cologne, one quart of alcohol, and three quarts of rain water. Bathe three times a day in a solution of two teaspoonfuls in two table-spoonfuls of water.

Ointment for Chapped Hands.—Take sweet oil, 3 ounces; spermaceti, 4 ounces, and pulverized camphor, 1 ounce. Mix them together in a clean earthenware vessel, by the aid of gentle heat, and apply it warm to the hands night and morning. Another very good ointment for chapped hands is made with a little fresh newly-churned butter and honey.

Cure for Bunions and Corns.—The tincture of iodine applied to bunions is said to afford great relief. A strong solution of pearlash, applied to corns, will soften them so that they may be easily drawn out.

To Remove Warts.—Take ashes made from burnt willow bark, and mix with sweet cider, and apply several times, and they will soon disappear.

Cure for Chilblains.—Apply a wash made of 1 part of muriatic acid and 7 parts of water.

To Destroy Flies.—To 1 pint of milk add ¼ pound of raw sugar and 2 ounces ground pepper; simmer them together eight or ten minutes, and place it about in shallow dishes. The flies attack it greedily, and are soon suffocated. By this method kitchens, &c., may be kept clear of flies all summer, whithout the danger attending poison.

Wash for Fruit Trees.—Take 3 gallons of lye, from wood ashes, strong enough to just float an egg; 1 pint of soft soap, ¼ pound of niter, and a handful of common salt. The niter should be dissolved in warm water; then add the salt and other ingredients, and stir until thoroughly incorporated. Apply it to the trunks and large branches of the trees with a common (painter's) brush. It should not be applied to very young branches, or the leaves.

Remedy for Curculio in Fruit Trees.—Sawdust, saturated with coal-oil, and placed at the roots of the tree, will be a sure preventive.

Another.—It is said that tansy, bound upon the limbs of plum-trees, will be an effectual antidote against the ravages of this insect.

To Take Out Stains.—Take half a pint of water, dissolve in it half an ounce of salt of sorrel; add 2 ounces of spirits of wine. Shake them well together. Rub the liquid on the stains with a sponge.

To Remove Stains from Broadcloth.—Take 1 ounce of pipe-clay, that has been ground fine, and mix it with 12 drops of alcohol, and the same quantity of spirits of turpentine. Whenever you wish to remove any stains from cloth, moisten a little of this mixture and rub it on the spots. Let it remain till dry, then rub it off with a woolen cloth, and the spots will disappear.

To Remove Black Stains from Scarlet Woolen Goods.—Mix tartaric acid with water, to give it a splendid acid taste, then saturate the black spot with it, taking care not to have it touch the clean part of the garment. Rinse the spots immediately in fair water. Weak pearlash water is good to remove stains of acids.

To Extract Grease from Silks, Woolen Goods, Paper, and Floors.—Grate on them very thick French chalk, (common will answer, but it is not so good,) cover the spots with brown paper, and set on a moderately warm iron, and let it remain till cool. Care must be taken not to have the iron so hot as to scorch or change the color of the cloth. If the grease does not appear to be out, on removing the iron, grate on more chalk, heat the iron again, and put it on. Repeat the process till the grease is entirely out. Strong pearlash water, mixed with sand, or the washing fluid used in washing, will remove grease spots from floors, if well scrubbed.

Another Method of Extracting Grease from Cloth.—Take ½ pint alcohol and add 10 grains carbonate of potash, ¼ ounce oil bergamot, and 1 ounce sulphuric ether; mix, and keep in a glass-stopped bottle. Apply with a piece of sponge, soaking the cloth thoroughly when the grease is not recent. The mixture emits a peculiarly fragrant odor, and being a fluid soap, chemically composed, will be found a perfect solvent for oily matter. This, probably, is the best remedy extant for removing grease spots.

Removing Stains.—Ox-gall is an excellent article for removing oil stains from delicate-colored fabrics. It often fixes and brightens colors, but will slightly soil pure white materials. Alcohol or strong whisky washes out stains of oil, wax, resin and pitchy or resinous substances; so also does spirits of turpentine, and generally without injury to colors. The turpentine may afterward be removed with alcohol or whisky. Common burning fluid, which is a mixture of alcohol and turpentine, (or camphene,) is an excellent solvent of oil, wax, tar, resin, etc., and it soon dries off after use. Ink stains, or iron mold, may generally be removed with the juice of lemons or of sorrel leaves. If these fail, oxalic acid is almost infallible. Moisten the stain spots with water and rub on a little powdered oxalic acid, which can be cheaply obtained at any druggist's. Wash off the acid very thoroughly, soon after it is put on, or it will eat the fabric. If children are present, remember that oxalic acid is poisonous in the mouth, though not so on the hands, if not kept long upon them.

Moistening a cloth and holding it a few minutes over the fumes of burning sulphur will bleach out most colors and stains. Be careful not to burn the fabrics. The fumes may be conducted to any particular spot by a paper roller, in funnel shape, (or a common tin funnel,) held over the fumes of sulphur burning upon a shovel. The sulphur fumes are especially applicable to stains of fruit, and of vegetable juices generally. These may frequently be removed by dipping the fabric in sour milk and

2

drying it in the sun, repeating the operation several times if needed. All oily substances (except paint oils,) can be expelled from carpets by holding a very hot iron as near as it can be placed without burning. Porous paper, or common brown paper laid upon a grease spot and run over several times with a hot sad-iron (flat-iron,) will absorb the oil.

Ox-gall has been used from time immemorial, by jobbing dyers, for removing grease stains from delicate colored woolen fabrics. It is mixed with cold water at the rate of about three gallons of water to the contents of one ox-gall.. The fabric is immersed in this and squeezed between the hands, or slightly pounded until the stains are removed. The fabric must then be very thoroughly washed in cold water, for if any of the gall is left in it the odor becomes very offensive. Strong cold soap suds, or a bath of dilute aqua ammonia, is preferable to ox-gall in cleaning such fabrics.

Oxalic, acetic, or any other acid must never be used to remove ink and iron stains from any kind of cloth but that which is white, because these acids will discharge pink, lilac, and other colors. The best way to use oxalic acid to remove ink stains from white muslin is to put some of the crystals of the salt upon the stain—making a small bag of the cloth between the fingers—and pour some hot water upon them until they are dissolved, when the stain will have disappeared with the crystals of the acid.

A mixture of alcohol and turpentine (burning fluid) is excellent for removing grease and other stains from light-colored gloves and silks. Benzole is also equally as good; but when using these substances beware of coming near a fire or a light of any kind, as they are very inflammable, and many painful accidents from burning have occurred by their careless use.

To Remove Resin Spots from Silk.—Many silk dresses receive stains from turpentine being spilled upon them. These stains are due to the resin which is held in solution by the turpentine, and which remains in the silk after the volatile or spirituous portion has evaporated. Alcohol, applied to the stains with a clean sponge, will remove the spots, because alcohol dissolves the resin. The silk stains should be moistened with the alcohol first, and allowed to remain soaked for a few minutes. Fresh alcohol is then applied with the sponge, and with a slight rubbing motion. It is then wiped as dry as possible and afterward permitted to dry perfectly in the open air. Alcohol also removes grease and oil spots from silk and woolen dresses, but oil generally leaves a yellow stain behind. A mixture of alcohol and the refined light petroleum, called benzone, is excellent for cleaning light kid gloves, ribbons, and silks. It is applied with a clean sponge. Persons who apply these liquors and mixtures to cleaning silks, gloves, &c., must be careful to do so in an apartment where there is neither fire nor lamp burning, under the penalty of an explosion.

To Remove Grease Spots from Wool.—In removing the grease from wool, use a very weak alkaline solution as a substitute for soap, because if the solution is too strong it will act chemically upon the wool, tending to dissolve it, and thus impair its strength and luster.

Solvent for Old Putty and Paint.—Soft soap mixed with a solution of potash or caustic soda; or pearlash and slaked lime mixed with sufficient water to form a paste. Either of these, laid on with an old brush or rag, and left for some hours, will render it easily removable.

To remove the stains on spoons caused by using them for boiled egg, take a little common salt, moist between the thumb and finger, and briskly rub the stain, which will soon disappear

To Clean Paint.—Smear a piece of flannel in common whiting, mixed to the consistency of common paste, in warm water. Rub the surface to be cleaned quite briskly, and wash off with pure cold water. Grease spots will, in this way, be almost instantly removed, as well as other filth, and the paint will retain its brilliancy and beauty unimpaired.

To Remove Ink Stains.—As soon as the ink is spilled, take a little milk and saturate the stain, soak it up with a rag. and apply a little more milk, rubbing it well. In a few minutes the ink will be completely removed.

To Remove Mildew.—Wet the cloth which contains the mildew with soft water; rub it well with white soap, then scrape some fine chalk to powder, and rub it well into the cloth; lay it out on the grass in the sunshine, watching it, to keep it damp with soft water. Repeat the process the next day, and in a few hours the mildew will all disappear.

To Keep Silk.—Silk articles should not be kept folded in white paper, as the chloride of lime used in bleaching the paper will probably impair the color of the silk. Brown or blue paper is better; the yellowish smooth India paper is best of all. Silk intended for dress should not be kept long in the house before it is made up, as lying in the folds will have a tendency to impair its durability by causing it to cut or split, particularly if the silk has been thickened by gum. Thread lace vails are very easily cut; satin and velvet being soft, are not easily cut, but dresses of velvet should not be laid by with any weight above them. If the nap of thin velvet is laid down, it is not possible to raise it up again. Hard silk should never be wrinkled, because the thread is easily broken in the crease, and it never can be rectified. The way to take the wrinkles out of silk scarfs or handkerchiefs is to moisten the surface evenly with a sponge and some weak glue, and then pin the silk with toilet pins around the selvages, on a mattress or feather bed, taking pains to draw out the silk as tight as possible. When dry, the wrinkles will have disappeared. The reason of this is obvious to every person. It is a nice job to dress light colored silk, and few should try it. Some silk articles may be moistened with weak glue or gum water, and the wrinkles ironed out on the wrong side by a hot flat iron.

To Prevent the Ravages of the Woolen Moth.—The ravages of the woolen moth may be prevented, in a measure, by the use of any of the following substances: camphor; and perhaps the most agreeable for wearing apparel, a mixture of one ounce of cloves, one ounce of rhubarb, and one ounce of cedar shavings, tied up in a bag, and kept in a box or drawer. If the substance be dry, scatter it in the folds of the cloth, carpet, blankets, or furs; if liquid, scatter it freely in the boxes, or on the cloth or wrapper, laid over and around it.

To Remove Foul Air from Wells.—It is well known that many accidents occur to persons going down into wells to clean them, owing to the noxious gas in such places. To remove the gas before descent is made into any well, a quantity of burned but unslaked lime should be thrown down. This, when it comes in contact with whatever water is below, sets free a great amount of heat in the water and lime, which rushes upward, carrying all the deleterious gases with it; after which descent may be made with perfect safety. The lime also absorbs carbonic acid in the well.

Disinfectants.—1. 1 pint of the liquor of chloride of zinc, in 1 pailful of water, and 1 pound of chloride of lime in another pailful of water. This is perhaps the most effective of any thing that can be used, and, when thrown upon decayed vegetable matter of any description, will effectually destroy all offensive odors. 2. 3 or 4 pounds of sulphate of iron (copperas) dissolved in a pailful of water will, in many cases, be sufficient to remove all offensive odors.   3. Chloride of lime is better to scatter about damp places, in yards, in damp cellars, and upon heaps of filth.

A Cheap and Truthful Barometer.—Put a small quantity of finely pulverized alum in a long, half-ounce phial, and fill it with spirits of wine; when the atmosphere is dry and clear, the spirits will be as clear as a crystal; but, on the approach of rain or foul weather, the alum will rise in the center, in the form of a spiral cloud, which is an infallible indication of rain or bad weather.

To Harden Lard or Tallow Candles.—To 5 pounds lard or tallow, add ¼ pound each, alum and saltpeter, first dissolved in a little water; then boil together till the water all evaporates.

Candles will burn much clearer, and the tallow will not "run," if you steep the wicks in lime water and saltpeter, and then dry them.

To Make Carmine.—Boil 1 pound 4 ounces of ground cochineal and a very little of the carbonate of soda in 4 gallons of soft water for twenty minutes; then take it from the fire, and add 6 drachms of alum, and stir the mixture for a few minutes, and let it stand for a quarter of an hour for the dregs to subside; then run off the clear liquor; strain the sediment through a fine sieve or cloth, and then, when cold, add the whites of two eggs to the sediment; fish-glue or isinglass will answer as well as the eggs. The muriate of tin may be used instead of alum.   The weight of the cochineal may be reduced to any amount to make a small quantity, if the proportions are preserved.

Preventing the Fracture of Glass Chimneys.—The glass chimneys which are now in such extensive use, not only for oil lamps, but also for the burners of oil and coal gas, very frequently break, and not only expose to danger those who are near them, but occasion very great expense and inconvenience, particularly to those who are resident in the country. The breaking of these glasses very often arises from knots in the glass where it is less perfectly annealed, and also from an inequality of thickness at their lower end, which prevents them from expanding uniformly by heat.   The evil arising from inequality of thickness may be cured by making a cut with a diamond in the bottom of the tube.

Teeth Set on Edge.—All acid, foods, drinks, medicines, and tooth-washes and powders, are very injurious to the teeth.   If a tooth is put in cider, vinegar, lemon juice, or tartaric acid, in a few hours the enamel will be completely destroyed, so that it can be removed by the finger nail as if it were chalk.   Most people have experienced what is commonly called teeth set on edge.   The explanation of it is, the acid of the fruit that has been eaten has so far softened the enamel of the tooth that the least pressure is felt by the exceedingly small nerves which pervade the thin membrane which connects the enamel and the bony part of the tooth.   Such an effect can not be produced without injuring the enamel.   True, it will become hard again, when the acid has been removed by the fluids of the mouth, just as an egg-shell that has been softened in this way becomes hard again by being put in the water.   When the effect of sour fruit on the teeth subsides, they feel as well as ever, but they are not as well. And the oftener it is repeated, the sooner the disastrous consequences will be manifested.

Yeast.—Those who are not in the neighborhood of bakers, and can not procure the fermentation called yeast, may make a better substitute as follows: boil 1 pound flour, ¼ pound brown sugar, and a little salt in 2 gallons water for an hour.   When milk-warm, bottle and cork it close, and it will be ready for use in twenty-four hours.

Preserving Paintings.—Many valuable paintings that are hung against soiled walls of masonry, in churches and other buildings, are subjected to a damp atmosphere, and the canvas becomes moldy. Old pictures, which have become blackened, are restored by washing them with deut-oxide of hydrogen, diluted in eight times its weight of water. The parts touched must be afterward wiped with a clean sponge and water.

Curing Rancid Butter.—A correspondent of the *Rural Register* gives the following recipe for curing rancid butter: For 100 pounds rancid butter, take 2 pounds fine white powdered sugar; 2 ounces saltpeter, finely pulverized, and as much fine dairy salt as you wish to add to the butter to make it to your taste. The butter has to be thoroughly washed in cold water before working in the above ingredients. The amount used should be in proportion to the strongness of the butter.

To Preserve Milk.—Put a spoonful of horseradish into a pan of milk, and it will remain sweet for several days, either in the open air or in the cellar, while other milk will sour.

Brilliant Whitewash.—Take half a bushel of nice unslaked lime; slack it with boiling water, cover it during the process to keep in the steam. Strain the liquid through a fine sieve or strainer, and add to it a peck of clean salt, previously well dissolved in warm water; 3 pounds of ground rice, boiled to a thin paste, and stirred in boiling hot; ½ pound powdered Spanish whiting, and 1 pint of clean glue, which has been previously dissolved by first soaking it well, and then hanging it over a slow fire, in a small kettle, with a large one filled with water. Add 5 gallons of hot water to the whole mixture, stir it well, and let it stand a few days covered from the dirt. It should be put on right hot; for this purpose, it can be kept in a kettle or a portable furnace. It is said that about 1 pint of this mixture will cover a square yard, if properly applied with a brush, as in painting. It answers as well as oil paint for wood, brick, or stone, and is the cheapest. It retains its brilliancy for many years. There is nothing of the kind that will compare with it, either for inside or outside walls. Coloring matter may be put in, and made of any shade you like.

Spanish brown stirred in will make red or pink, more or less, according to the quantity. A delicate tinge of this is very pretty for inside walls. Finely pulverized common clay, well mixed with Spanish brown, before it is stirred into the mixture, makes a lilac color. Lampblack in moderate quantities makes a slate color, very suitable for the outside of buildings. Lampblack and Spanish brown, mixed together, produce a reddish stone color. Yellow ochre stirred in makes yellow wash, but chrome goes farther, and makes a color generally esteemed prettier. In all these cases, the darkness of the shade will of course be determined by the quantity of coloring used. It is difficult to make a rule, because tastes are very different; it would be best to try experiments on a shingle, and let it dry. We have been told that green must not be mixed with lime. The lime destroys the color, and the color has an effect on the whitewash, which makes it crack and peel. If a larger quantity than five gallons is wanted, the same proportion should be observed.

Zinc Wash for Rooms.—Mix oxide of zinc with common size, and apply it with a brush, like lime whitewash, to the ceiling of a room. After this, apply a wash, in the same manner, of the chloride of zinc, which will combine with the oxide and form a smooth cement with a shining surface.

Preserving Butter.—Take two parts of the best common salt, one part of sugar, and one part of saltpeter, and blend the whole completely. Take 1 ounce of this composition for 1 pound of butter; work it well into a mass and close it up for use. Butter thus cured requires to stand three or four weeks before it is used.

To Make Butter Yellow, in Winter.—Just before the termination of churning, put in the yolks of eggs, and your butter will be as yellow as gold.

Water-proof Oil Blacking.—Take 2 ounces yellow beeswax, shaved fine, and 2 ounces pulverized resin, and melt in ½ pound currier's oil (lard will do,) over a slow fire, then add ½ pound fresh tallow and continue the heat till all are thoroughly incorporated. Apply this compound freely to all parts, the soles as well as the uppers, and dry in, by a moderate heat. Repeat the process as long as the leather will absorb the grease, and you will not be troubled with damp feet. While this compound is sufficiently water-proof, it does not, like India-rubber, and other compounds used for the same purpose, completely close the pores of the leather, making it impervious to the air, and thereby causing it to decay, but tends to preserve it to a period of double its natural wear. The process of alternately wetting and drying leather (by going out in wet weather and then drying) causes it do decay much sooner than it otherwise would; and if completely saturated with this composition two or three times before much worn, then occasionally afterward, so as to fill up the pores, and keep out the water, it would last twice as long.

Polish for Old Furniture.—Take 1 pint alcohol; 1 pint linseed oil; 1 ounce powdered gum arabic; ¼ ounce tincture red saunders; ¼ ounce bergamot. Put it on with cotton flannel, then rub it hard with another dry piece.

Another.—Dissolve beeswax in turpentine, and apply same way.

To Prevent Flies from Injuring Picture-frames, Glasses, etc.—Boil three or four onions in 1 pint of water; then, with a gilding brush do over your glass and frames, and the flies will not alight on the articles so washed. This may be used without apprehension, and it will not do the least injury to the frames.

To Clean Silver and Britannia.—Use whiting, finely-powdered, and moistened with alcohol.

To Make Cloth Fire-Proof.—Take 2½ pounds sugar of lead, ½ pound litharge, and boil them for half an hour in 4 gallons water, when the liquor is allowed to settle. Any quantity of the clear fluid that will suffice to cover the cloth to be operated upon, is now taken, and the cloth immersed and freely saturated in it; then dried in the open air.

The cloth is now immersed in a hot and moderately strong solution of silicate of soda, then thoroughly washed in cold water, and dried. Children's clothes prepared in this way will not take fire.

Porous Water-Proof Cloth.—This quality is given to cloth by simply passing it through a hot solution of weak glue and alum. This is what is done by paper-makers to make writing paper, the very thing which constitutes the difference between it and blotting paper, only on cloth the nap like the fur of a beaver, will preserve the cloth from being wet through, as the rain will not adhere, but trickle off as soon as it falls, and moisture will not adhere at all.

To apply it to the cloth, make up a weak solution of glue, and while it is hot, add a piece of alum, about an ounce to two quarts, and then brush it over the surface of the cloth while it is hot, and it is afterward dried. Cloth in pieces may be run through this solution, and then wrung out of it and dried. By adding a few pieces of soap to the glue the cloth will feel much softer. Goods in pieces may be run through a tubful of weak glue, soap, and alum, and squeezed between rollers. This would be a cheap and expeditious mode of preparing them. Woolen goods are prepared by brushing them with the above mixture, first on the inside, then with the grain or nap of the cloth, after which it is dried. It is best to dry this first in the air, and then in a stove room, at a low heat, but allow the cloth to remain for a considerable time, to expel the moisture completely. This kind of cloth, while it is sufficiently water-proof to keep out moisture and rain—being quite impervious to water—is pervious to the air. Many fishermen know that by boiling their pants, jackets, nets, and sails in a pot with oak bark and fish skins, and afterward drying them, they become waterproof. The composition mentioned above is of nearly the same nature as the fish-glue and oak bark, and, consequently, the same effects are produced. The composition is stated to be improved by adding about one-fourth the quantity of the sulphate of copper to the alum. Cloth made waterproof in this manner will resist the effects of water even if it is somewhat warm, but it loses its waterproof properties if boiled. Persons who are exposed to the inclemency of the weather will find it to their advantage, as a means of preserving health, to prepare their clothes in the way we have described. Several corps in the French army are provided with porous water-proof cloth tunics prepared in a similar manner. They have been found very beneficial when the troops are in active service.

Another.—Take 2¼ pounds of alum, and dissolve this in 10 gallons of boiling water; then, in a separate vessel, dissolve the same quantity of sugar of lead in 10 gallons of water, and mix the two solutions. The cloth is now well handled in this liquid until every part of it is penetrated; then it is squeezed and dried in the air, or in a warm apartment, then washed in cold water and dried again, when it is left for use. If necessary, the cloth may be dipped in the liquid and dried twice before being washed. The liquor appears curdled when the alum and lead solutions are mixed together. This is the result of double decomposition; the sulphate of lead, which is an insoluble salt, being formed. The sulphate of lead is taken up in the pores of the cloth, and it is unaffected by rain or moisture; and yet it does not render the cloth air-tight. Such cloth is also partially non-inflammable. A solution of alum itself will render cloth, prepared as described, partially waterproof; but it is not so good as the sulphate of lead. Such cloth—cotton or woolen—sheds rain like the feathers on the back of a duck.

To Soften Hard Water.—Dissolve 1 pound of sal soda in 1 gallon of boiling water, and to this add ¾ pound of fresh burned and slaked lime; agitate these together, and allow the water to rest for sediment to settle. The clear liquor is next poured off, and forms a caustic ley. A little of this ley is now placed in a glass tumbler, and a few drops of hydrochloric (muriatic) acid are added. If the liquor effervesces, a little more acid must be added. The acid is a test, and when the ley ceases to effervesce by adding a few drops of the acid, it is a sign that it is fit for use. This caustic ley will precipitate sulphates and carbonates in hard water, and render the latter soft and fit for feeding into boilers, or for washing purposes. A certain quantity of this ley is requisite to treat a certain quantity of hard water, and the way to determine this is as follows: Take a gallon of hard water to be softened; add 1 ounce of the prepared ley to it, and allow the sediment to settle for ten minutes; now add another ounce of the ley, and if no flocculent material, or precipitate, appears, it is a sign that one ounce of the ley will purify one gallon of the hard water.

The ley must be added until all the earthy impurities in the water are thrown down. From these data, a calculation can be made for thousands of gallons. Thus, for a 10-horse power boiler, 600 gallons of water will be required in 10 hours, and $3\frac{3}{4}$ gallons of this ley will be required to purify it. This should be done in a setting tank, and the purified water run off into a supply cistern for feeding the boiler. The water must not be rendered caustic, or it will act on the metal.

Fleas on Dogs.—I have found the following receipt most effectual in killing fleas on dogs, viz.: to rub them well over with whisky; it acts like magic, killing them *instanter;* if all are not polished off in one application, another will be necessary.

To Brighten Brass.—The pickle which is employed for brightening brass is made with equal parts of nitric and muriatic acids, diluted with four times their bulk of water. Sulphuric acid, diluted with three times its weight of water, and used hot, also makes a good brightening pickle for brass, which must be thoroughly washed in hot water afterward, and then dried in warm saw-dust.

To Keep Metals from Rusting.—A most excellent oil to preserve the locks of guns and bright iron from rusting, may be made as follows: Take some refined petroleum, and add about ten per cent. in measure, of castor oil, and stir together well, and it is ready for use. This is also a good lubricating oil for machinery.

To Brown Gun-Barrels.—Take tincture of iodine, and dilute with $\frac{1}{2}$ its bulk with water; apply it to the surface of the barrel with a clean rag; let it stand about six hours; then brush the metal, rub it over with some beeswax dissolved in turpentine, and it is done.

To Prevent Skippers in Ham.—Keep your smokehouse perfectly dark, and the moth which deposits the egg will never enter it. Smoke with, green hickory wood, and the flavor will be much better than by any other.

To Prevent Frost.—Frost can only occur where the atmosphere is dry and clear. Have a pile of straw or any other refuse matter, on hand, near your garden or orchard, and when there is any sign of frost, wet it and set it on fire about sundown, and the smoke and wind which it will create will effectually keep away all frost, especially if the fires be built on several sides of the area to be protected.

A Substitute for Coffee.—Take a peck of rye and cover it with water, let it steep or boil until the grain swells, or commences to burst; then drain and dry it. Now roast to a deep-brown color, and prepare as other coffee, allowing twice the time for boiling. This alone makes a very good coffee; but if mixed with equal parts of carrots or beets, sliced thin and dried in an oven till brown, it will make an article but little, if any, inferior to the genuine.

To Exterminate Rats.—Take about one-half a tea-cupful of potash, and wrap it in cotton batten, and place it in the holes in your cellars, and stop them up. They will take the batten to build nests, and burn their feet with the potash, whereupon they will quit the premises instanter.

Another.—Take equal parts of powdered nux vomica and oatmeal, and mix them thoroughly together, and put the mixture a short distance from the holes.

Poison Balls for Rats and Roaches.—Put a drachm of phosphorus in a bottle along with two ounces of water: cork it, and plunge it into a vessel of boiling water till the phosphorus is dissolved; then pour it into a mortar along with 3 ounces of lard, and rub it briskly, adding some water, about half a pound of flour, and 2 ounces of sugar. The whole is made into a paste, and divided into balls about the size of marbles. This is laid down on the floor, or shelves, for rats, cockroaches, or other vermin, who eat and are destroyed. For rats, cheese is better than sugar, and tallow better than lard. The cockroaches are fond of any thing sweet; hence sugar is a bait for them. Potatoes will answer as well as the flour. These balls should be laid down at night, and carefully lifted in the morning, taking care not to let any be touched by a child. They should be locked up through the day.

To Destroy Cockroaches and other Vermin.—An infallible means of destroying cockroaches, beetles, &c., is to strew the roots of black hellebore on the floor at night. Next morning the whole family of these insects will be found either dead or dying, for such is their avidity for the poisonous plant, that they never fail to eat it, when they can get it. Black hellebore grows in marshy grounds, and may be had at all herb-shops.

To Preserve Eggs.—Take 1 pint of good salt, 1 pint of slaked lime, and dissolve in 3 gallons of water. Put your eggs in this pickle, and keep them covered with it, and in a cool cellar.

Another.—Put your eggs in a basket, sieve, colander, or in a piece of thin muslin, and dip them into boiling water, and let them remain till you can count twenty. This forms a thin skin inside the shell, which makes them impervious to the air. Now pack them with the little end down, and keep in a cool place. If packed in salt, after having been subjected to this treatment, they will keep good two years.

How to Catch all the Fish you Want.—Take the juice of smallage or lovage, and mix it with any kind of bait. Bait your hooks and go to fishing, and you will catch all the fish you need. A few drops of oil of rhodium is also good.

Another.—Take cocculus indicus, pulverize, and mix with dough; then scatter broadcast over the water. This will be seized with great avidity by the fish, which will so completely intoxicate them that they will turn belly up on the surface of the water by hundreds. Now have a boat ready, and pick up what you want, and put them in a tub of fresh water, and in a few minutes they will be all right again.

How to Catch Wild Geese and other Wild Fowls Alive.—Soak wheat or other grain in strong alcohol or whisky, and strew it plentifully where they frequent, and it will intoxicate them so you can go up and catch them alive. Of course, they will have to be watched, so as to take them soon after eating.

Sealing-Wax for Bottles, Fruit-Cans, &c.—Melt together 6 ounces resin, 2 ounces shellac, 4 ounces Venice turpentine, and color with lampblack.

A Substitute for a Carpet.—Save all your old newspapers, and when you get enough for the purpose, make a paste, same as for putting on the wall, and lay them down, one by one, till your floor is covered. Let it dry; then lay down another coating in the same way. When again dry, get some good wall paper, of suitable color, and paste all over it. When dry, go over it with a good coat of varnish, and you will have a nice covering for your floor, which will wear as long as a carpet, and look as well as oil-cloths. This is a cheap method of covering bedroom floors, and other rooms which are not much used. When required to be cleaned, wipe it off with a wet cloth.

CULINARY DEPARTMENT.

General Remarks on Bread.—In order to secure good bread, it is the best economy to purchase the *best* flour, even at a greater cost. Newly-ground flour, which has never been packed, is much superior to barrel-flour. *Indian meal,* also, is much the best when freshly ground.

No one thing is of more importance in making bread than thoroughly kneading it. When bread is taken out of the oven hot, never set flat on a table, as it sweats the bottom, and acquires a bad taste from the wood. Take it out of the tins, wrap it in clean linen, and set it up on the end till cool. If it has a thick, hard crust, first wrap it with a wet cloth, then a dry one over it, and let it sweat till it becomes soft.

Wheat Bread.—Take 2 quarts of wheat flour, half a cup of molasses, a tea-cupful of lively yeast, mixed up with warm water; let it stand in a warm place an hour and a half; if necessary, add a little saleratus; bake an hour and a half.

Salt-rising Bread.—Take a little warm water, with a little salt in it, and mix with enough flour to make about a quart of batter (it will rise quicker with a handful of meal stirred in), and set in warm water, near the stove, where it will keep moderately warm. When it rises and comes up, near the point of running over, mix your bread, place in tins, and set near the stove to rise. When it comes up light, put in a hot oven, and bake till well done. Some prefer molding it over after it comes up, and then re-rising before baking.

Brown Bread.—Put the Indian meal in your bread-pan; sprinkle a little salt among it, and wet it thoroughly with scalding water. When it is cool, put in your rye, add 2 gills of lively yeast, and mix it with water as stiff as you can knead it. Let it stand an hour and a half, in a cool place in summer, on the hearth in winter. It should be put into a very hot oven, and baked three or four hours.

Rye and Indian Bread.—Take about 2 quarts of Indian meal, and scald it; then add as much rye meal, a tea-cupful of molasses, half a pint of lively yeast. If the yeast be sweet, no saleratus is necessary. If sour, put in a little; let it stand from one to two hours, till it rises; then bake it about three hours.

Light Biscuit.—Ten pounds flour, a pint of buttermilk, half a tea-spoonful of saleratus; put into the buttermilk a small piece of butter, or lard, rubbed into the flour; make it about the consistency of bread before baking.

Bread Biscuit.—Three pounds flour, half a pint of Indian meal, a little butter, 2 spoonfuls of lively yeast; set it before the fire, to rise over night; mix it with warm water.

Rolls.—Warm an ounce of butter in half a pint of milk, then add a spoonful and a half of yeast, and a little salt. Put 2 pounds of flour in a pan, and mix in the above ingredients. Let it rise an hour, or over night, in a cool place; knead it well, and make into seven rolls, and bake them in quick oven. Add half a tea-spoonful of saleratus just as you put into the baker.

Short Rolls.—Take about 5 pounds of flour, and a piece of butter half the size of an egg, two spoonfuls of yeast, and mix it with warm milk; make it into a light dough, and let it stand by the fire all night; should it sour, put in a little saleratus. Bake in a quick oven.

PUDDINGS.

Bread Pudding.—Take thin slices of bread (that which is a little dry is best) and put them in layers in your pan; now take a sufficient quantity of milk, eggs, and sugar, which has previously been well beaten together, and turn on till the bread is all well covered, then put in a hot oven and bake till well done. By no means ever beat or stir your bread all up like mush before it is baked, as it makes it heavy, and unfit to be eaten; but pour your milk, eggs, etc., on, and then bake without disturbing it. Add butter and fruit if you like.

Baked Rice Pudding.—Take a large coffee-cup of rice, and gradually heat on the stove in three pints of milk, for an hour or more; now beat up 4 eggs with another pint of milk, in which you have put sugar, seasoning, etc., and stir in and bake in a quick oven, three-quarters of an hour.

Baked Indian Pudding.—First make your meal into a boiled mush, then add your milk, eggs, sugar, and seasoning, well beat together, and bake same as rice or bread pudding.

Another—Always Good.—One quart of milk, 4 eggs, 5 large tea-spoonfuls of Indian meal, nutmeg and sugar to your taste. Boil the milk, and scald the Indian meal in it; then let it cool before you add the eggs. Bake three-quarters of an hour.

Cottage Pudding.—One pint-bowl flour, one teacup milk, one egg, half teacup sugar, one teaspoon soda dissolved in the milk, two teaspoons cream tartar rubbed in the flour. Bake twenty minutes or half an hour. Sauce.

Poor Man's Pudding.—Two quarts milk, one cup uncooked rice, half cup sugar, piece of butter size of walnut, 2 teaspoons salt. Spice to taste. Bake 3 hours, and stir several times during the first hours.

Apple Sago Pudding.—One cup sago, in water enough to swell it, i. e., about 6 cups. Put it on the stove and swell it. In the meantime stew 10 or 12 apples, mix with the swelled sago, and bake three-quarters of an hour. Eat with cream and sugar, or wine sauce.

Wedding Cake Pudding.—Two-thirds of a cup of butter, 1 cup of molasses, 2 cups of milk, 2 teaspoons of saleratus, 4 eggs, 2 pounds of raisins, stoned and chopped, 1 pound of currants, ¼ of a pound of citron. Flour to make a batter as thick as pound-cake; salt and all sorts of spices. Boil or steam five hours. To be eaten with wine sauce.

Salem Pudding.—One cup suet, chopped fine; one cup molasses, one cup milk, one teaspoon soda, three and a half cups flour, two teaspoons cream tartar, one cup raisins, one teaspoon cloves, a little salt. Steam three hours. Wine sauce.

Carrie's Apple Pudding.—Half pint milk, one egg, and flour to make a pretty stiff batter; a little salt. Fill your pudding-dish with sliced apples, pour your batter over them, and steam three hours. Sauce.

Green Corn Pudding.—Take half a dozen ears of green sweet corn, (good size,) and with a sharp-pointed knife split each row of kernels, and scrape from the ear. Mix with this pulp 2 eggs, well beaten, 2 tablespoons sugar, 1 of butter, 1 saltspoon of salt, ½ pint sweet cream, (milk may be substituted, with an extra spoonful of butter,) and one dozen crackers, grated or pounded very fine. Mix well together, and bake three hours, if in a pudding-dish—or two, in custard cups. Use the corn raw.

Baked Plum-Pudding.—Two quarts milk, ten soft crackers, eight eggs, one pound stoned raisins. Spice to taste. Bake from three to four hours. Sauce.

Sunderland Pudding, No. 1.—One quart milk, four eggs, six tablespoons flour, a little salt. Bake in cups twenty minutes. Sauce.

Sunderland Pudding, No. 2.—One pint milk, one pint flour, three eggs, salt.

Quaking Plum Pudding.—Take slices of light bread, spread thin with butter, and lay in a pudding-dish layers of this bread, and raisins, till within an inch of the top. Add 5 eggs, well beaten, and a quart of milk, and pour over the pudding; salt and spice to taste. Bake it twenty or twenty-five minutes, and eat with liquid sauce. Before using the raisins, boil them in a little water, and put it all in.

Mrs. Weston's Baked Indian Pudding.—Take 6 table-spoonfuls of meal, and stir molasses or sirup enough in it to have the meal all wet, and no more; that will sweeten enough: then take 1 quart of milk, and boil it; pour it boiling hot on the meal; stir the meal while pouring the milk on to it, so as not to make it lumpy. Stir in 3 table-spoonfuls of wheat flour, wet with a little cold milk; salt and spice to the taste, and bake two hours; and it will be equal to any meal pudding with eggs and suet that can be made.

Fig Pudding.—Half pound of figs, ½ pound of flour, two eggs, ¼ pound of suet, a little sugar, and a little wine, salt, and various spices. To be boiled in a tin shape for four hours.

Mrs. Hamlin's Pudding.—One pint sweet milk, 1 tea-spoonful soda, ½ cup molasses, 2 cups Indian meal, 1 cup flour. Steam two hours.

Bird's-Nest Pudding.—Put into 3 pints of boiling milk 6 crackers, pounded fine, and 1 cup of raisins; when cool, add 4 eggs, well beaten, a little sugar, and four good-sized apples, pared and cored. To be baked and eaten with warm sauce.

Carrot Pudding.—Half pound grated carrot, half pound grated potato, half pound suet chopped fine, half pound flour, spices of all sorts, salt, raisins, and citron to taste. Steam five hours. To be eaten with wine sauce.

Corn Starch Pudding.—Let those who are fond of good dessert puddings get the Oswego Corn Starch, and make according to the directions accompanying each package. An excellent diet for the sick.

Tapioca Pudding.—Six table-spoonfuls of tapioca, one quart of milk, three eggs, sugar and spice to your taste; heat the milk and tapioca moderately; bake it one hour.

Mrs. Meacham's Boiled Indian Pudding.—Two cups Indian meal, two cups flour, one egg, half cup molasses, one teaspoon soda, two teaspoons cream tartar. Wet with milk till about as thick as cake. Steam three hours. Never lift the cover while it is cooking, or it will not be light. Sauce.

Mrs. H.'s Berry Pudding.—Coffee-cup sweet milk, one-third cup molasses, one egg, a little salt, a little saleratus, three and a half teacups flour. Beat all with a spoon. Flour, three pints berries, and stir in with a knife. Steam three hours. Sauce.

Madame F.'s Pudding Sauce.—Large coffee-cup powdered sugar, quarter pound butter. Beat together very light; then add one egg, but do not beat much after the egg is in. Stir in one glass of wine. Take off the tea-kettle cover, set the sauce in, and let it melt till as thick as cream, stirring it occasionally.

Hasty Pudding.—Boil water, a quart, three pints, or two quarts, according to the size of your family; sift your meal, stir five or six spoonfuls of it thoroughly into a bowl of water; when the water in the kettle boils, pour into it the contents of the bowl; stir it well and let it boil up thick·

put in salt to suit your own taste, then stand over the kettle, and sprinkle in meal, handful after handful, stirring it very thoroughly all the time, and letting it boil between whiles. When it is so thick that you stir it with difficulty, it is about right. It takes about half an hour's cooking. Eat it with milk or molasses. Either Indian meal or rye meal may be used. If the system is in a restricted state, nothing can be better than *rye* hasty pudding and good molasses. This diet would save many a one the horrors of dyspepsia.

A Good Sauce for Baked Puddings.—Take 1 pint of water, a large tea-cup of sugar, piece of butter size of a large egg, a little nutmeg and essence of lemon, and bring to a boil. Now take a little flour, or corn-starch, (which is best,) well beat into a paste, and thinned, and stir in gradually, till of the consistency of cream, or as thick as you like; then add a large table-spoonful of vinegar or brandy.

Sauce for Boiled Puddings.—Equal parts of butter and white sugar well beaten together, till it becomes light; then seasoned with nutmeg, and wine or brandy.

PIES AND PASTRY.

Common Paste for Pies.—Take a quantity of flour proportioned to the number of pies you wish to make, then rub in some lard and salt, and stir it with cold water; then roll it out, and spread on some lard, and scatter over some dry flour; then double it together, and cut it to pieces, and roll it to the thickness you wish to use it.

Good common Pie Crust.—Allow one hand as full of flour as you can take it up for each pie; and for each three handfuls, allow two heaping spoonfuls of lard or butter; rub in a part, as directed, and roll in the rest.

Cream Crust.—This is the most healthy pie crust that is made. Take cream, sour or sweet, add salt, and stir in flour to make it stiff: if the cream is sour, add saleratus in proportion of one tea-spoonful to a pint; if sweet, use very little saleratus. Mold it as little as you can.

Rich Puff Paste.—Weigh an equal quantity of butter with as much fine flour as you judge necessary, mix a little of the former with the latter, and wet it with as little butter as will make it into a stiff paste. Roll it out, and put all the butter over it in slices, turn in the ends, and roll it thin; do this twice, and touch it no more than can possible be avoided.

Paste for a Good Dumpling.—Rub into a pound of flour six ounces of butter; then work it into a paste, with two well-beaten eggs and a little water. If you bake this paste, a large table-spoonful of loaf sugar may be added to it.

Paste for Family Pies.—Rub into one pound and a half of flour half a pound of butter; wet it with cold water sufficient to make a stiff paste, work it well, and roll it out two or three times.

Plain Mince Pies.—These may be made of almost any cheap pieces of meat, boiled till tender; add suet or salt pork chopped very fine; two-thirds as much apple as meat; sugar and spice to your taste. If mince pies are eaten cold, it is better to use salt pork than suet. A lemon and a little syrup of sweetmeats will greatly improve them. Clove is the most important spice.

Apple Mince Pies.—To twelve apples chopped fine, add six beaten eggs, and half a pint of cream. Put in spice, sugar, raisins or currants, just as you would for meat mince pies. They are very good.

Cherry Pies.—The common red cherry makes the best pie. A large deep dish is best. Use sugar in the proportion directed for black-berries.

Whortleberry or Blackberry Pies.—Fill the dish not quite even full, and to each pie of the size of a soup plate, add four large spoonfuls of sugar, for blackberries and blueberries; dredge a very little flour over the fruit before you lay on the upper crust.

Apple Pie.—Peel the apples, slice them thin, pour a little molasses, and sprinkle some sugar over them; grate on some lemon peel or nutmeg. If you wish to make richer, put a little butter on the top.

Cocoa Nut Pie.—One good-sized cocoa-nut peeled and grated, 1 quart of milk sweetened like custard, a piece of butter the size of a walnut in each pie; four eggs to the quart.

Mince Pies.—Meat finely chopped, five pounds; good apples, 7 pounds; sugar, 3 pounds; raisins, 3 pounds; currant jelly, 1 pound; butter, 4 ounces; mace or cinnamon, 1 ounce. When this is prepared, make a crust of two-thirds the usual quantity of lard, and one-third of fat salt pork, very finely chopped; all of which should be rubbed in flour and wet with cold water. Bake in a slow oven one hour.

Pineapple Pie.—Pare and grate large pineapples, and to every teacup of grated pineapple, add half a tea-cupful of fine white sugar; turn the pineapple and sugar into dishes lined with paste; put a strip of the paste around the dish; cover the pie with paste, wet and press together the edges of the paste; cut a slit in the center of the cover, through which the vapor may escape. Bake thirty minutes.

Augusta's Lemon Pie.—Juice and grated rind of three lemons, 3 eggs, and three tablespoons sugar to a lemon. Bake in puff paste.

Mrs. C.'s Pumpkin Pie.—Stew a large-sized pumpkin in about 1 pint of water till dry, sift through a colander; add 2 quarts milk scalded, 6 eggs, heaped tablespoon ginger, half as much cinnamon, 2 coffee-cups molasses, 2 coffee-cups sugar, 2 teaspoons salt. Bake in a pretty hot oven, one hour at least.

Jane P.'s Lemon Cream Pie.—One cup sugar, 1 cup water, 1 raw potato, grated, juice, grated rind of 1 lemon; bake in pastry top and bottom. This will make one pie.

Dedham Cream Pie.—Bake your paste not too rich, in a common pie plate *first.* Boil 1 pint of milk; when boiling, stir in half cup flour, one cup of sugar, and the yolks of two eggs; beat well together. Cook long enough not to have a raw taste; add juice and grated rind of one lemon, and a little salt; beat the whites of the 2 eggs, with a cup of sugar, to a stiff froth; spread over the pie when filled, and brown in the oven.

German Puffs.—One pint milk, five eggs, two ounces butter, ten spoon-fuls flour. Bake in cups. Sauce.

Rhubarb Pie.—Take the tender stalks of rhubarb, strip off the skin, and cut the stalks into very thin slices. Line deep the plates with pie crust, then put in the rhubarb in layers, each layer to be covered with a thick coating of sugar. Put on your crust, press it down tight around the edge of the plate, and prick the crust with a fork, so it will not burst in baking, and let out the juices of the pie. Bake in a slow oven. Never stew rhu-barb for pies before baking.

Custard Pie.—For a large pie, put in three eggs, a heaping table-spoon-ful of sugar, one pint and a half of milk, a little salt, and some nutmeg grated on. For crust, use common pastry.

Rice Pie.—Boil your rice soft; put one egg to each pie, one table-spoon-ful of sugar, a little salt, and nutmeg.

Lemon Pie.—Take one lemon and a half, cut them up fine, one cup of molasses, half a cup of sugar, two eggs; mix them together; prepare your plate, with a crust in the bottom; put in half the materials, lay over a crust; then put in the rest of the materials, and cover the whole with another crust.

CUSTARDS.

In making custards always avoid stale eggs. Never put eggs in very hot milk, as it will poach them. Always boil custards in a vessel set in boiling water.

Boiled Custards.—Boil a quart of milk with a bit of cinnamon and half a lemon peel; sweeten it with nice white sugar; strain it, and when a little cooled, mix in gradually seven well-beaten eggs, and a table-spoonful of rose-water; stir all together over a slow fire till it is of proper thickness, and then pour it into your glasses. This makes good boiled custards.

Another Way.—Take six eggs, leave out the whites, mix your eggs and sugar together, with some rose-water; then boil a pint of rich milk, and put in the eggs; let it simmer a minute or two, and stir it, to prevent its curdling.

Baked Custard.—Two quarts of milk, twelve eggs, twelve ounces of sugar, four spoonfuls of rose-water, one nutmeg.

Cream Custard.—Eight eggs, beat, and put into two quarts of cream; sweeten to taste; add nutmeg and cinnamon.

Custard to turn out.—Mix with the well-beaten yolks of four eggs, a pint of new milk, half an ounce of dissolved isinglass; sweeten with loaf sugar, and stir over a slow fire till it thickens; pour it into a basin, and stir it till a little cooled; then pour into cups, to turn out when quite cold. Add spice as you like, to the beaten eggs.

CAKE.

Composition Cake.—Two and a quarter pounds of flour, one and three-quarter pounds of sugar, one and a half pounds of butter, three pounds of fruit, six eggs, one pint of milk, one cup of molasses, two glasses of wine, two glasses of brandy, two teaspoons saleratus. Cloves, cinnamon, nutmeg, &c.

Spice Cake.—One pound flour, one pound sugar, half pound butter, four eggs, teacup cream, teaspoon soda, teaspoon cloves, one nutmeg, teaspoon cinnamon, one pound raisins, one glass wine or brandy.

Cream Cake.—One teacup cream, two teacups sugar, three well-beaten eggs, teaspoon saleratus dissolved in wineglass of milk, piece butter, size half an egg, flour to make as thick as pound cake; add raisins, and spice to taste; wine and brandy, if you like.

Gingerbread.—One pound flour, half pound sugar, the yolks of three eggs, half pound of butter; ginger to taste.

Laura Keene's Jelly Cake.—One teacup of sugar, one teacup of milk, two teaspoon of cream of tartar, one pint of flour, one teaspoons of soda, one egg, one tablespoon of melted butter; salt, spice, and bake in thin sheets; when baked, spread jelly of any sort between the sheets. This receipt makes one cake, in three small divisions.

A Philadelphia Sponge Cake.—Take ten eggs, one pound sugar, half pound flour, and lemon juice, or extract, to flavor. Beat the whites to a stiff froth, warm and sift the flour; stir the yolks and sugar together, till light, and add the whites and flour, half at a time, alternately. Stir the whole gently, till bubbles rise to the surface. Bake in a modern oven.

Cider Cake.—Two pounds flour, half pound butter, one pound sugar, teaspoon saleratus, dissolved in one pint of cider; fruit and spice to taste.

An Excellent Plain Tea Cake.—1 cup of white sugar, half a cup of butter, 1 cup of sweet milk, 1 egg, one-half tea-spoonful of soda, 1 of cream tartar, and flour enough to make it like soft gingerbread. Flavor with the juice of a small lemon. This makes one good-sized loaf.

Another Fruit Cake.—1½ pounds of sugar, 1½ pounds of flour, ¾ pounds of butter, 6 eggs, 1 tea-spoon of soda, 1 glass of wine, 1 of brandy, and as much fruit and spice as you can afford, and no more.

Doughnuts.—2 cups sugar, 2 cups milk, 1 teaspoon saleratus, 3 eggs, and a piece of butter half as large as a small hen's egg.

Crullers.—6 tablespoons melted butter, 6 tablespoons sugar, 6 eggs, and flour to roll.

Gingerbread Loaf.—1 pound of flour, 1 pound of treacle, ¼ pound of butter, 1 egg, 1 ounce of ginger, some candied peel, and a few caraway-seeds, *ground*, a tea-spoonful of soda. To be baked in a slow oven. The flour to be mixed in gradually; the butter and treacle to be milk-warm; the soda to be put in last. Let it stand half an hour, to rise.

Corn-Starch Cake.—¾ pound sugar, 4 ounces butter, 5 eggs, 1 tea-spoonful cream tartar, ½ a tea-spoonful of soda, ½ pound of corn-starch, ½ a gill of sweet milk.

Short Cake.—3 pounds flour, ½ pound of butter, ½ pound lard. 1 tea-spoonful of soda, 2 of cream tartar; mix with cold milk.

For Strawberry Cake, open these when first baked; take out some of the crumb, and fill the inside with ripe strawberries, sugared; close, and bake the cakes five minutes longer.

Railroad Cake.—A pint of flour, 3 eggs, 1 tea-spoonful of cream of tartar, half a tea-spoonful of soda, a table-spoonful of butter, a tea-spoonful of sugar; bake the butter in a square pan twenty minutes.

Mrs. Gaubert's Coffee Cake.—1 cup coffee, 1 cup of molasses, 1 cup sugar, half cup butter, 1 teaspoon saleratus, 1 egg; spice and raisins to suit the taste.

Soda Cake.—4 eggs, 1 pint of sugar, 1 teacup of butter, 1 cup of sweet milk, 1 quart of flour, 1 tea-spoonful of soda, 2 of cream tartar.

White Cake.—3 cups of sifted flour, 1½ cups of sugar, 1 cup of sweet milk, 1 egg, 2 table-spoonfuls of butter, 2 tea-spoonfuls of cream tartar, 1 tea-spoonful of essence of lemon. Beat the butter and sugar to a cream; then add the milk (in which the soda should be dissolved), the egg, well beaten, and the essence. Mix with the above 2 cups of the flour; and lastly, add the third cup, in which the cream of tartar has been stirred; then bake in pans, or basins, in a quick oven.

Mountain Cake.—1 cup of sugar, 2 eggs, half cup of butter, half cup of milk or water, 2 of flour, tea-spoonful of cream tartar, half tea-spoonful of soda, nutmeg.

Jumbles.—1 pound of butter, 1 of sugar, 2 of flour, 3 eggs, half cup of sour milk, 1 tea-spoonful of soda; roll in white coffee sugar. This will make a large batch. If a small quantity be wanted, take proportionately less of material.

Ginger Snaps—1 cup of butter, 1 of sugar, 1 of molasses, half cup of ginger, tea-spoonful of soda; mix stiff.

A Small Sponge Cake.—One cup of sugar, half cup of milk, one egg, two tea-spoonfuls of cream tartar, one of soda; butter, size of an egg.

Whigs.—Mix half a pound of sugar with six ounces of butter, two eggs, tea-spoonful cinnamon. Stir in two pounds flour, a teacup of yeast, milk enough to make a stiff batter; when light, bake in cups.

Poor Man's Cake.—One cup sugar, half cup butter, one cup sour cream, one egg, flour enough to make a good batter, half tea-spoonful saleratus.

Fruit Cake.—1½ pounds sugar, 1½ pounds flour, ¾ of a pound butter, 6 eggs, a pint sweet milk, 1 tea-spoonful saleratus, 1 glass wine, 1 of brandy, and as much fruit and spice as you can afford, and no more.

Cup Cake.—5 cups flour, 3 cups nice sugar, 1 cup of butter, 4 eggs, 1 cup of good buttermilk, with saleratus enough to sweeten it; 1 nutmeg.

Cookies.—1 cup of butter, 2 cups sugar, 1 cup of cold water, ½ tea-spoonful of saleratus, 2 eggs; flour enough to roll, and no more.

Soft Gingerbread.—1 cup of molasses, 1 cup of sugar, 1 cup of butter, 1 cup of buttermilk, 1 egg, saleratus and cloves. Mix pretty stiff.

Delicate Cake.—Nearly 3 cups flour, 2 cups sugar, ¾ of a cup of sweet milk, whites of 6 eggs, 1 tea-spoonful of cream tartar, ½ tea-spoonful of soda, ½ cup of butter, lemon for flavoring.

Cream Cake.—1 cup of cream, 1 cup of sugar, 2 cups flour, 2 eggs, tea-spoonful of saleratus; flavor with lemon.

Sugar Gingerbread.—1 pound of flour, three-quarters of a pound of sugar, half a pound of butter, 5 eggs; roll very thin on flat tins; do not grease the tins, but slip off the cake, when baked, with a knife.

Waffles.—1 pound of flour, half pound butter, 4 eggs, 1 quart of milk, 1 tea-spoonful of yeast; boil the milk; stir in the butter; beat up warm, and rise them.

Old Colony Cake.—Three eggs, one scant cup of butter, two and a half cups of sugar, one cup of sour milk, three and two-thirds cups of flour, even tea-spoonful of soda; spice to taste; sift a little powdered sugar over the top.

Mrs Work's Sponge Cake.—One coffee-cup flour, one coffee-cup sugar, four eggs, one lemon.

Sponge Cake.—One pound powdered sugar, one pound flour, six eggs, beaten separately, grated rind of one lemon, and part of the juice; one tea-spoonful cream tartar, rubbed with the flour, half tea-spoonful soda, dissolved in half tea-cupful cold water.

Every-day Fruit Cake.—One cup butter, two cups sugar, two cups sour milk, two cups raisins, five cups flour, tea-spoonful saleratus. Salt, cinnamon, cloves, citron, and wine to taste. ✱

Rice Cake.—Three-quarters pound rice flour, half pound butter, eight fresh eggs, one pound sugar, half glass brandy.

Mrs. Holmes' Liberty Cake.—One cup butter, two cups sugar, one cup milk, one pint and a half flour, three eggs, salt and spices, three tea-spoons Babbit's yeast powders.

Pound Cake.—One pound of flour, one pound of sugar, one pound of butter, eight eggs, three spoonfuls rose-water, mace or other spice.

Measure Cake.—Four teacups of flour, two teacups of sugar, one and a half teacups of butter, one glass of brandy, four eggs, and one nutmeg.

Soft Gingerbread.—Two teacups of molasses, one teacup of milk, two eggs, one teaspoon saleratus, and flour to make it thick.

Fannie's Cake.—Half a pound of butter, three quarters of a pound of sugar, one pound of flour, four eggs, one cup of milk, one teaspoon of soda. Cloves, cinnamon, mace, to taste, with or without fruit, as you choose. Bake in a slow oven.

3

BREAKFAST AND TEA CAKES.

Mrs. Moulton's New England Brown Bread.—To four cups of Indian meal, and two of rye meal, add one quart of milk, (skimmed will do, if perfectly sweet,) one cup of molasses, one tea-spoonful of saleratus, and one dessert-spoonful of salt. Stir with a spoon, and bake without rising.

Crackers.—One pint of water, one teacup of butter, one teaspoonful of soda, two of cream tartar, flour enough to make as stiff as biscuit. Let them stand in the oven until dried through. They do not need pounding.

Pop Overs.—Four cups of flour, four eggs, four cups of milk, piece of butter size of two nutmegs, half teaspoon of salt, melt the butter.

Bread Cakes.—Soak some crusts of bread in milk, strain them through the colender very fine, beat in four eggs, and a little flour, just sufficient to thicken the substance; add one tea-spoonful of saleratus. Mix all to make a thin batter, and bake on the griddle.

Artificial Oysters.—Grate as many ears of green corn as will make one pint of pulp; add one tea-cupful of flour, half teacup butter, one egg, and pepper and salt to suit your taste. Dropped and fried in butter.

Rye and Indian Johnny Cakes.—Two cups of rye, two cups of Indian meal, a small tea-spoonful of saleratus, a little salt, sufficient sour milk to make a stiff batter. .Bake in cakes on a griddle; split open and butter them; send to table hot.

Pan Doddlings.—Three teacups of fine rye meal, three teacups of Indian meal, one egg, three table-spoonfuls of molasses; add a little salt and all-spice; sufficient sweet milk to form a batter stiff enough to drop from a spoon. Fry them in hot lard until a nice brown.

Plain Corn Bread, but very Good.—One pint of sour milk, two eggs, one tea-spoonful of saleratus, a little salt; make soft enough to pour out.

Corn Bread.—One quart of sour milk, 2 tea-spoonfuls of saleratus. 4 ounces of butter, three eggs, three table-spoonfuls of flour, and corn meal sufficient to make a stiff batter.

Fruit Fritters.—Make a batter of flour, milk, and eggs, of whatever richness you desire; stir into.it either raspberries, currants, or any other fruit. Fry in hot lard, the same as pancakes.

Mrs. Roberts' Boston Brown Bread.—One heaping quart of rye flour, 1 do. of Graham flour, scanty quart of milk, same quantity of warm water, coffee-cup of molasses, one penny's worth of baker's yeast, or one coffee-cup of home-made yeast, teaspoon saleratus, dessert-spoon of salt. Grease an iron kettle, put in the mixture, and place immediately in a slow oven. Bake six or seven hours.

Ground Rice Griddle Cakes.—Boil a quart of milk; rub smooth a tea-cupful of ground rice, in a gill or two of cold milk, and stir it into the boiling milk; add a little salt, and while it is scalding hot, stir in flour enough to make the right thickness for baking. When cool, add a teacup of yeast, and four eggs. Let it rise light.

Rice Griddle Cakes.—Put a tea-cupful of rice into two tea-cupfuls of water, and boil it till the water is nearly absorbed, and then add a pint and a half of milk. Boil it slowly, until the rice is very soft.

Muffins.—Melt half a teacup of butter in a pint and a half of milk; add a little salt; a gill of yeast, and four eggs; stir in flour enough to make a batter rather stiffer than for griddle cakes. If kept in a moderately warm place, it will rise sufficiently in eight or nine hours.

Rye Cake.—Four and a half cups rye meal, three eggs, one and a half teaspoons cream tartar, one teaspoon soda. Mix with milk, till about as thick as fritters; little salt. To be eaten hot.

Widow's Cake.—Two cups of Indian meal, three cups of wheat flour, one pint of buttermilk, four table-spoons of molasses, two tea-spoons of saleratus. To be eaten hot, with butter, for tea or breakfast.

Boiled Bread.—Two cups of Indian meal, two cups of rye, one of flour, two-thirds cup of molasses, pint and a half of milk; a little salt, and a large tea-spoonful of saleratus; pour it into a long tin pail; put it into a pot; have just enough water to keep it boiling; cover tight, and not boil into the pail, and keep it boiling three hours, and you will have a loaf of bread without any crust.

Rice Cakes for Breakfast.—Put half a pound of rice in soak over night. Early in the morning, boil it very soft, drain it from the water, mix with it a quarter of a pound of butter, and set it away to cool. When it is cold, stir it into a quart of milk, and add a very little salt. Beat six eggs, and sift half a pint of flour. Stir the egg and flour alternately into the rice and milk. Having beaten the whole very well, bake it on the griddle, in cakes about the size of a small dessert-plate. Butter them, and send them to table hot.

Lucy's Rye Cakes.—Four and a half cups rye meal, three eggs, one and a half teaspoon cream tartar, one teaspoon soda; salt, mix with meal till as thick as pound cake.

To Make Good Rusk.—Take a piece of bread dough large enough to fill a quart bowl, one teacup of melted butter, one egg, one tea-spoonful of saleratus; knead quite hard, roll out thin, lap it together, roll to the thickness of a thin biscuit, cut out with a biscuit mold, and set it to raise in a warm place. From twenty to thirty minutes will generally be sufficient. Bake them, and dry thoroughly through, and you will have an excellent rusk to eat with your coffee. You can make them with hop-yeast, and sweeten them, too, if you please. I use milk yeast.

Corn Bread.—Two cups Indian meal, one cup flour, two eggs, large tea-spoonful melted butter, two small tea-spoonfuls cream tartar, one small tea-spoonful soda, one large spoonful brown sugar dissolved in milk; of which add enough to make it as soft as gingerbread.

Cocoa-Nut Cake, No. 1.—One pound of butter, two pounds of sugar, two grated cocoa-nuts—mixed well; one cup of milk and the milk of the cocoa-nuts, one pound and three-quarters of flour, ten eggs, nutmeg if desired, half tea-spoonful of soda. This quantity will make two loaves.

Cocoa-Nut Cake, No. 2.—One pound sugar, half pound butter, three-quarters of a pound flour, six eggs, and one cocoa-nut grated. Cream the butter and sugar, add the yolks well beaten, next the whites well beaten, then the flour, and last the cocoa-nut.

Seed Cakes.—Eight cups of flour, three cups of sugar, one cup of butter, one cup of cream—or milk, if you cannot get cream—one tea-spoonful saleratus, one egg, carraway seed to suit your taste.

Ginger Snaps.—Boil together one pint of molasses and tea-cupful of butter. Let it stand till cool; add two tablespoons of ginger, and one tea-spoonful of soda; flour to roll. Bake quick, in thin rounds, on a flat sheet.

Buns.—One cup butter, one cup sugar, half cup of yeast, half pint of milk; make it stiff with flour; add, if you like, nutmeg.

Silver Cake and Gold Cake.—One cup white sugar, half cup butter, whites of five well-beaten eggs, quarter tea-spoonful soda dissolved in half tea-cupful milk, three-quarters tea-spoonful cream tartar mixed with two cups of flour. Flavor with extract of bitter almonds. The yolks of these five eggs, and the same ingredients, make Gold Cake.

MEATS.

Roast Beef.—The tender-loin, and first and second cuts off the rack, are the best roasting pieces—the third and fourth cuts are good. When the meat is put in the oven, a little salt should be sprinkled on it, and the bony side turned toward the heat first. When the bones get well heated through, turn the meat, and keep a brisk fire; baste it *frequently* while roasting. There should be a little water put into the dripping pan when the meat is put down to roast. If it is a thick piece, allow fifteen minutes to each pound to roast it in—if thin, less time will be required.

Roast Veal.—Veal should be roasted brown, and if a filter or loin, be sure and paper the fat, that as little of it may be lost as possible. When nearly done, baste it with butter and dredge it with flour.

Roast Pork.—Pork should be well done, and requires to be baked a long time. Before roasting, score the skin across with a sharp knife, or it will be difficult to carve. A spare-rib should be basted with a little butter and flour, and sweet herbs, or sage and onions, as best suits the taste.

Roast Turkey.—Let the turkey be picked clean, and washed and wiped dry, inside and out. Have your stuffing prepared, fill the skin of the crop, and also the inside; sew it up, put it in the oven, and roast moderately for three hours. Put a little water in the pan, and baste the outside with a little flour.

Chickens.—Prepare them as above, and bake in a quick oven for one hour, more or less, according to size and age.

To Roast Geese and Ducks.—Boiling water should be poured all over and inside of a goose or duck, before you prepare them for cooking, to take out the strong oily taste. Let the fowl be picked clean, and wiped dry with a cloth, inside and out; fill the body and crop with stuffing; if you prefer not to stuff it, put an onion inside, and roast it brown. It will take about two hours and a half.

Wild Fowls.—These fowls always require a brisk fire, and should be roasted till they are a light brown, but not too much, otherwise they lose their flavor by letting the gravy run out.

Stuffing.—Take dry pieces of bread or crackers, chop them fine, put in a small piece of butter, or a little cream, with sage, pepper, and salt, one egg, and a small quantity of flour, moistened with milk.

Baked Tongue.—Season with common salt and saltpeter, brown sugar, pepper, cloves, mace, and allspice, in fine powder, for a fortnight; then take away the pickle, put the tongue into a small pan, lay some butter on it, cover it with brown crust, and bake slowly, till so tender that a straw would go through it. To be eaten when cold. It will keep a week.

To Boil a Calf's Head and Pluck.—Clean the head very nicely, and soak it in water till it looks very white. The tongue and heart need longer cooking than the rest. Boil these an hour and a half, the head an hour and a quarter, and the liver an hour; tie the brains in a bag, and boil them one hour. Take up all at the same time; serve up the brains with pounded cracker, butter, pepper, vinegar, and salt. To be eaten with butter gravy.

To Boil a Turkey.—Stuff a young turkey, weighing six or seven pounds, with bread, butter, salt, pepper, and minced parsley; skewer up the legs and wings as if to roast; flour a cloth, and pin around it. Boil it forty minutes, then set off the kettle and let it stand, close covered, half an hour more. The steam will cook it sufficiently. To be eaten with drawn butter and stewed oysters.

Beefsteak.—The tender loin is the best piece for broiling. A steak from the round or shoulder clod is good, and comes cheaper. If the beef is not very tender, it should be laid on a board and pounded, before broiling or frying it. Lay it on a gridiron, place it on a hot bed of coals, and broil it as quickly as possible, without burning it. If broiled slow, it will not be good. It takes from fifteen to twenty minutes to broil a steak. For seven or eight pounds of beef, cut up about a quarter of a pound of butter. Heat the platter very hot that the steak is to be put on, lay the butter on it, take up the steak, salt and pepper it on both sides. Beefsteak, to be good, should be eaten as soon as cooked.

Beef Sausages.—To three pounds of beef, very lean, put one pound and a half of suet, and chop very finely; season with sage in powder, allspice, pepper and salt; have skins thoroughly cleaned, and force the meat into them.

Mrs. Pegg's Potted Veal.—Three and a half pounds raw leg of veal chopped, one heaping tablespoon salt, one do. black pepper, eight do. pounded butter cracker, three do. cream or milk, piece butter size of an egg, two eggs, one nutmeg; mold into a loaf, and put in a pan with a little water, and sprinkle over it bits of butter, and some more pounded cracker: bake two hours, and eat cold.

A Nice Way to Cook Chickens.—The following is highly recommended: "Cut the chicken up, put it in a pan, and cover it over with water; let it stew as usual, and when done, make a thickening of cream and flour, adding a piece of butter, and pepper and salt; have made and baked a couple of short cakes, made as for pie-crust, but rolled thin, and cut in small squares. This is much better than chicken pie, and more simple to make. The crust should be laid on a dish, and the chicken gravy put over it while both are hot.

Pork Sausages, fine.—Have two-thirds lean and one-third fat pork; chop very fine. Season with nine tea-spoonfuls of pepper, nine of salt, three of powdered sage, to every pound of meat. Warm the meat, that you can mix it well with your hands; do up a part in small patties, with a little flour mixed with them, and the rest pack in jars. When used, do it up in small cakes, and flour the outside, and fry in butter, or alone. They should not be covered, or they will fall to pieces. A little cinnamon to a part of them will be a pleasant addition. They should be kept where it is cool, but not damp. They are very nice for breakfast.

Meat Pie.—Cut your meat (be it beef, veal, or mutton) into small pieces, and stew till it is very tender; season with salt and pepper, and, if lean, also a little butter, and thicken with flour, so as to make a tolerably thick gravy. Now place between two crusts, in a deep dish, and bake till the crust is well done. Cold roast and boiled meats may be disposed of in this way to very good advantage. Chicken pie is made in the same way.

Chicken Corn Pie.—A lady contributor sends us the following: First, prepare two chickens as for frying; then put them down, and let them stew in a great deal of good, rich, highly-seasoned gravy, until they are just done; then have ready picked two dozen ears of corn; take a very sharp knife and shave them down once or twice, and then scrape the heart out, with the rest already shaved down; then get a baking-pan (a deep one); place a layer of corn on the bottom of the pan, or dish, then a layer of the chicken, and so on, until you get all the chicken in; then cover with the corn, and pour in all the gravy, and put a small lump of butter on the top, and set it to baking, in a not very hot oven. It does not take long to cook: as soon as the corn is cooked, it will be ready to send to the table. It can either be sent in the pan it is baked in, or turned out into another dish. There must be a great deal of gravy, or it will cook too dry.

A New Receipt for Welch Rabbit.—Cut your cheese into small slips, if soft; if hard, grate it down. Have ready a spirit of wine lamp, &c., and deep block tin dish; put in the cheese, with a lump of butter, and set it over the lamp. Have ready the yolk of an egg whipped, with half a glass of Madeira, and as much ale or beer. Stir your cheese, when melted, till it is thoroughly mixed with the butter; then add, gradually, the egg and wine; keep stirring till it forms a smooth mass. Season with cayenne and grated nutmeg. To be eaten with a thin, hot toast.

To Cook a Ham.—An excellent manner of cooking a ham is the following: Boil it three or four hours, according to size; then skin the whole, and fit it for the table; then set in the oven for half an hour, cover it thickly with pounded rusk, or bread-crumbs, and set back for half an hour longer. Boiled ham is always improved by setting it in an oven for nearly an hour, until much of the fat dries out, and it also makes it more tender.

To have Good Corned Beef.—Select a good, nice piece of fresh beef (a briscott or flank piece is best), and put it in a pot of boiling water, and throw in a handful of salt, or enough to make it sufficiently salt to taste, and boil till tender. This will be far superior to any beef pickled in brine.

Mock Terrapin—A Supper Dish.—Half a calf's liver; season and fry brown. Hash it, not very fine; dust thickly with flour; a teaspoon mixed mustard; as much cayenne pepper as will lie on a half-dime; two hard eggs, chopped fine; a lump of butter as large as an egg; a teacup of water. Let it boil together a minute or two. Cold veal will do, if liver is not liked.

Mutton Haricot.—Take a loin of mutton, cut it into small chops, season it with ground pepper, allspice, and salt; let it stand a night, and then fry it. Have good gravy, well seasoned with flour, butter, catsup, and pepper, if necessary. Boil turnips and carrots, cut them small, and add to the mutton, stewed in the gravy, with the yolks of hard-boiled eggs and forcemeat balls. Some green pickles will be an improvement.

Chicken Jelly.—For chicken jelly, take a large chicken, cut it up into very small pieces; bruise the bones, and put the whole into a stone jar, with a cover that will make it water-tight. Set the jar in a large kettle of boiling water, and keep it boiling for three hours. Then strain off the liquid, and season it slightly with salt, pepper, and mace; or with loaf-sugar and lemon juice, according to the taste of the person for whom it is intended. Return the fragments of the chicken to the jar, and set it again in a kettle of boiling water. You will find that you can collect nearly as much jelly by the second boiling. This jelly may be made of an old fowl.

FISH, OYSTERS, ETC.

To Boil Fish.—Fill the fish with a stuffing of chopped salt pork and bread, or bread and butter, seasoned with salt and pepper, and sew it up; then sew it into a cloth, or you can not take it up well. Put it in cold water, with water enough to cover it, salted at the rate of a tea-spoonful of salt to each pound of fish; add about three table-spoonfuls of vinegar. Boil it slowly for twenty or thirty minutes, or till the fin is easily drawn out. Serve with drawn butter and eggs, with capers or nasturtion in it.

Fish can be baked in the same way, except sewing it up in a cloth. Instead of this, cover it with egg and cracker, or butter crumbs.

To Broil Fish.—Let it have been caught one day; lay the inside on the gridiron, and not turn it till it is nearly done.

Fried Eels.—Parboil them a few minutes, then have your fat ready and fry them. An improvement is to dip them into an egg, and crumbs of bread.

To Make a Chowder.—Lay some slices of good fat pork in the bottom of your pot, cut a fresh cod into thin slices, and lay them top of the pork; then a layer of biscuit, and alternately the other materials, till you have used them all; then put in a quart of water. Let it simmer till the fish is done. Previously to its being thoroughly done, add pepper, salt, and such seasoning as you like, and a thickening of flour, with a coffee-cup of good cream, or rich milk.

Clam Chowder is made in the same way, only the heads and hard leathery parts must be cut off.

Oyster Soup.—Bring your water to a boil, and put in your oysters, and let them boil up for a minute or so; season with butter, pepper, and salt. You can use all water, all milk, or a part of both, for the soup.

To Stew Oysters.—Put the liquor in a sauce-pan, and when it all boils up, add the oysters, and pour in a little milk; or, if you choose, water, about a teacup to a quart of oysters. Let them boil up a minute, not more; meantime, put in a small piece of butter, and dredge in some flour; set the saucepan off, and stir the oysters till the butter is melted. Lay some crackers or toasted bread in the dish, and pour on the oysters. They are very fine with roast or boiled turkey.

To Fry Oysters.—Make a batter of two eggs, three gills of milk, two spoonfuls of flour, and some fine bread-crumbs; beat it well; dip each oyster into the batter, and fry in lard.

Oyster Sauce.—When your oysters are opened, take care of all the liquor, and give them one boil in it. Then take the oysters out, and put to the liquor three or four blades of mace; add to it some melted butter, and some good cream; put in oysters, and give them a boil.

Oyster Toast—Bruise one anchovy fine in a mortar; take twenty oysters, cut off their beards, and chop them small. Mix the anchovy and chopped oysters in a saucepan, with as much cream as will make them of a good consistency; add a little cayenne pepper; spread them, when quite hot, on a round of hot, well-buttered toast, cut as for anchovy toast.

Gratin of Lobster.—Take out all the meat from a large lobster; then wash the body, tail, and shells, if the lobster is first cut in halves down the back; then dry and butter them, and sprinkle them with bread-crumbs; chop up the meat fine, with a little parsley and chalot, a few drops of essence of anchovies, a spoonful of vinegar, cayenne pepper, and salt; a little bechamel sauce, and boil all well together: then add the yolk of an egg; put it to cool; then fill your shells, or paper-cases; cover it with bread-crumbs and some pieces of butter; brown them in the oven, and dish on a napkin.

PRESERVES, JELLIES, JAMS, AND PICKLES.

Remarks.—Brass, iron, and copper kettles should never be used for making preserves. Iron-ware, lined with porcelain or tin, is far preferable, and not subject to the verdigris which acids produce on the others. If obliged to use a brass or copper kettle, scour it perfectly clean, and don't let your preserves stand in it one minute after they are done. It is bad economy to use too little sugar in the preservation of fruit. When it once begins to spoil, it can never be reinstated. Jellies, without sufficient sugar, will not congeal. Preserves, to look clear and handsome, should be made with loaf sugar. Small jars are preferable to large ones in putting away preserves, as frequent exposure to the air is not good. After pouring the preserves into jars, cut several round pieces of paper, made to fit the mouth of the jar, and after laying one or two of them over the fruit, pour upon it a tea-spoonful of good brandy; then cover the jar closely with some paper, or bladder-skin, and tie it down in a manner which will entirely exclude the air. If the preserves candy, after being kept a short time, the jar should be placed in a kettle of water, and permitted to boil from half to three-quarters of an hour.

To Preserve Citron.—Pare and cut open the citron; clean out all, except the rind; boil it till soft. To a pound of citron, add a pound of sugar, and a lemon to each pound; put the sugar and lemon together, and boil it till it becomes a sirup, skimming it well; then put the sirup and citron together, and boil it an hour.

Another.—Cut off the hard rind of the melon (which should be preserving citron, not the green cantalope), and cut it in pieces of any size and shape you choose; the slices should be from a quarter to half an inch thick. Weigh your fruit, and to every pound add one of sugar. Put the sugar in a preserving kettle, with a gill of water to each pound of sugar, and some isinglass dissolved in warm water; it will require a quarter of an ounce of isinglass to every five pounds of fruit. When the sugar is dissolved, put it over the fire, and boil and skim it. Then pour the sirup out of the kettle, wash it, and return the sirup to it. Now put in the fruit, and set it over a brisk fire, where it will boil rapidly. When the fruit appears translucent when held up toward the light, it is done. It will take from an hour and a quarter to an hour and a half to cook it. Then take it out, a piece at a time, spread it on dishes, and strain the sirup in a pan. When the sirup is lukewarm, put your fruit in the jars, and pour it over. Let them stand till next day; put brandy paper over it, and paste them. This fruit may be flavored with lemons, sliced, and preserved with it. Do not peel the lemons; cut them in thin slices, and cook them with the fruit. To three pounds of fruit add one lemon. As the citron makes a beautiful but tasteless preserve, it is necessary to flavor it with lemon, orange, or some other fruit. If, when it is a little cool, it should not taste sufficiently of the lemon, a few drops of the essence of lemon may be added.

Good Receipt for Citron Preserves.—Prepare the rind, cut into any form you desire; boil very hard for thirty or forty minutes in alum water, tolerably strong; take them from the alum water, and put into clear cold water; allow them to stand over night; in the morning, change the water, and put them to boil; let them cook until they have entirely changed color, and are quite soft; then make your sirup, allowing one and a-half pounds of white sugar to one pound of fruit; then add your fruit, which needs but little more cooking. Mace, ginger, or lemon flavors nicely. This receipt is the best we ever saw.

To Preserve Watermelon Rinds.—Cut the melon rinds into strips, boil them in weak pearlash water fifteen minutes; then drain out the liquor. Add a pound of loaf sugar to a pound of rind, and boil the whole about two minutes. The sirup will require to be scalded several times.

Cherries.—To a pound of cherries allow three-quarters of a pound of fine loaf sugar; carefully stone them, and as they are done, throw part of the sugar over them; boil them fast with the remainder of the sugar, till the fruit is clear, and the sirup thick. Take off the scum as it rises.

Black Currants.—Gather the currants upon a dry day; to every pound allow half a pint of red currant juice, and a pound and a half of finely pounded loaf sugar. With scissors, clip off the heads and stalks: put the juice, currants, and sugar in a preserving-pan: shake it frequently, till it boils: carefully remove the fruit from the sides of the pan, and take off the scum as it rises: let it boil for ten or fifteen minutes. This preserve is excellent, eaten with cream.

Preserved Apples.—Weigh equal quantities of good brown sugar and of apples: peel, core, and slice them thin. Boil the sugar, allowing to every three pounds a pint of water: skim it well, and boil it pretty thick: then add the apples, the grated peel of one or two lemons, and two or three pieces of white ginger, if you have it: boil till the apples fall, and look clear and yellow. This preserve will keep for years.

Peach Preserves.—Three-quarters of a pound of sugar to a pound of peaches; put your sugar in the kettle, and put on water enough to make a thick sirup; boil and skim it; then put in your fruit, and cook till done. White sugar is best, but brown will do.

Quince Preserves.—Pare your fruit and cut into the proper size, and boil in a very little water till they become sufficiently soft to run a brown-straw through. Now put your sugar in the same water in which your fruit was boiled, bring it to a boil, and skim; then add your fruit, and cook till done, using the same proportion of sugar as in the peach preserves.

Blackberry and Raspberry Preserves.—To every pound of fruit, use three-quarters of a pound of sugar. Make a sirup of your sugar, boil and skim; then add your fruit, and cook till done.

To Preserve Plums.—Make a sirup of clean, brown sugar; clarify it; when perfectly clear, and boiling hot, pour it over the plums, having picked out all the unsound ones, and stems; let them remain in the sirup two days, then drain it off; make it boiling hot, skim it, and pour it over again; let them remain another day or two, then pour them in a preserving kettle, over the fire, and simmer gently, until the sirup is reduced, and thick or rich. One pound of sugar to each pound of plums. Small damsons are very fine, preserved as cherries, or any other ripe fruit; clarify the sirup, and, when boiling hot, put in the plums; let them boil very gently until they are cooked, and the sirup rich. Put them in pots or jars; the next day secure as directed.

Tomato Preserves.—Take the round yellow variety of tomato, as soon as they are ripe, scald and peel; then, to seven pounds of tomatoes add seven pounds of white sugar, and let them stand over night. Take the tomatoes out of the sugar, and boil the sirup, removing the scum. Put in the tomatoes, and boil gently fifteen or twenty minutes; remove the fruit again, and boil until the sirup thickens.· On cooling, put the fruit into jars, and pour the sirup over it, and add a few slices of lemon to each jar, and you will have something to please the taste of the most fastidious.

Crab-Apple Jelly.—Jelly from any other tart apples can be made in the same way as the following. The apples, however, should be sliced. The crab-apples have a very delicate flavor—better for jelly than that of other apples. Pour them in a kettle with just enough water to cover them, and let them boil four hours; then take them off the fire and rub them through a colender; this will separate the seeds and skin from the pulp; then strain them through a flannel bag. Then, to each pint of the juice thus strained, add a pound of white sugar, and boil for twenty minutes; meanwhile skim, if necessary; then fill your glasses or molds, and let them stand for two or three days in the sun, till sufficiently hardened. Dip in brandy a piece of unsized paper, and lay on the top of the jelly; then paste over the top of the mold a piece of letter paper, to keep out the air, and the jelly is ready to be put away for use.

To make Good Apple Jelly.—Take apples of the best quality and good flavor, (not sweet), cut them in quarters or slices, and stew them till soft; then strain out the juice, being very careful not to let any of the pulp go through the strainer. Boil it to the consistency of molasses, then weigh it, and add as many pounds of crushed sugar, stirring it constantly till the sugar is dissolved. Add one ounce of extract of lemon to every twenty pounds of jelly, and when cold, set it away in close jars. It will keep good for years. Those who have not made jelly in this way will do well to try it; they will find it superior to currant jelly.

Currant Jelly.—Pick fine red, but long, ripe currants from the stem; bruise them, and strain the juice from a quart at a time through a thin muslin; wring it gently, to get all the liquid; put a pound of white sugar to each pound of juice; stir it until it is all dissolved; set it over a gentle fire; let it become hot, and boil for fifteen minutes; then try it by taking a spoonful into a saucer; when cold, if it is not quite firm enough, boil it for a few minutes longer. Or, pick the fruit from the stems; weigh it and put into a stone pot; set it in a kettle of hot water, reaching nearly to the top; let it boil till the fruit is hot through, then crush them, and strain the juice from them; put a pound of white sugar to each pint of it; put it over the fire, and boil for fifteen minutes; try some in a saucer; when the jelly is thick enough, strain it into small white jars, or glass tumblers; when it is cold, cover with tissue paper, as directed. Glass should be tempered by keeping it in warm water for a short time before pouring any hot liquid into it; otherwise it will crack.

Currant Jelly without Cooking.—Press the juice from the currants, and strain it; to every pint put a pound of fine white sugar; mix them together until the sugar is dissolved, then put it into jars, seal them, and expose them.

Cranberry Jelly, excellent.—Take any quantity of cranberries, and stew them in a sufficient quantity of water till they are well done. Now strain them through a piece of linen, or a sieve, and to each pint of the juice, add one pound of white sugar, and boil till it jellies. This is superior to any jelly ever made.

Compote of Apples.—Pare six large apples, cut them in half, and put them into a pan, with a little water and lemon juice. Next, clarify half a pound of sugar, skim it, and put the apples into it, adding the juice of a lemon. Set the whole on a fire. Turn the apples frequently, and cook them until they are sufficiently soft to be easily penetrated by a fork. Then take them out; strain the sirup, and reduce it by boiling; strain it again, and pour it over the apples. They may be served either hot or cold. Cut the peel of a rosy apple into various devices, and lay them on the apples, as a garnish.

Dried Apple Jelly.—One quart of apples put in four quarts of water, and allowed to stand all night; boil till the goodness is out of the apple; strain to a quart of juice, add a pint of sugar, and boil till it comes to a jelly.

Raspberry, Red Currant, and Strawberry Jellies may be made by putting the fruit into an earthen pan, bruising it with a wooden spoon, adding a little cold water and some finely-powdered loaf sugar. In an hour or two, strain it through a jelly bag, and to a quart of the juice add one ounce of isinglass which has been dissolved in half a pint of water, well skimmed, strained, and allowed to cool; mix all well, and pour into an earthen mold. Lemon juice should be added to jellies, in proportion to their acidity.

Apple Jelly, No. 2.—Pare, core, and cut thirteen good apples into small bits; as they are cut, throw them into two quarts of cold water; boil them in this, with the peel of a lemon, till the substance is extracted, and nearly half the liquor wasted; drain them through a hair sieve, and to a pint of the liquid add one pound of loaf sugar, pounded, the juice of one lemon, and the beaten whites of one or two eggs; put it into a saucepan, stir it till it boils, take off the scum, and let it boil till clear, and then pour it into a mold.

Raspberry Jam.—Weigh equal proportions of pounded loaf sugar and raspberries; put the fruit into a preserving pan, and with a silver spoon mash it well; let it boil six minutes; add the sugar, and stir well with the fruit. When it boils, skim it, and let it boil for fifteen minutes.

Strawberry Jam.—Gather the scarlet strawberries, when perfectly ripe, bruise them well, and add the juice of other strawberries; take an equal weight of lump sugar, pound and sift it, stir it thoroughly into the fruit, and set on a slow fire; boil it twenty minutes, taking off the scum as it rises; pour it into glasses or jars, and, when cold, tie them down.

White or Red Currant Jam.—Pick the fruit very nicely, and allow an equal quantity of finely-pounded loaf sugar; put a layer of each alternately, into a preserving pan, and boil for ten minutes; or they may be boiled the same length of time in sugar previously clarified, and boiled like candy.

Currant Jam.—Pick the currants free from stems; weigh three-quarters of a pound of sugar for each pound of fruit; strain the juice from half of them, then crush the remainder and the sugar together, and put them with the juice in a kettle, and boil until it is a smooth jellied mass; have a moderate fire, that it may not burn the preserves.

To Keep Red Gooseberries.—Pick gooseberries when fully ripe, and for each quart take a quarter of a pound of sugar and a gill of water; boil together until quite a sirup; then put in the fruit, and continue to boil gently for fifteen minutes; then put them into small stone jars; when cold, cover them close; keep them for making tarts or pies.

Dried Peaches.—Peaches, as usually dried, are a very good fruit, but can be made vastly better, if treated the right way. Last season, the receipts which had quite a circulation in the papers, of drying the fruit by a stove, after halving it, and sprinkling a little sugar into the cavity left by the extracted pits, was tried in our family. The fruit was found to be most excellent; better, to the taste of nine persons out of ten, than of any other peach preserves, by far. The peaches, however, were good ones before drying; for it is doubtful whether poor fruit can be made good by that process, or any other.

Tomato Sauce.—Gather your tomatoes when fully ripe, and, after washing them, mash them in some suitable vessel. Then place them in a kettle over a moderate fire, and when just warmed through, press a colender down upon them—then dipping from the colender all the watery juice possible. After boiling a short time, strain the mass through a wire sieve, just fine enough to retain the rind of the fruit; then return it to the kettle, and boil it down to the desired consistency, (some prefer it thin, as it retains more of the flavor,) taking all care that it does not become scorched in the process. Heat the bottles you intend to use in a steamer, to boiling heat, and while they retain this heat, fill them with sauce in a boiling state. Then cork them immediately with good corks, and place them where they will cool slowly. Tomatoes, thus prepared, will keep good, and retain all their original freshness and flavor, until their season comes round again.

Tomato Cutsup.—Wash your tomatoes and cut them up; boil and strain them through a sieve. To two quarts of the juice, add 1 pint of strong cider vinegar, and mace, cloves, spice, and cayenne to taste. Boil 15 or 20 minutes, and, when cool, bottle for use.

To Pickle Cucumbers.—Wipe and put them in salt water, strong enough to bear an egg, in which let them remain six or seven days; then scald in vinegar to green them; after which put them in cold, spiced vinegar. Beans are done the same.

Superior Method.—Put them into salt water for three days, then scald weak vinegar and turn to them, and let them remain three more days, when you must scald your new vinegar, with a few onions, ginger-root, and horseradish, and set them in a cool place for use.

To Pickle Tomatoes.—Always use those which are thoroughly ripe. The small round ones are decidedly the best. Do not prick them, as most receipt-books direct. Let them lie in strong brine three or four days; then put them in layers in your jars, mixing them with small onions and pieces of horseradish. Then pour on the vinegar, (cold), which should be first spiced, as in the receipt given for peppers; let there be a spice-bag to throw into every pot. Cover them carefully, and set them by in the cellar for a full month before using.

To Keep Jams, Jellies, and Preserves from Mold.—The closet in which sweetmeats are kept should be perfectly dry and cool. If that is the case, and the following receipts used, preserves will keep for years. Cut a round circle of writing paper, the size of the interior of the pot, and one about an inch and a half larger. Take the white of an egg, and a paste-brush, and lay a coating of white of egg over the surface of the smaller circle, and then lay that piece on the top of the jam, with the untouched side of the paper next to the jam. Take the larger piece, and coat that on one side with white of egg, and let the surface thus coated be the one turned inward. This circle is to cover the pot; and the white of egg renders it adhesive, and pastes it firmly down all around the edge of the crack.

Patent Honey.—Take five pounds of good common sugar, two pounds of water, gradually bring to a boil, skimming well; when cold, add one pound bee's honey, and four drops essence of peppermint.

Preserves without Fruit or Sugar.—Boil one pint of molasses from five to twenty minutes, (according to its consistency,) stir in three finely beaten eggs, and boil a few minutes longer; season with lemon and nutmeg if you like.

Clarified Molasses.—Common molasses may be clarified and rendered much more palatable by heating it over the fire and pouring in sweet milk in the proportion of one pint to a gallon of molasses. When the molasses boils up once, the albumen in the milk collects all the impurities in a thick scum upon the top, which must be carefully removed, and the molasses is then fit for use. Bullock's blood is also used for this purpose, but milk is more agreeable, in many ways, for domestic use.

Watery Potatoes.—If your potatoes are watery, put a piece of lime, about as large as a hen's egg, in the pot, and boil with them, and they will come out as mealy as you please.

HINTS TO HOUSEKEEPERS.

If your flat-irons are rough and smoky, lay a little fine salt on a flat surface, and rub them well; it will prevent them from sticking to anything starched, and make them smooth.

Rub your griddle with fine salt before you grease it, and your cake will not stick.

When walnuts have been kept until the meat is too much dried to be good, let them stand in milk and water eight hours, and dry them, and they will be as fresh as when new.

It is a good plan to keep your different kinds of pieces tape, thread, &c., in separate bags, and there is no time lost in looking for them.

Oats straw is best for filling of beds, and it is well to change it as often as once a year.

Cedar chests are best to keep flannels, for cloth moths are never found in them. Red cedar chips are good to keep in drawers, wardrobes, closets, trunks, &c., to keep out moths.

When cloths have acquired an unpleasant odor by being kept from the air, charcoal, laid in the folds, will soon remove it.

If black dresses have been stained, boil a handful of fig-leaves in a quart of water, and reduce it to a pint. A sponge dipped in this liquid and rubbed upon them, will entirely remove stains from crapes, bombazines, &c.

In laying up furs for summer, lay a tallow candle in or near them, and danger from worms will be obviated.

To prevent metals from rusting, melt together three parts of lard and one of resin, and apply a very thin coating. It will preserve Russia iron stoves and grates from rusting during summer, even in damp situations. The effect is equally good on brass, copper, steel, &c.

MEDICAL DEPARTMENT.

In giving this department to the public, we do not intend to give specifics for every disease to which human flesh is heir; but only a limited number of prescriptions, which have been thoroughly tested and proved successful in the treatment of well-known diseases, which seem to baffle the skill of the " Regular Faculty;" and also a few plain directions to be pursued, in cases of emergency, where the services of a physician can not be immediately procured. In the first place, the limits which we have set for the work will not admit of the space necessary for a detailed description of all diseases and their remedies, as this would require a volume of several hundred pages. Then, again, no one but a regular physician is competent to decide upon the nature of all diseases, and to prescribe their remedies under the existing circumstances, as there are scarcely two cases, even in the same disease, that require to be treated exactly alike. Those, however, which we have given, are the best that can be compounded for the purposes for which they are designed; as they are composed of nearly all plants known to the materia medica, the properties of which act specifically upon the functions of the organs designed to be affected. Being purely vegetable, no harm can result from their use; besides, they are far more efficacious than the " mineral poisons" usually employed by the Faculty for the same purpose.

The vegetable materia medica, which we have compiled from the United States Dispensatory, gives the reader a knowledge of the properties of the remedies which he employs; besides, it supplies him with a basis, or the data, for compounding remedies for the treatment of other diseases than those here prescribed for.

Cough Sirup.—Make a strong decoction of hoarhound, liverwort, ground ivy, and licorice root; sweeten with honey and loaf sugar, to make a thick sirup, and then boil for fifteen or twenty minutes. If the cough be severe, take a table-spoonful very often. If the throat be sore, add a little gum camphor to the mixture.

A Sure Cure for Fever and Ague.—Take best Peruvian bark, two ounces; wild cherry-tree bark, two ounces; poplar, one ounce; ginger, one table-spoonful; cinnamon, one drachm; balmony, one ounce; capsicum, one table-spoonful; cloves, quarter ounce. Have all finely pulverized, and put in two quarts good port wine, and let it stand one or two days before using. Take a wine-glassful four or five times a day, and the disease will soon disappear. Much better and safer than quinine.

The Best Tonic and Cathartic for Liver Complaint and Dyspepsia extant. —Chamomile flowers, two ounces; dandelion root, four ounces; yellow dock root, three ounces; burdock root, three ounces; sarsaparilla, three ounces; blood root, two ounces; liverwort, one ounce; hops, two ounces; wild cherry-tree bark, two ounces. Put all these together (in a crude state) in one vessel, and cover with water, at least three quarts or more, and steep (not boil) for several hours; then strain through a piece of muslin. There should be at least three pints of the liquid after it is strained, and it must not be allowed to evaporate while steeping, so there will be a less quantity; if it should, add a little more water before straining. The safest way is to keep on water enough while steeping, so that when you

46

press down with the bowl of a spoon, the water will always come over the place so pressed. Having strained the liquor from the dregs, add three-fourths of a pint of London Dock or Holland gin, one and a-half ounces rhubarb, and two table-spoonfuls of ground ginger. Take one or two table-spoonfuls night and morning (on retiring and getting up), or just enough to keep the bowels gently open.

Let dyspeptics persevere in taking this regularly, live upon a light and nourishing diet, keep the body clean, by frequent ablutions, and take plenty of exercise in the open air, and their ailments will soon disappear.

This cured my dyspepsia and liver complaint of fifteen years standing, raised me from a mere living skeleton, with my weight less than ninety pounds, to one hundred and fifty-five pounds, being twenty pounds more than I had ever before weighed.

A Pleasant and Healthy Tonic for Restoring the Appetite.—Take one ounce pulverized golden seal, one ounce pulverized balmony, one ounce pulverized poplar, half ounce pulverized cloves, and put into one quart of good wine (currant or rhubarb is best), with a tea-cupful of loaf sugar. Let it stand a day or two, shaking it occasionally, and take a wine-glassful three times a day, before meals. This is an excellent tonic, and may be taken with advantage in connection with the one above.

Nervine for Female Weakness and Nervous Debility.—Take one ounce valerian, one ounce yarrow, one ounce golden rod, one ounce unicorn, one ounce lady's slipper, one ounce scull-cap, one ounce ginseng (all in a crude state), and steep in three pints of water till evaporated to one, when strained. Then mix with one quart good port wine, and add one ounce pulverized golden seal, half ounce pulverized cloves, and sweeten with loaf sugar to taste.

Dose—Half a wine-glass three times a day, before meals. Good in colic, pains in the stomach, flatulency, &c.

Alterative Sirup for Scrofula, and all Diseases arising from Impurity of the Blood.—Yellow dock, two ounces; sarsaparilla, two ounces; prickly ash, two ounces; wintergreen, two ounces; blue flag, two ounces; bitter-sweet, two ounces. Put all together, in a crude state, and steep in three quarts of water till evaporated to one, when strained. Now add one pint good London Dock, or Holland gin, one ounce extract of dandelion, and one ounce of sulphur; sweeten with loaf sugar to taste. Dose—A table-spoonful three times a day before meals. If the bowels be costive, add one ounce pulverized rhubarb to the mixture.

Rheumatic Drops, or No. 6.—Take gum-myrrh, one pound; golden seal, four ounces; African cayenne, one ounce; put these into a jug, with two quarts best brandy; shake several times a day for eight or ten days, when it is fit for use. This is a stimulant and tonic, and an excellent remedy for rheumatism, fresh wounds, bruises, sores, and sprains. It is also used in hemorrhage, mortification, &c. Dose—from one to two tea-spoonfuls in warm water.

Composition Powders.—Take one pound fine bayberry bark; one-half pound ginger; three ounces of common cayenne, and mix them all together. Dose—A tea-spoonful in a cup two-thirds full of boiling water; sweeten, and add a little milk.

An Excellent Liniment for Cuts, Bruises, Sores, &c.—Take four ounces balm gilead buds, and steep for two or three days in one quart of alcohol; then turn off the liquor, and add three ounces turpentine, four ounces gum camphor, three ounces oil arganum, two ounces sweet oil. For cuts, bruises, wounds, &c., in either man or beast, it has no equal. For old sores and ulcers, first cleanse them thoroughly with a wash made of witch hazel, sumach, and elder bark; then use the liniment. If they result from impurity of the blood, or are of long standing, then use the alterative sirup in connection with it.

Diarrhea Cordial and Cholera Sirup.—Take three ounces blackberry root, one ounce golden seal, one ounce gum myrrh, one ounce bayberry, one ounce evan root, one ounce sumach (leaves and berries), one ounce valerian, one ounce capsicum, one ounce allspice, one ounce ginger root. Put all, in a crude state, together, and steep in six quarts of water till evaporated to two after it is strained; then add two quarts of good brandy, two ounces extract of dandelion, from three to four ounces of pulverized cloves, and six or eight ounces of loaf sugar. Dose—for an adult, from one to two table-spoonfuls, in a little warm water, as often as the severity of the case may require. If taken freely, in large doses, in cases of cholera, it is a sure cure. Every person having a friend in the army should make up a good-sized bottle, and send it to him. (If all the ingredients can not at all times be obtained in compounding medicines from these receipts, it will not always matter particularly if a portion be left out, as the properties of many are identical. By reference to the Materia Medica here appended, it can be seen what the properties of each are, and then determined whether it be absolutely essential.) This medicine is a powerful tonic and astringent; but an astringent is not to be taken in all cases where there is looseness of the bowels. If the discharges be dark-colored, and of an offensive character, they show a bilious and morbid condition of the stomach and bowels, which require to be thoroughly cleansed with some mild cathartic before any attempt is made to check them, when, as a general thing, the bowels will regulate themselves without any further treatment. If, however, watery discharges continue after the bilious matter has all passed off, then some astringent is necessary. Dysentery is a disease of the colon (lower bowel), caused by morbid irritation and inflammation, producing hemorrhage and intense pain, and bearing down; in which case astringents, especially those of a hot and irritating nature, are not to be taken, as they only serve to keep up the inflammation and enhance the difficulty; but soothing emolients, in the form of clysters, must be given in their stead. For this purpose, infuse one tea-spoonful of the pulverized leaves of lobelia in one pint of slippery-elm water, and inject into the bowels about six ounces (a common tumbler full) at a time. If the bloody discharges and pains continue, also apply warm fomentations to the bowels, and give freely of hot ginger tea, so as to get up an action on the surface, which will withdraw the blood from within, and allows the inflammation to subside. If the slippery-elm water and lobelia can not be obtained right away, use starch-water. A lobelia emetic, for the purpose of cleansing the stomach, can be taken with advantage in this, and nearly all diseases of the bowels. If these simple rules were strictly observed in all cases of dysentery, many valuable lives might be saved, that otherwise would be sacrificed by the ignorance of the patient's friends, or the empiricism of "quacks," who make no distinction in the treatment of diarrhea and dysentery.

The following receipts, for the cure of hydrophobia, diphtheria, &c., are taken from the papers designated in their respective headings, and we give them for what they are worth:

Remedy for Diphtheria.—The following receipt for diphtheria—a disease that is becoming dangerously prevalent throughout the country—we copy from the New York *Tribune:* We have received a receipt for the cure of diphtheria from a physician, who says that of one thousand cases in which it has been used, not a single patient has been lost. The treatment consists in thoroughly swabbing the back of the mouth and throat with a wash made thus: Table-salt, two drachms; black pepper, golden seal, nitrate of potash, alum, one drachm each. Mix and pulverize; put into a teacup, which half fill with boiling water; stir well, and then fill up with good vinegar. Use every half hour, one, two, and four hours, as recovery progresses. The patient may swallow a little each time. Apply one ounce each of spirits of turpentine, sweet oil, and aqua ammonia, mixed, to the whole of the throat, and to the breast-bone every four hours, keeping flannel to the part.

Cure of Hydrophobia.—The New York *World's* Paris correspondence says: Some of the medical journals are giving publicity now to an alleged cure for this terrible disease, which is communicated to them by the Rev. R. P. Legrand, who has been for many years a missionary in Syria, where hydrophobia is quite common, and where, he says, he has tried this remedy in sixty different cases, and performed sixty cures. If this be so, and there certainly is no reason to doubt the good father's word, the simple remedy which he proposes should be made known all over the world. It is this: take three handfuls of the leaves of *datura stramonium*, boil them in a quart of water till it is reduced to a pint, and make the patient drink the whole as soon as possible after the bite. A violent madness will ensue, but this is of short duration. A profuse perspiration follows, and in twenty-four hours the patient is cured. Cauterization should also be resorted to as quickly as possible, although the reverend father states that he has seen many cures effected where this has not been done.

Important Medical Discovery.—A London correspondent of the *Liberator* gives this account:—A great discovery is just now engaging the attention of the scientific and medical world. Few English names are more familiar to Americans than that of Dr. John Chapman, once the leading publisher of heretical books, now editor of the *Westminister*, and always a devotee of science and medicine. He is well acquainted with many scientific and literary Americans; and many of them, among others Mr. Emerson, have resided in his house when in England. This Dr. Chapman has for years engaged in studies and experiments connected with the nervous system alone, with such men as Dr. Brown, Sequard, and Claud Bernard, of Paris. For the past year he has been proving a tremendous discovery—namely the cure of epilepsy, and many diseases hitherto deemed incurable, by means of an external application of ice and hot water, in India rubber bags, at various parts of the spinal cord, acting thus upon the sympathetic nerve, and, through it, upon the most important and vital regions of the body. Many eminent physicians have accompanied Dr. Chapman to see the marvels which he had wrought upon patient, who had long ago despaired of health. Some physicians, among others Dr. Wilkinson (though a homeopathist) have so recognized the importance of the discovery as to commit to Dr. Chapman's care some of their patients. Cases are attested where a man for six years had three fits (on an average) daily, and a girl who had two from the ages of thirteen to seventeen, had been entirely cured by ice. Just as wonderful have been the cures of paralysis. Many of the worst and most inveterate female diseases have yielded to the new cure. The treatment is as simple as it is grand. Any one who is troubled by the pressure of blood on the brain, will find that by holding a bag of ice on the nape of the neck ten minutes, an equable flow of blood can be secured. Those who are troubled with habitual cold feet, may find relief by applying ice to the small of the back in the lumbar regions. It is hard to estimate the importance

4

of this discovery, which will, ere long, be ranked by the side of Jenner. Several hospitals are already under Dr. Chapman's practice, and as yet no one can bring forward an instance of failure.

Cure for Small-Pox.—The German *Reformed Messenger* has received a letter from a friend in China, in which it is stated a great discovery is reported to have recently been made by a surgeon of the English army in China, in the way of an effectual cure of small-pox. The mode of treatment is as follows: When the preceding fever is at its hight, and just before the eruption appears, the chest is rubbed with croton oil and tartaric ointment. This causes the whole of the eruption to appear on that part of the body, to the relief of the rest. It also secures a full and complete eruption, and thus prevents the disease from attacking the internal organs. This is said to be the established mode of treatment in the English army in China, by general orders, and is regarded as a permanent cure.

How to Prevent the Defacing Marks of Small-Pox.—While it is known to medical men that a total suppression of the eruption of small-pox will endanger the life of the sufferer, it is proved, by experience, that such a suppression can be undertaken on small portions of the body, for instance the face, without harm. The pomade of Baudeloque, made of six parts of pitch, (pix nigra), ten parts of yellow wax, and twenty-four parts of mercurial ointment, will answer that purpose. When used, it should be warmed and all parts of the skin of the face be covered, and kept covered, continually, for the space of four days; the salve, if it proves efficacious, must be applied on the first or second day the eruption has broken out. Four days after the application, when removed, the eruption will have remained papulose, and the spots will disappear in time, without leaving any marks behind. Having experienced the good effects from the administration of this remedy, we hope the press of this city will promulgate it by publication, and earn their thanks from the smiling faces of those whom it will have spared a frightful disfiguration.

The French Physicians are now using gutta-percha, dissolved in chloroform, in the same way, which is more simple, and answers every purpose.—*N. O. True Delta.*

RULES FOR THE PRESERVATION OF THE HEALTH.

"Always keep the head cool, and the feet warm." Go to bed early, and get up at the peep of day. Never be in a hurry when you eat, but masticate your food well, and thoroughly mix it with the saliva of the mouth before swallowing, which is one-half the process of digestion. Above all never wash your food down, half masticated, with a pint or more of tea or coffee. Too much fluid on the stomach dilutes the gastric juice, prevents its direct and immediate action, on the food, and, consequently, retards the process of digestion till the fluids have been absorbed. Drink very moderately with your meals, and nothing for two and a-half or three hours afterward. Avoid too much greasy and fatty substances. The too common practice of eating fat pork is the cause of more scrofula than all other causes combined. Fresh bread and hot biscuits are decidedly injurious, and unfit to be eaten. Eat regularly, and never between meals.

Whatever may be your occupation, take plenty of daily exercise in the open air. If you can not work in the garden, saw and split wood, or do something else useful; walk and run briskly, or ride on horseback. Don't say that you have not time; for, in the long run, you will find it the best "put in" of any thing which you have done.

Always have your house, especially the sleeping apartment, well ventilated, be it warm or cold weather.

Never sit in a room, on a cold or damp day, without a fire, if you are in any degree chilly and uncomfortable without one. But few causes are more productive of disease than this practice, which is almost universal. People generally take their stoves down too early in the spring, and neglect putting them up till late in the fall; some, in fact, till dire necessity actually drives them to it. This is more particularly the case in hotels and boarding-houses, which is not only a great inconvenience, but an actual injustice to guests and boarders. Better to save the "almighty dollar" by robbing them of one-half their meals, than to deprive them of the comforts of a warm and comfortable room, on a cold, chilly day.

Avoid contracting colds as much as possible; and when taken, endeavor to break them up as soon as you can. If you have been caught in a rain-storm, and your clothes have become drenched through, never sit down, or remain idle one minute after you get where you can exchange them for dry ones. As soon as you discover that your pores are closed, from having allowed any part of your body to become chilled, keep yourself comfortably warm, within doors, till the difficulty has been removed. Drink plentifully of warm ginger, pennyroyal, or sage-tea; evacuate the bowels by enemas, and live upon warm broths and gruels. Vapor baths are excellent in removing colds. Attend to these conditions promptly, and no permanent injury will ensue; but if neglected, pulmonary diseases, which will ultimate in consumption, will often be the result, to say nothing of the dangers of pneumonia, congestions, &c.

Avoid sleeping on feather-beds, and under too much clothing, as it retains the perspiration and noxious exhalations from the body, and prevents a free circulation of the air. Woolen blankets are preferable to cotton comforts.

Never allow yourself to become passionately angry, or unduly excited; but uniformly endeavor to preserve an equanimity and serenity of mind, which will greatly tend to the promotion of your health and happiness.

Never indulge in the filthy, disgusting, and enervating practice (now a universal crime among all so-called civilized nations) of smoking and chewing tobacco, as no other cause is more prolific of deleterious effects upon both mind and body.

If you have become so thoroughly wedded to the "weed" that you can not give it up yourself, for heaven's sake, and the sake of humanity, don't permit your darling boy to imitate your bad example, so long as he remains under your guardianship; and when he arrives at man's estate, the chances are, if he be possessed of a reasonable share of common sense, that he will not then take it up. Mothers, see to it, that your boys do not acquire this man-killing habit before you are aware of it.

Keep the body clean by frequent ablutions. Never go more than one week in cold weather, and not more than one or two days in warm weather, without washing your person all over.

Regulate the temperature of the water by that of the weather, and the constitution and vitality of the system. If the constitution be feeble, with but little vitality in the system, never, especially in winter, use water with the temperature much below the heat of the body—that is, 96 deg. Fahrenheit; then wipe yourself perfectly dry, and rub briskly with the hand, or a dry towel. Persons of strong, robust constitutions, may use cold water, as the superabundance of animal heat will be sufficient to get up a reaction, and carry off the excessive cold. Were the above rules universally and strictly observed, nine-tenths of the "ills" and "ails" to which human flesh is heir, would disappear from the face of our beautiful earth.

WATER AS A REMEDIAL AGENT.

The "Water-cure," as it is called, is good as an auxiliary in the treatment of nearly all diseases, especially those of a febrile nature; but it is not, as the hydropathics claim, a universal panacea, and will not do to depend upon, unaided by other remedies. The wise physician makes his selection from the entire Laboratory of Nature, using *all* remedies which experience has proved to be beneficial, instead of confining himself exclusively to any particular one-idea system; though the hydropathic, as an exclusive system, is, undoubtedly, preferable to the old system of poisoning with calomel, cupping and bleeding, which is now fast going out of use among more *enlightened* minds, in the old, or Alopathic school of practice.

Water requires to be employed with discretion, or much harm may result from its use. However, it may be used by almost any person without danger, in nearly all cases of febrile attacks, where there is severe local inflammation or general fever.

If the disease be local, and the parts much swollen and highly inflamed, bathe frequently in cold water, and apply cloths wet in cold water as often as they become warm, till the inflammation subsides. In cases of general fever, where the pulse ranges from 90 up to 120, sponge the surface all over with water more or less cold, according to the constitution, *general* health, and present condition of the patient. The safest rule is, to use it of such a temperature as will feel cool, refreshing, and agreeable when applied; but never when it produces a chilly sensation, and a shrinking from it. This last rule will apply to consumptives, and all persons in feeble health. Observe these rules strictly, and no harm will result from its use; but, in most of cases, much good will come therefrom.

Pure fresh air is another very important consideration in the treatment of the sick. Always have the chamber of the sick well ventilated, but not in such manner as to bring the bed into a direct draft, as there will be danger of taking cold.

Sunlight is the next consideration of importance, both to the sick and the healthy. Persons, as well as plants, can not thrive well when deprived of the vivifying and genial influence of the direct rays of the sun; hence it is highly injurious to have your house all hemmed in with shade-trees, or the walls of adjoining buildings. This is evident from the fact that in all large towns and cities, the buildings on the south side of the street, where the rays of the sun never penetrate in midday, are the most unhealthy; and that in times of prevailing epidemics, by far the largest percentage of mortality is in buildings so situated. Therefore, keep your shade-trees at a proper distance from your building, throw open your blinds, and, as nearly as possible, admit the direct rays of the sun into every part of your house daily.

In the treatment of nearly all diseases, whether acute or chronic, more depends upon these conditions of pure, fresh air, sunlight, exercise, diet, and cleanliness, than in the skill of physicians and the potency of medicines; which, however, are right and proper, when *properly* used.

DIET AND BEVERAGES FOR THE SICK.

Remarks.—Where persons have become very weak and much prostrated from the effects of fevers and other diseases, nothing, especially after the disease is broken, and the patient is beginning to be convalescent, is of so much importance as suitable food and drinks; as the least indiscretion, in this respect, will often bring on a relapse, which will be apt to prove fatal. Therefore, avoid all hard and indigestible substances, such as pastry of every kind and description; crude and uncooked vegetables; hard and unripe fruit; tough and fatty meats; highly-seasoned and rich soups, and all strong and intoxicating beverages.

Beef Tea.—This is the most proper food that can be given where the patient is in a low, prostrate condition, with but little recuperative power left in the system. It is made as follows: Take a piece of tender, lean beef, large enough, when cut up, to fill a large coffee-cup; cut it very fine, almost into mince; put it into two cups, or double its own bulk of cold water; bring it to a boil, skimming it as the skum rises to the top; continue the boiling till one-half of the water has been evaporated, when it is ready for use. Use no seasoning, except a very little salt. If the patient be much reduced, from the effects of prostrating fevers, or other causes, this is to be given, at first, in teaspoon quantities; then gradually increased in quantity, as the patient gains strength—taking care that no more is taken at a time than the stomach is able to bear. Better give a little, often, than to overload the stomach with more than it can manage. As soon as the patient recovers sufficiently to require something solid, a little toasted soda-cracker, or nice wheaten bread, may be crumbed in with the broth. If beef can not always be procured, the next best thing is mutton, wild fowls, squirrels, rabbits, and, last of all, chickens. Wild fowls are much healthier than domestic ones, and venison is healthier than beef or mutton.

Broths made from boiling mutton, or other meat, with pearl-barley, till the latter becomes a jelly, is an excellent diet for the sick. First soak the barley several hours in cold water, then put the water and barley, together with the meat, in the pot, and boil till sufficiently done. Rice, cooked in the same way, is also good.

Corn-Starch.—Get the Oswego corn-starch, and make into light, boiled puddings. Take all milk, or part milk and part water, and bring to a boil; then stir in corn-starch, which has been beaten into a paste, and thinned with milk or water, till it is of the proper consistency. Cook for fifteen or twenty minutes over a moderate fire, stirring it all the while, to prevent its burning. For sick people, do not put in eggs, according to the directions accompanying each package, as the eggs, when cooked hard, are too hard to digest. This is as good as the Bermuda arrow-root, and is much cheaper.

Sago.—Wash it clean, and soak in cold water for one hour; now put in a stew-pan, in the same water, and cook gently till it is done. Season with a little nutmeg and lemon, and also add wine and sugar, if you like. If preferred, it can be boiled the same way in new milk.

Meal Gruel.—Stir a little Indian-meal, or oatmeal, with water, and boil thoroughly till well done, stirring it so it will not burn.

Milk Porridge.—Bring one quart of milk to a boil, and stir in a little flour, which has been well beaten into a paste, and thinned, till it is of the desired consistency. Cook till well done. Roast and baked potatoes, baked apples, and soft-boiled eggs, are good for sick persons when in an advanced state of convalescence, but are not good to be eaten at first, as they would prove too much for the digestive organs.

Toast.—Take good, nice wheaten bread, and cut in slices, and toast till a little brown; now put a slice on a plate, and turn on a little hot water, and allow it to remain long enough to moisten it all through, but no

longer; then sprinkle a little salt over it, spread it with a little fresh butter, or sweet cream.   Prepare what you want in the same way; and,
having put all the slices together on the same plate, set it in the oven, and
allow it to remain till it becomes well heated all through, but not long
enough to bake and become dry. This is not a bad dish for well people
to take.

Toast Water.—Toast two or three slices of bread till well browned all
through, but not burned in the least. Put in a pitcher, and turn on one
pint of hot water, and let it stand for half an hour or so, when it is ready
for use. Sweeten with loaf sugar, if you like. This is cool and nourishing.

Slippery Elm and Date-Water is also cool and nourishing for sick people.   Take a tumblerful of nice plump dates, or of slippery elm, and put
into a pint of cold water, and let it stand till it becomes thick, like mucilage or gum-water. People have been known to live for weeks upon this,
when the stomach was unable to bear any thing else.

Lemon and Orange-ade is a good beverage for persons sick with a fever.

Why Children Die.—One reason why children die is because they are
not taken care of. From the day of birth, they are stuffed with food,
and choked with physic, sloshed with water, suffocated in hot rooms,
steamed in bed-clothes. So much for in-door. When permitted to breathe
a breath of pure air once a week in summer, and once or twice during
the colder months, only the nose is permitted to peer into daylight. A
little later, they are sent out with no clothing at all on the parts of the
body which most need protection. Bare legs, bare arms, bare necks, girted
middle, with an inverted umbrella to collect the air and chill the other
parts of the body. A stout, strong man goes out on a cold day with gloves
and overcoat, woolen stockings, and thick, double-soled boots, with cork
between and rubbers over. The same day a child of three years old, an
infant flesh, blood, bone, and constitution, goes out with shoes as thin as
paper, cotton socks, legs uncovered to the knees, neck bare; an exposure
which would disable the nurse, kill the mother outright, and make the
father an invalid for weeks. And why? To harden them to a mode of
dress which they are never expected to practice; to accustom them to
exposure which, a dozen years later, would be considered downright fool-
ery. To rear children thus for the slaughter-pen, and then lay it on the
Lord, is too bad. We don't think the Almighty had any hand in it.
And to draw comfort from the presumption that He had an agency in
the death of the child is a profanation.—*Journal of Health.*

Dieting.—Dieting is usually considered to mean the same thing as a
kind of starvation. The idea which the educated physician attaches to
the term is a judicious regulation of the quantity and quality of the food,
according to the circumstances of each case. A healthy man may diet
himself in order to keep well; an invalid may diet with a view to the
recovery of his health; yet the things eaten by the two will widely differ
in their nature, bulk, and mode of preparation. A vast multitude are
suffering hourly by the horrors of dyspepsia; no two are precisely alike
in all points, since there is an endless variety of combinations as to age,
sex, occupation, air, exercise, mode of eating, sleeping, constitution, tem-
perament, etc. Yet dyspepsia is always brought on by over and irregular
eating; it could be banished from the world in a generation, if the children were educated to eat moderately, regularly, and slowly; the parents
who do this will do their offspring a higher good than by leaving them
large fortunes, which, in three cases out of four, foster idleness, gluttony
and every evil thing. As the rich can get any thing to eat or drink when

wanted, they, with indulged children, bring on dyspepsia by eating irregularly and without an appetite. The poor—those who have to work for a living—induce the horrible disease by eating too rapidly and at unseasonable hours; mainly by eating heartily at supper, and going to bed within an hour or two afterward. In the heyday of youth and manly vigor there may not for a while be noticed any special ill effect from such a practice—in truth, it is at first inappreciable, but it is cumulative, and impossible not to manifest itself in due time. Infinite Benevolence forgives a moral delinquency; but Omnipotent as He is, and loving towards all, it is not in the nature of His government of created things to work a miracle, to suspend a natural law, in order to shield one of his creatures from the legitimate effects of a violence offered the physical system by excesses in eating, drinking, or exercise.

Perhaps hearty suppers make more dyspeptics than any or all other causes combined. If dinner is at noon, nothing should be taken for supper but a single cup of weak tea or other hot drink, and a piece of stale bread and butter. After forty years of age, those who live in-doors, sedentary persons—that is, all who do not work with their hands as laborers—would do better not to take any supper at all. Half the time the sedentary, who eat at noon, do not feel hungry at supper; especially if they see nothing on the table but bread and butter and tea. But Nature is goaded on to act against her instincts in almost every family in the nation by "relishes" being placed on the supper-table, in the shape of chipped beef, salt fish, cake, preserves or other kinds of sweetmeats, and before the person is aware, a hearty meal has been taken, resulting in present uncomfortableness, in disturbed sleep, in a weary waking in the morning, bad taste in the mouth, and little or no appetite for breakfast, all of which can be avoided by beginning early to eat habitually, according to the suggestions above made.—*Hall's Journal of Health.*

POISONS AND THEIR ANTIDOTES.

It not unfrequently happens that serious and distressing results are occasioned by the accidental employment of poisons; and we herewith submit a compendious list of the more common poisons, and the remedies for them most likely to be at hand:

Acids.—These cause great heat and sensation of burning pain, from the mouth down to the stomach. Remedies: Magnesia, soda, pearlash or soap dissolved in water; then use stomach-pump or emetics.

Alkalies.—The best remedy is ginger.

Ammonia.—Remedy: Lemon-juice or ginger; afterward milk and water, or flaxseed tea.

Alcohol.—First cleanse out the stomach by an emetic; then dash cold water on the head, and give ammonia (spirits of hartshorn).

Arsenic.—Remedies: In the first place evacuate the stomach; then give the white of eggs, lime-water, or chalk and water, charcoal, and the preparations of iron, particularly hydrate.

Lead.—White lead and sugar of lead. Remedies: Alum, cathartic, such as castor oil and Epsom salts especially.

Charcoal.—In poison by carbonic gas, remove the patient to the open air, dash cold water on the head and body, and stimulate the nostrils and lungs by hartshorn, at the same time rubbing the chest briskly.

Corrosive Sublimate.—Give the white of eggs freshly mixed with water, or give wheat flour and water, or soap and water freely.

Creosote.—White of eggs and emetics.

Belladona or night Henbane.—Give emetics, and then plenty of vinegar and water, or lemonade.

Mushrooms, when Poisonous.—Give emetics, and then plenty of vinegar and water, with dose of either, if handy.

Nitrate of Silver (Lunar Caustic.)—Give a strong solution of common salt, and then emetics.

Opium.—First give a strong emetic of mustard and water, then strong coffee and acid drinks; dash cold water on the head.

Laudanum.—Same as opium.

Nux Vomica.—First emetics, then brandy.

Oxalic Acid.—Frequently mistaken for Epsom salts. Remedies: Chalk, magnesia, or soap and water freely, then emetics.

Nitrate of Potash, or Saltpeter.—Give emetics, then copious draughts of flaxseed tea, milk and water, and other soothing drinks.

Prussic Acid.—When there is tim, administer chlorine in the shape of soda or lime; hot brandy and water. Hartshorn and turpentine are also useful.

Snake-bites, etc.—Apply, immediately, strong hartshorn, and take it internally. Also give sweet oil and stimulants freely. Apply a ligature tight above the part bitten, and then apply a cupping glass.

Tartar Emetic.—Give large doses of tea made out of galls, Peruvian bark, or white-oak bark.

Tobacco.—First an emetic, then a stringent tea, then stimulants.

Verdigris.—Plenty of the white of eggs and water.

White Vitriol.—Give the patient plenty of milk and water.

In almost all cases of poisons, emetics are highly useful, and of these, one of the very best, because most prompt and ready, is the common mustard flour or powder, a tea-spoonful of which, stirred up in warm water, may be give every five minutes, until free vomiting can be obtained.

Emetics and warm demulcent drinks, such as milk and water, flaxseed or slippery-elm tea, chalk-water, etc., should be administered without delay. The subsequent management of the case will, of course, be left to a physician.

VEGETABLE MATERIA MEDICA.

Lobelia Inflata.—The properties of this plant have long been known to the Aborigines of this country, but Dr. Samuel Thompson has the honor of bringing it into general use, and of establishing its efficacy in the treatment of various diseases. This herb, properly administered, will subdue diseases of long standing, which have resisted the power of every other remedy. It is one of the most powerful and effective emetics that can be given, and is of incalculable value in the treatment of all morbid affections of the stomach, poisonings, etc. There is scarcely a case arising from a morbid and bilious condition of the stomach, and other viscera, in which an emetic may not be taken with great advantage to the patient, as it expels all morbific matter, and removes all obstructions which retard the process of digestion. It may be administered occasionally in all cases of dyspepsia and indigestion, cholera-morbus, diarrhea, dysentery, etc. I have seen persons lingering along with a poor appetite, or none at all, with constant nausea at the stomach, in spite of the most powerful remedies administered by skillful hands, take one or two lobelia emetics and throw up nearly a pint of phlegm and slimy matter, which had lain on the stomach so long that it had become tough and ropy, so that when lifted up it would hang in strings ten or twelve inches long. This "sliming," as it is sometimes termed, adheres closely to the coatings of the stomach, and almost entirely prevents the action of the gastric juice upon the food; and nothing will so effectually dislodge and expel it, as a good lobelia emetic. Whatever may be the prejudices of the patient against this harmless but powerful remedy, it will all be removed on taking one or two doses, followed with the expulsion from the stomach of half a pint or more of morbific or bilious matter, the speedy return of his appetite, and a feeling better generally, and at the stomach particularly.

The following is the best method of administering it: Take one tea-spoonful of ginger and put in a pitcher and pour on one quart of hot water. When a little cool, take a tea-cupful (with sugar if you like,) and repeat every five minutes till all is drunk up; now put a tea-spoonful of a mixture (equal parts,) of bayberry bark and ginger into the pitcher, and pour on another quart of boiling water; let it steep a few moments, and then take a tea-spoonful of the pulverized leaves of lobelia and put into a teacup, which fill two-thirds full of the tea from the pitcher; let it stand covered for five minutes, then give the patient one-half of it, to be followed by more of the new tea. If, after the lapse of five or ten minutes, vomiting does not ensue, give the balance of the lobelia, and drink again of the tea till it commences, and the stomach becomes thoroughly evacuated. Should the first dose produce the desired effect, then pour more water on the grounds in the pitcher, drink again of the tea, and take the remaining portion of the lobelia, as in the first dose. If the bayberry and ginger can not at all times be had, use pennyroyal tea in the same manner. This emetic is simple, and can be administered by almost any adult person, and, in nine cases out of ten, will be sufficient to completely evacuate the stomach, while now and then a case will require double the quantity of lobelia.

Skunk Cabbage.—The root is stimulant and expectorant; useful in coughs, asthma, and all pulmonary complaints. It is also given to children, to destroy worms.

Alder.—This is an astringent, useful in bleeding at the lungs, or as a wash for ulcers.

Motherwort.—This will ease the pain in the nervous headache.

Balm Gilead Buds.—Steeped in spirits, excellent for bathing wounds.

Mullen.—This is physical; good, simmered in lard, for piles.

Burdock.—This is a cathartic; it will produce perspiration. The leaves are good in fevers, to bind upon the head and feet.

Blackberry.—This is astringent; very valuable in dysentery.

Plantain.—Good, combined with lard, for the salt-rheum; its juice will cure the bite of snakes.

Blueflag.—Useful in fevers, or to expel humors from the system. Dose—half a tea-spoonful three times a day.

Prickly Ash.—The bark and berries of the prickly ash are stimulant and tonic. They are almost a sovereign remedy for cold feet and hands, and all diseases dependent on a sluggish or languid circulation. Dose—from half to a tea-spoonful of the powdered bark and berries.

Smart Weed.—This herb produces powerful sweating; is an excellent remedy to break up a cold when threatened with a fever. It may be drank in tea at liberty.

May Weed.—It is a stimulant and tonic, useful in febrile attacks, sudden colds, cough, etc. This is commonly used in the form of tea, induces perspiration, and sometimes vomiting.

Chamomile.—It is a stimulant and tonic, useful in colds, febrile attacks, debility, and in all cases the same as May weed.

Pipsissewa— Winter Green.—The pipsissewa is a stimulant, diuretic, astringent, and tonic; useful in scrofulas, tumors, cancers, and kidney complaints. The tea is also useful as a wash for ill-conditioned sores and cutaneous eruptions.

Peppermint.—Is a pleasant stimulant, promotes perspiration, and may be administered in all cases of colds, pain in the stomach and bowels, flatulency, headache, nausea, etc.

Spearmint.—Is a tonic and stimulant, and is employed to stop vomiting, and allay nausea. It is an excellent carminative, induces perspiration, warms and invigorates the system, and quiets pain in the stomach and bowels.

Ginseng.—The root is tonic and nervine. It is useful in all cases of debility, loss of appetite, neuralgic affections, and dyspepsia. Dose—half a tea-spoonful of the powdered root, more or less.

Beth Root.—Beth root is astringent, tonic, and antiseptic, may be employed in all cases of hemorrhage, leucorrhea, asthma, and coughs. Dose —half a tea-spoonful.

Scullcap.—Scullcap is a most valuable nervine, and antispasmodic. It may be used successfully in delirium tremens, fits, locked-jaw, St. Vitus' dance, and all nervous diseases. It is also recommended in hydrophobia. Dose—a tea-spoonful of the powdered herb.

Ladies Slipper.—Is a valuable nervine, quiets nervous excitement, eases pain, and induces sleep. It may be used freely in all nervous and hysterical affections, without incurring the least danger, or producing unpleasant consequences. Dose—a tea-spoonful of the powdered root may be taken three or four times a day, or until relief is obtained.

Slippery Elm.—The inner bark is mucilaginous and nutritious, and may be employed in all cases of inflammation, debility, diseases of the urinary passages, diarrhea, dysentery, pleurisy, and sore throat.

Pennyroyal.—Is an agreeable stimulant, and, if convenient, should always be used in giving an emetic. It promotes perspiration, and facilitates the operation of lobelia. It is also a valuable carminative, and may be freely used in all slight attacks of disease.

Gum Myrrh.—It is astringent, antiseptic, and tonic. It is useful in pulmonary complaints, loss of appetite, sore mouth, and offensive breath. It is also useful in dysentery and diarrhea, and to cleanse offensive ulcers, putrid and ill-conditioned sores. Dose—a tea-spoonful of the tincture, or fourth of a tea-spoonful of the powder.

Cayenne.—Is a pure, powerful, and healthy stimulant, and produces, when introduced into the stomach, a sensation of warmth, which diffuses itself gradually through the system, but without any narcotic effect. It is an excellent remedy in all cases of colds, coughs, flatulency, congestion, dyspepsia, etc. It should not be taken in very large doses upon a cold or empty stomach, but in small quantities at first, gradually increasing the dose.

Balmony.—It serves as a tonic laxative, and may be used in debility, costiveness, dyspepsia, jaundice, coughs, and colds. There are but few forms of disease in which this article may not be used to advantage. Dose— an even tea-spoonful of the powdered herb.

Poplar.—The bark is a pleasant tonic, useful in loss of appetite, indigestion, diarrhea, worms, and headache. It possesses diuretic properties, and may be employed in strangury, and all diseases of the urinary passages. Dose—a tea-spoonful of the powdered bark.

Unicorn.—The root of this plant is a valuable tonic, beneficial in all female complaints, particularly so in leucorrhea; also in pleurisy, general debility, weakness of the digestive organs, and coughs. Dose—from half to a tea-spoonful of the powdered root.

Boneset.—Is laxative, tonic, and expectorant. A decoction of the leaves and flowers, taken while warm, and in large quantities, will evacuate the stomach in a very gentle and safe manner; administered cold, it acts as a tonic and laxative. It is useful in coughs, colds, and pulmonary complaints.

Bayberry.—The bark of bayberry is powerfully astringent, and slightly stimulating; useful for cleansing the stomach and bowels from canker, scarlatina, dysentery, and diarrhea. A decoction of the bark is also useful as a gargle for sore throat, and as a wash for ill-conditioned sores.

Hemlock Bark.—It is astringent and tonic. Enemas composed of a strong tea of this article may be used with advantage in all cases of prolapsus.

Marsh Rosemary.—The root of the marsh rosemary is astringent and tonic, and may be used in all cases where these properties are required. A decoction of this is an excellent wash for canker-sores, sore mouth, etc.

Witch Hazel.—The bark and leaves are astringent and tonic. May be used in all cases of hemorrhage, debility, and for cleansing irritable sores.

Evan Root.—Evan root is a valuable tonic and astringent; useful for diarrhea, dysentery, sore mouth, debility, etc.

White Pond-Lily.—The root of this plant is a pleasant astringent useful in bowel complaints, and as a gargle for putrid and ulcerated sore throat. Combined with slippery-elm, it forms an excellent poultice for cleansing old sores, ulcers, etc.

Gold Thread.—It is astringent and tonic, useful as a gargle for sore throat, and is much used for that purpose. It may also be employed in debility and loss of appetite, and in all cases where golden seal and poplar bark are recommended.

Sumach.—The leaves and berries are stimulant, astringent, and tonic, beneficial in dysentery, stranguary, sore mouth, also for washing offensive sores and ring-worms.

Golden Seal—It is a laxative and tonic, and an excellent remedy in costiveness, loss of appetite, jaundice, debility, liver complaint, and faintness at the stomach. Taken in doses of an even tea-spoonful, it is efficacious in relieving unpleasant sensations occasioned by a hearty meal.

Barberry.—The bark is tonic and laxative, useful in jaundice, loss of appetite, weakness of the digestive organs, and in all cases where golden seal is recommended. Dose—a tea-spoonful of the powdered bark.

Hoarhound.—The root is stimulant and tonic, useful in coughs, colds, asthmatic affections, and in pulmonary diseases. It may be prepared with honey or molasses.

Fir Balsam.—Is a valuable expectorant and tonic, beneficial in coughs, colds, and all affections of the lungs.

Yarrow.—This plant is a valuable stimulant, an excellent remedy in all cases of female weakness, colic, and intermittent fevers. A decoction of the herb is also used as a wash for sores, salt-rheum, and piles.

Golden Rod.—Is aromatic and slightly stimulant; is used for quieting pains in the stomach and bowels, flatulency, and for scenting other medicines.

Cleavers.—Are useful on account of their diuretic properties; also in inflammation of the kidneys and urinary obstructions.

Dandelion.—Is tonic and diuretic, an excellent corrector of the bile, and an invaluable remedy in hepatic diseases.

Sassafras.—Steeped in water, it is an excellent wash for all kinds of humors.

Catnip.—Valuable for injections. In fevers, it promotes perspiration without raising the heat of the body.

Sage.—Useful in fevers, and for worms in children. Good substitute for tea.

Comfrey.—This is mucilaginous; valuable in coughs and all consumptive complaints.

Saffron.—Makes a valuable tea for children afflicted with the measles, chicken-pox, and all eruptive diseases.

Coltsfoot.—A tea of this is good for hoarseness.

Valerian.—Good in all nervous complaints; a swallow or two taken occasionally will produce the same effect as paregoric, and is every way preferable to it.

Wild Cherry-Tree Bark.—A tea made of this is said to have cured consumption, if taken in season.

PROF. A. CURTIS, M. D.,

Office at Hill's Drug Store, corner Fifth and Race Sts.,

CINCINNATI, OHIO,

Is prepared to treat all forms of disease, medical and surgical, in the best manner. His practice is purely physiological, embracing hygienic agencies, as pure air, proper food, and exercise; and water, caloric, electricity, and galvanism, in their appropriate applications, as in baths, simple, medicated, and chemical.

He uses innocent and powerful medicines, rejecting all poisonous substances; and all violence, as bleeding and blistering. In an extensive practice for thirty years, he has not lost a case of scarlet fever, measles, nor small-pox, summer complaint nor dysentery, nor one of typhoid, remittent, intermittent, continued, nor bilious fever; not a single case in parturition, nor in consequence of it, in which he was the only physician. He has cured, in a few minutes, without medicines or pain, many a severe case of disease, both acute and chronic, some of years duration; and, by the aid of magnetism and chloroform, performed severe surgical operations without producing suffering or injury.

He has lately performed, with complete success, some of the most difficult and dangerous operations. Among them are the removal of a diseased femur, a cancerous breast, a fungus hematodes or melanosis, from the cavity of the eye, and an ovarian tumor which weighed over thirty pounds. In thirty years practice he has never lost a surgical patient.

He does not promise to cure every case, but believes that he can cure all that are curable by any other practice or physician. Examinations free; charges for prescriptions moderate.

Having able assistants at home, he can visit important cases at a distance, where rail-cars can carry him without much loss of time. But it is better, if they can, that they come to him, as he desires to attend as much as possible to his friends in the city.

He receives students, male and female, and teaches them the true science of life, and the divine art of preventing and curing disease. The Regular Lectures in the PHYSIO-MEDICAL COLLEGE will commence on the 20th of October, and continue sixteen weeks.

Dr. Curtis's Medical Books for sale as above.

MECHANICS' DEPARTMENT.

Painting Glass Transparencies.—Provide a small muller and a piece of thick ground glass, five or six inches square, to grind the colors on; also a small pallet knife, and a few bottles to put the colors in. For a red color get a little scarlet lake, and for blue a little Prussian blue. For green use purified verdigris ground with a quarter of its bulk of gamboge, and for brown use burnt umber, and for black, burnt sienna black. These colors are truly transparent. Having all these colors ready, grind them in the balsam of fir mixed with half its bulk of turpentine; mastic varnish will do very well, but the balsam is the most beautiful. To coat the glass black round the painting, dissolve asphaltum in turpentine, and mix with lampblack. When the colors are all ground they must be put in separate bottles and sealed, and when they are to be used, a little bit is taken out at once on a piece of glass, just as much as is needed at once, as it quickly dries. If the color is too thick, it must be diluted with turpentine. To paint glass sliders, the subject must be designed on paper, and the paper put under the glass, and the glass painted above it according to the design of the paper underneath.

Varnish for Wood Patterns.—The most simple varnish, combined with adaptation, is the following: One quart of alcohol and a quarter of a pound of gum shellac. This put into a bottle, and when wanted for use, mix up with a little lampblack to about the thickness of cream, and varnish the pattern over, rubbing it into the grain of the wood, until a slight friction produces a polish. This varnish makes a smooth surface on the pattern, rendering it more easily drawn from the sand, and it fills up all pores, or worm-holes, that may be in the wood; consequently, a cleaner and smoother casting is produced.

Crystal Varnish.—First, genuine pale Canada balsam and rectified oil of turpentine, equal parts; mix, place the bottle in warm water, agitate well, set it aside in a moderately warm place, and in a week pour off the clear. Used for maps, prints, drawings, and other articles on paper, and also to prepare tracing paper, and to transfer engraving. Second, mastic, three ounces; alcohol, one pint, dissolved. Used to fix pencil drawings.

Etching Varnish.—First, white wax, two ounces; black and Burgundy pitch, of each half an ounce; melt together, add, by degrees, powdered asphaltum, two ounces, and boil till a drop taken out on a plate will break, when cold, by being bent double two or three times between the fingers; it must then be poured into warm water, and made into small balls for use. Second, linseed oil and mastic, of each four ounces; melt together. Third, soft linseed oil, four ounces; gum benzoin and white wax, of each half an ounce; boil to two-thirds.

Flexible Varnish.—First, India-rubber in shaving, one ounce; mineral naphtha, two pounds; digest, at a gentle heat, in a close vessel, till dissolved, and strain. Second, India-rubber, one ounce; drying oil, one quart; dissolve by as little heat as possible, employing constant stirring; then strain. Third, linseed oil, one gallon; dried white copperas and sugar of lead, each three ounces; litharge, eight ounces; boil, with constant agitation, till it strings well; then cool slowly, and decant the clear. If too thick, thin it with quick-drying linseed oil. These are used for balloors, gas-bags, &c.

Varnish for Iron Work.—The beautiful, glossy, black varnish for iron work may be made by fusing one pound of amber in an iron vessel, and adding, while hot, one quart of boiled linseed oil and three ounces each of dark rosin and asphaltum, in powder. When the whole is thoroughly incorporated, take it off; and, when cool, add about one pint of turpentine. Several coats of this varnish are put on, and the articles are dried, after each application, in a warm oven.

Another.—To make a good black varnish for iron work, take eight pounds of asphaltum, and fuse it in an iron kettle, then add five gallons of boiled linseed oil, one pound of litharge, half a pound of sulphate of zinc (add these slowly, or it will fume over), and boil them for about three hours. Now add one and a-half pounds of dark gum-amber, and boil for two hours longer, or until the mass will become quite thick, when cool; after which, it should be thinned with turpentine to due consistency.

Varnish for Iron Castings.—Heavy petroleum, mixed with coal tar, and applied warm, is an excellent varnish for iron castings.

Black Japanning.—Black grounds for japan may be made by mixing ivory black with shellac varnish; or, for coarse work, lampblack, and the top coating of common seedlac varnish. A common black japan may be made by painting a piece of work with drying oil, and putting said work into an oven, not too hot; then gradually raising the heat, and keeping it up for a long time, so as not to burn the oil and make it blister.

Tortoise-Shell Japan.—This varnish is prepared by taking of good linseed oil one gallon, and of umber, half a pound, and boiling them together until the oil becomes very brown and thick, when they are strained through a cloth, and boiled again until the composition is about the consistence of pitch, when it is fit for use. Having prepared this varnish, clean well the vessel that is to be varnished (japanned), and then lay vermilion, mixed with shellac varnish, or with drying oil diluted with good turpentine, very thinly on the places intended to imitate the clear parts of the tortoise-shell. When the vermillion is dry, brush over the whole with the above umber varnish, diluted to a due consistence with turpentine; and when it is set and firm, it must be put into an oven, and undergo a strong heat for a long time. This is the ground for those beautiful tea-boards which are so much admired. The work is all the better to be finished in an annealing oven.

Painting Japan Work.—The colors to be painted are tempered generally in oil, which should have at least one-fourth of its weight of gum sanderac, or mastic, dissolved in it, and it should be well diluted with turpentine, that the colors may be laid on thin and evenly. In some instances it does well to put on water-colors, or grounds of gold, which a skillful hand can do, and manage so as to make the work as if it were embossed. These water-colors are best prepared by means of isinglass size, mixed with honey, or sugar-candy. These colors, when laid on, must receive a number of upper coats of the varnish above described.

Transparent Painting on Linen.—Very fine muslin is the best material for painting upon; and before you begin to paint, a straining-frame must be made, of beech or hard wood. It should consist of two upright bars mortised at each end, with holes, into which top and bottom cross-bars, tenoned at the sides, can slide, much after the same pattern as the ordinary embroidery frame; but it is rarely required larger than suitable for a window blind. Along the inner edge of the frame a strip of webbing is permanently nailed, and to this the muslin must be sewed before it is stretched. Having stretched the muslin, it is ready for the first preparation, which is sizing. The best size is that made from parchment cuttings; you must have a pipkin, to hold about a quart of water. Having cut up the parchment into small strips, fill the pipkin with water, and put them to simmer, but not to boil. When this operation has gone on for a couple of hours, you will have sufficient size, which should be allowed to cool, and then you will have a clear, transparent jelly. Remove the dregs from it, and boil in a clean pipkin as much as you will require; but recollect the more careful you are in the preparation of the size, the better will be the result of your workmanship.

After the muslin is sized, it will be found to relax in the frame, and has, therefore, to be again fully tightened. A second, or even a third coating of size is to be applied, when the former is dry, and the muslin again stretched, if it slackens. After a couple of days or more, when the size is quite hard, it must be rubbed smooth with pumice-stone; a smooth face may be obtained to the pumice-stone by grinding it on a stone flag with water. This operation of smoothing the size is very necessary, as the colors take better to the material than when this process is omitted. The muslin being now in a fit state to receive the paint, the subject of the design must be drawn upon it. In order to secure accuracy—for no "rubbing out" can be effected on muslin—it is a common practice to draw the intended outline first upon cartridge-paper, with a bold stroke, in ink, so that when fixed to the back of the muslin with threads, it can be seen through the fabric, and the picture be traced out on the muslin with a dark pencil. Another way of tracing a design is to employ the pounce-bag and a perforated pattern; thus, for instance, take a natural leaf, such as that of the vine or ivy, lay it upon a strip of cartridge-paper; then perforate the paper all round the leaf with a pointer, or a thick needle fastened into a handle. On removing the leaf, a few perforation may be made, to indicate the arteries. If several strips of paper are placed under the leaf at once, repetitions of the designs can be readily obtained.

The best pounce-bag is made of a couple of folds of muslin tied up like a laundress's blue-bag, and filled with a finely-powdered charcoal. The perforated paper patterns being placed on the muslin, they are then pounced over, when the charcoal dust falls through the holes on to the muslin, and thus transfers the design of the leaf. If a border of leaves is required, it is only necessary to repeat the same leaf, but placed in different positions—now left, now right, then overlapping each other. The same may also be done with a butterfly, or any similar object. Having perforated the design of a bird on the wing, it will not look like the same, if its position is considerably altered, now flying up in mid-air, now alighting on to a bough, then descending; the subsequent coloring of the leaves, birds, and butterflies being also modified, changes their general appearance.

Transferring Prints to Glass, Wood, &c.—When it is desired to transfer a steel, copper, or lithographic print to glass, the first operation is to coat the glass with dilute lac, or clear copal varnish. The print is then moistened with water, and while the varnish remains sticky, the paper is placed on the glass with the print side upon the varnish; it is then pressed gently, to make it adhere. Several folds of white paper are now placed upon the back of the print, also a board, with a light weight thereon, to keep the print and varnish in contact till both are dry. After this the paper is moistened, and rubbed off gently with the fingers, when the ink composing the print is left adhering to the glass. The several parts of the print may then be painted with appropriate colors, and then finished with a ground-coat over all. Prints may be transferred to wood in the same manner. The common mode of transferring prints to wooden blocks, for engraving, is to immerse a print for a short period in a solution of potash, then place it upon the block and press it. The potash softens the ink on the paper of the print, and when placed upon the block of wood and pressed, the impression is made in the same manner as printing in the usual way. Prints are also transferred thus to stones for lithographic printing; also to plates of zinc for printing in a lithographic press.

Many very elegant designs can be perforated by folding the paper once, twice, or four times; thus, whatever pattern is perforated will then be repeated through the other sections. In this way corners and centers are formed. The design, thus placed in outline on the linen, is now to be colored. We, of course, presume that persons employing themselves thus will have some knowledge of art, and it is now that their taste can be displayed. The rules which govern art are applicable to transparent painting, but our observations are limited to the specialities required to put it in practice. A fine sponge forms a good tool to lay on the tints for clouds and sky, or distant hills, and coarse honey-comb sponge does well for luxurious foliage, rocks, &c. Flat hog's-hair brushes, the same as are used for oil-painting, do admirably for this work. Varnish colors, tempered with japanners' gold size and turpentine, are the best; the paints sold in tubes will be found convenient—copal varnish and pale-drying oil being used as a vehicle.

Young persons who can draw, and are in want of a little occupation, either for amusement or as a means of income, can now, from these hints, turn their attention to transparent painting; and there are too many ugly back windows to hide in every town for them to fear any lack of employment.

Colors for Stamping Muslin for Embroidery.—Lamp-black, mixed with a solution of gum arabic or starch, will make a very good composition for stamping white muslin for embroidery. Prussian-blue, ground to powder, and mixed with a little boiled starch, answers for stamping blue on white muslin. All colors used for stamping should be of such a nature that they will wash out easily with soap and water; hence those fast colors, which are used to print on calicoes, are unsuitable. For stamping on a black ground—such as a piece of black cloth or velvet, common pipe-clay, mixed with a little starch, makes a white stamping composition. Lamp-black, mixed with resin in a molten condition, then cooled and ground to powder, with a little water, makes a good black for stamping.

Collodion Formulæ.—The following two receipts are from the *Photographic News:* Those who are in the habit of experimenting in the preparation of collodion for photographs will, probably, like to try the following formula, communicated by M. Jeanrenaud to the *Moniteur de la Photographie.* To counterbalance the drawback of complexity which seems to characterize it, is the strong recommendation of the author, who possesses a high reputation. It is stated to give delicate results, to be very rapid and durable, improving rather than deteriorating with age. Here is the formula: Soluble cotton, 8 parts; pure ether, 800 parts; alcohol (sp. gr. 830), 250 parts; iodide of cadmium, 9 parts. Dissolve, and add to 35 ounces of collodion 25 of pure bromine. To 3 ounces of the collodion then add 12 drops of strong liquid ammonia. A deposit is thrown down, which may be redissolved by adding a few drops of glacial acetic acid. The 3 ounces are then added to the remainder of 35 ounces, and the whole left to settle for a fortnight. If it retains a straw color, it is fit for use; if it be colorless, add a few drops of bromine.

M. Jeanrenaud also gives a formula for dry collodion, as follows: Take ordinary collodion, and add to it 5 per cent. of a solution of ether, saturated with yellow amber; the sensitizing bath consists of from 7 to 8 per cent. of nitrate of silver, and 2 per cent. of glacial acetic acid; the plate is then washed in four or five waters. The development may be effected either by the ordinary bath of sulphate of iron, or with pyrogallic acid. When the plates are large, it is necessary to fix the film around the edges by means of some varnish, either with alcohol or chloroform. M. Jeanrenaud found plates, so prepared, as sensitive, after the lapse of a month, as when first fixed. The time required is about double that of the wet process, and, for landscapes, varies from three to seven minutes, according to the light and the season.

Dammara Varnish.—"Gum Dammara," as it is called, is a resin, not a gum. It is employed for making varnish, by dissolving it in turpentine. The resin should be first well-dried, for, if it contains any moisture, it will tend to make the varnish opaque. A common way to prepare it is to boil the resin in the turpentine in an open vessel; but if the resin is thoroughly dried, it will dissolve slowly in cold turpentine, and form a clear varnish.

A good way to prepare it, on a large scale, is to use an enameled cast-iron vessel, capable of containing about fifty pounds, for making twenty-five pounds of the varnish. The dammara resin is put into the vessel in a solid state, the proper quantity of turpentine (five parts to four parts of resin) is then poured in, and the whole put upon the fire. As soon as the boiling begins, the water, originally included in the resin, is dissipated in the form of vapor, and the resin acquires a softer consistence. When all the water is expelled, and the varnish boils quietly, the solution is completed, and the vessel may be removed from the fire. As long as traces of water exist in the varnish, its boiling is attended with a bubbling movement; but as soon as all the water is got rid of, the varnish boils quite quietly. When the varnish is prepared, it is poured through a fine wire-sieve, and then allowed to settle sufficiently. If it be desired to give the varnish a tougher consistence, two or three per cent. of good bleached linseed oil (not boiled with oxide of lead) must be added to it before boiling. This communicates great toughness to it.

Alloy for Journal Boxes.—Take seven and a-half pounds of pure copper and melt it in a crucible; then gradually add, in small pieces, ninety-two and a half pounds of zinc; when this is melted, and the two metals thoroughly mixed, the alloy is to be run into molds for journal boxes. A patent was granted May 1, 1855, for this alloy, to Thomas Forth, of Cincinnati, Ohio.

Babbitt Metal.—Take twenty-four pounds of copper, and melt it first in a crucible; then add, gradually, twenty-four parts of pure tin and eight of antimony. Great care must be exercised in adding the tin to the copper. This composition is rendered softer by the use of a greater quantity of tin. It is first run into ingots, then melted and cast, to form the journal boxes, &c.

Fine Polishing Powder.—Professor Vogel, of England, states, that the finest powder for polishing optical glasses and fine metals, is made by calcining the oxalate of iron. It is superior to the common polishing-powder for glass, made of lixiviated colcothar.

Consolidating Cast-steel.—Mr. J. M. Rowan, of Glasgow, proposes to consolidate cast-steel, or metal produced by the pneumatic process, by com-

5

pressing it while still liquid, or nearly so, whereby it is rendered much better adapted for subsequent processes.

A harmless green, for coloring confectionery, may be made as follows: Take thirty-two parts of saffron, and infuse it in seven parts of water, to which add twenty-six parts of the carmine of indigo in fifteen parts of water. The yellow saffron and blue indigo, when mixed, form a beautiful green color, which will combine with sugar solutions.

A most excellent Furniture Paste is made, by dissolving one part resin and one part beeswax in two parts of benzine.

Refined Glycerine is a very suitable lubricator for clock-work. It does not freeze in cold weather.

To Clean Brass.—Rub the surface of the metal with rotten-stone and sweet oil, then rub off with a piece of cotton flannel and polish with soft leather. A solution of oxalic acid rubbed over tarnished brass, with a cotton rag, soon removes the tarnish, rendering the metal bright. The acid must be washed off with water, and the brass rubbed with whitening in powder, and soft leather. When acids are employed for removing the oxide from brass, the metal must be thoroughly washed afterwards, or it will tarnish in a few minutes after being exposed to the air. A mixture of muriatic acid and alum dissolved in water imparts a golden color to brass articles that are steeped in it for a few seconds.

Cleaning Tinware.—Acids should never be employed to clean tinware. because they attack the metal, and remove it from the iron of which it forms a thin coat. We refer to articles made of tin plate, which consists of iron covered with tin. Rub the article first with rotten-stone and sweet oil, the same as recommended for brass, then finish with whitening and a piece of soft leather. Articles made wholly of tin should be cleaned in the same manner. In a dry atmosphere, planished tinware will remain bright for a long period, but will soon become tarnished in moist air.

Cleaning Silver-plated Articles.—White metal articles electro-plated with silver are now very common, and great care is required in cleaning them when tarnished. No powder must be used for this purpose which has the least grit in it, or the silver will be scratched and soon worn off. The finest impalpable whitening should be employed, with a little soft, water, in removing the tarnish. They are next washed with rain water, dried and polished with a piece of soft leather, some rouge powder, or fine whitening, then finally rubbed down with the hand, which forms a most excellent polisher.

Black on Gun-Barrels.—The following mode of producing a black coating on gun-barrels is taken from Mr. Wells's "Annual of Scientific Discovery" for the present year: First, take chloride of mercury and sal ammoniac; second, perchloride of iron, sulphate of copper, nitric acid, alcohol and water; third, perchloride and proto-chloride of iron, alcohol and water; fourth, weak solution of the sulphide of potassium. These solutions are successively applied, each becoming dry before the other is used. No. 3 is applied twice, and a bath of boiling water follows Nos. 3 and 4. The shade of color is fixed by active friction, with a pad of woolen cloth, and a little oil. The shade thus obtained is a beautiful black, of uniform appearance. This process is used in the manufacture of arms at St. Etienne, France. We regret that the proportions of the different ingredients are not given. Several of our gunsmiths have made many inquiries as to the mode of producing the blue-black coating on the Whitworth and other English rifles. Perhaps the above solution will effect the object. The alcohol is used to make the application dry quickly. The perchloride of iron and the sulphate of copper in No. 2 should be used only in a moderately strong solution, and only about 10 per cent. of nitric acid added to the water. We hope that our gunsmiths will meet with success in using these solutions. No. 2, applied in three or four coats, will form the common brown coating for gun-barrels. After the last application has become dry, it is rubbed with a wire scratch brush, washed with warm water, then dried, and afterward rubbed down with a composition of beeswax dissolved in turpentine.

Aluminum Bronze.—Experiments have been made at the Royal Gun Factory, Woolwich, England, by Mr. J. Anderson, to test the comparative strength, &c., of aluminum bronze. Its average breaking tensile strength was found to be 73,185 lbs per square inch, while that of common gun metal is but 35,040 lbs. Its composition is 90 per cent. of copper, 10 per cent. of aluminum. The purest copper that can be obtained, such as that of Lake Superior, is the best to employ. It requires to be remelted three times before it becomes fit for practical purposes. The specific gravity of this alloy is said to be about that of cast-iron. It is far more rigid than brass or common gun-metal. It produces good castings; it can be drawn into tubes, rolled into sheets, and hammered like iron, and it is also capable of being soldered with brass.

Bronzing Metals.—The production of different colors on the surface of metals, such as works of fine art, &c., is called bronzing. Mere surface-coloring is executed with metallic powders mixed and applied with a varnish. But the most perfect bronzing is produced by chemical action on the metal itself—its own surface being thus made to form the bronze color. Dr. Ure says, respecting this art: "Coins and metals may be handsomely bronzed as follows: 2 parts of verdigris and 1 part of sal-ammoniac are to be dissolved in vinegar; the solution is to be boiled, skimmed, and diluted with water, till it has only a weak metallic taste, and, upon further dilution, lets fall no white precipitate. This solution is now made to boil briskly, and is poured upon the objects to be bronzed. These objects must have been previously cleaned and made perfectly free from grease, and set in a copper pan. This pan, with the articles now in it, is put on a fire, and the solution made to boil for some time. The articles, if made of copper, will acquire an agreeable reddish-brown hue, without losing their luster; but if they are boiled too long, the coat of oxide upon them becomes too thick, and looks scaly and dull; and if the solution is too strong, the copper becomes covered with a white powder, which becomes green on exposure to the air. The pieces thus bronzed must be washed well in warm soft water, and then carefully dried, or they will turn green. The antique appearance is given with a solution of three-quarters of an ounce of sal ammoniac and a drachm and a half of binoxalate of potash (salt of sorrel) dissolved in a quart of vinegar. It is applied with a soft rag to the surface of the metal, then allowed to dry. Several applications are thus made, until a coating of sufficient thickness is obtained. "Copper acquires a brown color by rubbing it with a solution of the common liver of sulphur, or sulphuret of potash.

The Chinese are said to bronze their copper vessels by taking 2 ounces of verdigris, 2 ounces of cinnamon, 5 ounces of sal ammoniac, and 5 ounces of alum, all in powder, making these into a paste with vinegar, and spreading it upon the surface of the article, which should be previously brightened. The article is then held over a fire, till it become uniformly heated, then it is cooled, washed, and dried. It thus receives one, two, or several of such coats, until the desired color is obtained. An addition of sulphate of copper to the mixture makes the color chesnut-brown.

A good method of bronzing copper articles, such as tea-urns, to prevent them tarnishing, is described in most all the best treatises on chemistry. It is as follows: The copper is first cleaned, then brushed over with peroxide of iron (generally colcothar) made into a paste with water or with a dilute solution of the acetate of copper. The article is then placed in a muffle in a furnace, and heated cautiously for some time, then taken out and cooled. Upon brushing off the oxide, the surface underneath is found to have acquired the desired hue.

Another method of bronzing copper is to brush it over with a paste of black lead, place it over a clear fire till moderately heated, then brush it off. A very beautiful bronze is thus produced. The surface of the copper must be perfectly bright when the black lead is applied. A thin film of wax or tallow applied to copper, and the article placed on a clear fire until the wax or grease begins to smoke, produces a bronzed surface. In all these operations great care is necessary in managing the articles properly when subjecting them to the action of heat.

The following is a receipt which we have been told will produce a beautiful dark bronze on brass: To 1 pound of muriatic acid add 6 ounces of the peroxide of iron and 3 ounces of yellow arsenic; mix these together and let the solution stand for about two days, shaking it occasionally. The brass article, perfectly free from dirt and grease, is now to be immersed in it, and allowed to stand for about three hours, when it turns perfectly black. It is then lifted out, and washed well in soft water, and dried in sawdust. After this it is coated with a paste of black lead used for iron stoves, and when dry, it is polished with a brush. After this it may receive a thin coat of lac-varnish.

Dull Black Color on Brass.—The *Practical Mechanic's Journal* (Glasgow) states that the dull black so frequently employed for brass optical instruments, may be produced as follows: First rub the brass with tripoli, then wash it with a dilute solution of a mixture of one part of neutral nitrate of tin, and two parts of chloride of gold; allow the brass to remain without wiping for about ten minutes, after which wipe it off with a wet cloth. If there has been an excess of acid, the surface will have assumed a dull black appearance. The neutral nitrate of tin is prepared by decomposing perchloride of tin in ammonia, and dissolving the precipitated oxide thus obtained in nitric acid.

Staining Marble.—A solution of the nitrate of silver stains marble black; a solution of verdigris applied hot stains it green; a concentrated solution of carmine applied hot stains it red; orpiment dissolved in ammonia stains it yellow; the sulphate of copper, blue; and a solution of magenta, purple. The marble should be warmed before any of these solutions are applied, so as to open its pores, and enable it to absorb more of the coloring matter. Marble may be stained according to beautiful designs with such colors. This art was more extensively practiced in Italy during former ages than it is at present.

Hardening Wood for Pulleys.—After a wooden pulley is turned and rubbed smooth, boil it for about eight minutes in olive oil, then allow it to dry, after which it will ultimately become almost as hard as copper.

Case-hardening Iron.—The hardness and polish of steel may be united, in a certain degree, with the firmness and cheapness of malleable iron, by case-hardening; it is a superficial conversion of iron into steel.

The articles intended to be case-hardened, being previously finished, with the exception of polishing, are stratified with animal carbon, and the box containing them luted with equal parts of sand and clay. They are then placed in the fire, and kept at a light, red heat for half an hour when the contents of the box are emptied into water. Delicate articles may be preserved by a saturated solution of common salt, with any vegetable mucilage, to give it a pulpy consistence. The animal carbon is nothing more than any animal matter—such as horns, hoofs, skins, or leather—sufficiently burned to admit of being reduced to powder. The box is commonly made of iron; but the use of it, for occasional case-hardening upon a small scale, may easily be dispensed with, as it will answer the same end to envelop the articles with the composition above directed to be used as a lute; dry it, gradually, before it is exposed to a red heat, otherwise it will probably crack. The depth of the steel, induced by case-hardening, will vary with the time the operation is continued.

A very speedy and most excellent method of case-hardening is effected by reducing some of the prussiate of potash to powder, and making it into paste, rubbing it over the finished iron while it is at a red heat, and then putting it in the fire again, and plunging it into water when the iron is at a blood-red heat. Another method consists in covering the polished iron with a paste of the prussiate of potash and flour, allowing it to dry, then placing it in a clear fire until it becomes red hot, when it is plunged into cold water. This may be repeated, to insure a greater depth of hardening.

Enameling Cast-iron Vessels.—Reduce into fine powder and grind together nine parts of red lead, six parts of flint glass, two parts of purified pearlash, two parts of purified saltpeter, and one part of borax. This is put into a large crucible about half full, and melted until a clear glass is obtained. This glass is then ground with water, and the cast-iron vessel is covered with a coating of it, and then heated in a muffle in a furnace. This will melt in a very short time if the furnace is at a good heat, and the cast-iron vessel will be covered with a very fine black enamel of a shining appearance. To make it tough, it should be put into an annealing oven.

Another very fine enamel for iron vessels is made as follows: Twelve parts of flint glass, four parts of pearlash, four parts of saltpeter, two parts of borax, and three parts of the oxide of tin calcined with common salt. This is treated the same as described above, and makes a white enamel.

The cast-iron articles to be enameled are scoured bright with sand and dilute sulphuric acid, then dried, and the enamel paste put on with a brush, or poured on the surface, and the excess dripped off. This paste is dried slowly in the air, and the articles baked in a hot oven until the paste fuses. The heat is gradually raised to the melting point.

Silvering by Powdered Tin.—A quantity of pure tin is melted and poured into a box, which is then violently shaken; the metal assumes, when cold, the form of a very fine gray powder. This is sifted, to separate any coarse particles, and is mixed with melted glue. When it is to be applied, it should be reduced, by the addition of water, to the consistence of thin cream, and is laid on with a soft brush, like paint. It appears, when dry, like a coat of gray water color; but when it is gone over with an agate brusher, it exhibits a bright surface of polished tin. If the glue is too strong, the burnisher has no effect; and if too weak, the tin crumbles off under the burnisher. A coating of white or gold-colored oil varnish, or lacquer, is immediately laid over it, according as it may be intended to imitate silvering or gilding. This kind of gilding is often used for covering wood, leather, iron, or other articles in constant wear. It is very ornamental.

Composition for Welding Cast-steel.—Take ten parts of borax and one part of sal ammoniac; grind them together and fuse them in a metal-pot over a clear fire, taking care to continue the heat until all spume has disappeared from the surface. When the liquid appears clear, the composition is ready to be poured out to cool and concrete, when it is ground to a fine powder and is ready for use. To use this composition the steel is put into the fire and raised to a bright yellow heat; it is then dipped into the welding powder, and again placed into the fire, until it attains the same degree of heat as before, when it is ready to be placed under the hammer.

To Tin Small Articles.—To tin small articles, prepare a solution of the chloride of zinc, which is done by feeding muriatic acid with scraps of zinc until it will take up no more. A strong glass bottle is the best vessel for this purpose. Let the solution settle, and then decant the clear, and it is ready for use. Next prepare an iron pot, of such size as will suit the purpose for the work to be done. Next put the pot on the fire, and put in a sufficient quantity of tin to cover the work. When the tin is melted, put in as much beef or mutton tallow as will cover it about one quarter of an inch thick, which must remain in a clear melted state, taking care not to let it get on fire. The iron, or any other metal to be tinned, must be well cleaned, either by filing or scraping, or polishing with sand. Let the article to be tinned be then wet with the chloride of zinc and carefully immersed in the tallow and melted tin, and if the article be well cleaned, it will, in a very short time, be fairly and perfectly covered with the tin, when it may be taken out.

To tin a piece of plated metal, say a piece of copper plated on one side with silver, prepare a paste, which may be of common pipe-clay, and a very little wheaten flour wet up with water. Then take a soft brush and lay an even coat of the paste over the silver side, and lay it in a warm place to dry; then, when dry, it may be immersed in the pot of melted tallow and tin, as already described, and the copper side will be covered with tin; but the silver will be protected from the tin by the paste, which may be removed by washing in water.

To Gild Steel.—Make a neutral solution of gold in nitro-muriatic acid (aqua regia), and pour into it a quantity of sulphuric ether; the ether will take up the gold and float upon the denser acid. The article is then to be washed with this auriferous ether (with a hair pencil); the ether flies off, and the gold adheres.

To Silver Brass.—Take one part of chloride of silver (the white precipitate which falls when a solution of common salt is poured into a solution of nitrate of silver or lunar caustic), three parts of pearlash, one of whiting, and one and a half of common salt, or one part of chloride of silver, and ten parts of cream of tartar, and rub the brass with a moistened piece of cork dipped in the powder.

Tinning Cast-iron Articles.—Many articles, such as bridle-bits, small nails, &c., are manufactured of tinned cast-iron. Saucepans, goblets, and other hollow ironware, are tinned upon their inner surfaces. They are first scoured bright with sand and dilute sulphuric or muriatic acid, then washed thoroughly in soft water and dried. They are then placed over a fire and heated, when grain tin is poured in, and the vessel moved so as to roll the molten tin over the surface. Some powdered rosin is added, to prevent oxide forming on the surface of the iron. Hollow vessels of copper and brass are tinned in the inside in the same manner.

Tinning Iron.—Cast-iron articles to be tinned, are first scoured bright with sulphuric acid and sand, then washed in clean warm water, and dried. They are afterward coated with zinc, and a coat of tin is put upon the top of the zinc, by dipping the articles in molten tin. When the tinning operation is finished, the articles are placed in boiling water, and allowed to cool slowly.

Coloring Gold.—A solution of two ounces of alum, two of saltpeter and one of sal ammoniac is used for coloring gold. Another pickle, used for coloring gold, consists of nitric acid eight ounces, muriatic acid one quart, sal ammoniac two ounces, alum one ounce, and water two gallons. The articles of gold are dipped in this for a few seconds, then washed thoroughly in pure water, and dried. Pale, brassy gold may be made to assume a deep reddish shade by using such a pickle or "dip."

Preparing Kid Leather.—Yolk of egg is largely used in the preparation of kid leather for gloves, in France, to give it the requisite softness and elasticity. The treatment of the skins in this manner is called by the French glove-makers *nourriture.* As a substitute for the yolk of egg, the brains of certain animals, which, in chemical nature, closely resemble the yolk of egg, have been used. For this purpose the brain is mixed in hot water, passed through a sieve, and then made into dough with flour and the lye of wood ashes. The glove-leather is also steeped for a short period in a weak solution of alum. The Indians of our forests employ the brains of deer and buffalo, mixed with a weak lye of wood ashes, and, after this, they smoke the skins; the pyroligneous acid of the wood in the smoke accomplishes the same object as the alum used by the French skin-dressers. Indian-prepared skins stand the action of water in a superior manner to the French kid. Furs dressed in the same manner resist the attacks of insects. It is believed that the carbonic acid in the smoke is the preservative principle which renders the skins tanned by the Indians superior to those tanned with alum and sumac in the usual way. The skins are rubbed with the mixture of the brains of the animals and the lye, by the squaws; then dried in the open air. Three or four such applications are necessary before they are smoked in pits covered with the bark of trees.

Tanning Nets, Sails, and Cordage.—The cloth of awnings and sails, also of nets and cordage, may be prepared in a simple manner to endure for a far greater length of time than is usual with such articles. Take about 100 pounds of oak or hemlock bark, and boil it in 90 gallons of water, until the quantity is reduced to 70 gallons; then take out the bark and steep the cloth, sails, or cordage in the clear liquor for about twelve hours; then take it out and dry it thoroughly in the atmosphere or in a warm apartment. The cloth should be entirely covered with the tan liquor, and should lie loose in it, so as not to press the folds too closely together. By boiling the cloth or cordage in the tan liquor, it will be ready in a shorter period. Sail and awning cloth, so prepared, will resist the action of damp for years, in situations where unprepared cloth will decay in a few months.

Glazed Leather.—The basis for glazed, or what is called "enameled leather," is boiled linseed oil. The oil is prepared by boiling it with metallic oxides, such as litharge (oxide of lead) and white copperas (sulphate of zinc) until it acquires a sirupy consistency. Five gallons of linseed oil are boiled with four and a half pounds of white lead and the same weight of litharge, until the whole becomes thick like cream. This mixture is then combined with chalk in powder, or with yellow ocher, is spread upon the leather, and worked into the pores with appropriate tools. Three thin coats are thus applied, each dried before the other is put on, and when the last is perfectly dry, the surface is rubbed down with pumice-stone until it is quite smooth. A mixture of the prepared oil, without ocher or chalk, but rendered black with ivory-black and thinned with turpentine, is now put on in one or two thin coats, according to circumstances; then dried. The final coating consists of boiled linseed oil and copal varnish, thinned with turpentine, and colored with lamp-black. The apartment in which such leather is dried is maintained at a temperature ranging from 134 to 170 deg. F. White enameled leather is prepared in the same manner; but white lead and chalk are exclusively used to thicken the oil. Copal varnish colored with lamp-black, will make very good enameled leather, if it is put on in several thin coats, and dried after each application.

Sulphurized Oil for Wood.—M. Lapparent, inspector of timber for the French navy, states that he prepared a paint for preserving timber, composed of linseed oil, sulphur, and manganese, which was found very effectual. The flowers of sulphur were stirred into linseed oil in about equal quantities, by weight, and about twelve per cent. of the oxide of manganese added. This was applied to some oak logs, which were buried in a manure heap for six months, when the wood was found to be uninjured —no fungi being formed upon it. Unprepared wood subjected to the same treatment was covered with fungi.

Nitrate of Silver.—The nitrate of silver is prepared by adding small pieces of pure silver to nitric acid (aquafortis) until effervescence ceases. The solution then formed is clear and caustic. It stains the hair, skin, and almost all animal substances, black. When boiled for a considerable period, it deposits beautiful clear crystals. It is very poisonous. Stains of the nitrate of silver may be removed by the cyanide of potassium.

Cement for Mending Steam Boilers.—Mix two parts of finely-powdered litharge with one part of very fine sand, and one part of-quicklime, which has been allowed to slake spontaneously by exposure to the air. This mixture may be kept for any length of time without injury. In using it, a portion is mixed into paste with linseed oil, or, still better, boiled in linseed oil. In this state it must be quickly applied, as it soon becomes hard.

Cement for Joints of Petroleum Stills.—Take six pounds graphite (black lead), three pounds of dry slaked lime, eight pounds of the sulphate of barytes, and three pounds of boiled linseed oil, and mix them thoroughly together. The solid materials must be reduced to fine powder before being stirred among the linseed oil. If the above quantity of oil is not sufficient for making the cement sufficiently thin, add more, until the proper consistency is obtained.

Linseed meal cake, reduced to powder, and mixed with water so as to make it into a paste, makes a good luto for stills which are not subjected to a temperature above 260 deg. F.

Marine Glue.—Dissolve four parts of India rubber in thirty-four parts of coal-tar naphtha—aiding the solution with heat and agitation. The solution is then thick as cream, and it should be added to sixty-four parts of powdered shellac, which must be heated in the mixture till all is dissolved. While the mixture is hot, it is poured on plates of metal in sheets like leather. It can be kept in that state, and when it is required to be used, it is put into a pot and heated till it is soft, and then applied with a brush to the surface to be joined. Two pieces of wood joined with this cement can scarcely be sundered; it is about as easy to break the wood as the joint.

Cement for Leather Belts.—A strong solution of isinglass is the best cement for joining leather bands. It may be kept from becoming moldy by adding to it some whisky and a little of the essential oil of cloves, or a little camphorated spirits.

Cement for Attaching Ornaments to Wood.—A cement composed of glue, chalk, and paper pulp, is sometimes used for making architectural ornaments, to be attached to wood. Another cement, used for the same purpose is composed of fine sifted chalk, beeswax, and resin. Use equal parts of resin and wax, then melt them, and add the chalk until the composition attains the proper consistency. A strong solution of glue and whiting makes a very good cement for ivory.

Rubber Cement.—Shreds of India-rubber or gutta-percha dissolved in refined turpentine, or good naphtha, will make a good cement for rubber shoes, shoe soles, etc.

Boot and Shoe Edge Blacking.—Bring half a gallon soft water to a boil, and put in three-fourths of an ounce extract of logwood, and boil three minutes; then remove from the fire, and stir in forty-eight grains bichromate of potash, eight grains prussiate of potash, and one hundred grains powdered gum arabic.

Varnish Blacking for Harness, etc.—Take one gallon alcohol and put in half pound orange shellac, and let stand, tightly corked, till the gum is all cut; then put in a tin vessel, which is to be set in boiling water over the fire, and add one and a half pounds pine pitch, one gill sweet oil, one gill Venice turpentine, and two ounces lamp-black, and beat till all are well mixed and thoroughly incorporated; then remove from the fire, and continue stirring till cool.

Cement for Brick Walls.—Bricks are very porous, and absorb moisture freely; hence brick walls, exposed to long and severe rain-storms, frequently become penetrated, so as to dampen the plastering inside, which renders the room damp and unhealthy, besides injuring the wall. The best water-tight composition that can be employed for such a purpose, is a mixture of hydraulic cement and boiled linseed oil.

To Gild Iron and Steel with Gold.—Make a solution of eight ounces of niter and common salt, with five ounces of crude alum, in a sufficient quantity of water; dissolve half an ounce of gold, thinly plated and cut; then evaporate to dryness. Now dissolve in rectified spirit of wine, or ether, which will perfectly abstract the gold. The iron or steel is brushed over with this solution, and takes on a fine gilt resembling gold.

To Silver Iron and other Metals.—Dissolve pure silver in nitric acid (aquafortis), and precipitate the silver with common salt; make this precipitate into a paste, by adding a little more salt and cream of tartar. Apply to the surface of the article to be silvered with a cork.

To Stain Wood a Mahogany Dark.—Boil half a pound of madder and two ounces logwood in one gallon water, and brush the wood well over with the hot liquid. When dry, go over the whole with a solution of two drachms of pearlash in one quart of water.

To Stain Mahogany Light.—Brush over the surface with dilute nitrous acid, and, when dry, apply the following with a soft brush: Dragon's blood, four ounces; common soda, one ounce; spirit of wine, three pints. Let it stand in a warm place, shaking frequently; then strain. Repeat the application until the proper color is attained.

To Stain Maple a Mahogany Color.—Dragon's blood, half ounce; alkanet, one-fourth ounce; alaco, one drachm; spirit of wine, sixteen ounces. Apply with a sponge or brush.

Rosewood.—Boil eight ounces of logwood in three pints of water until reduced one-half; apply it, boiling hot, two or three times, letting it dry between each application. Afterward put in the streaks with a camel-bair pencil, dipped in a solution of copperas and verdigris, in a decoction of logwood.

Ebony.—Wash the wood repeatedly with a solution of sulphate of iron. Let it dry; then apply a hot decoction of logwood and nutgalls for two or three times. When dry, wipe it with a wet sponge; and when it is again dried, polish with linseed oil.

To Stain Wood Red.—Use a strong decoction of Brazil wood and alum.

To Stain Pine Black.—The pine should be perfectly free from knots (as they will not color), and a strong solution of hot logwood rubbed carefully all over the board, and then it is allowed to dry. Another coat may be given, or a number, according to the shade wanted. After the logwood is dried, a solution of copperas should be applied in the same way as the logwood.

Solders.—Soldering is the art of uniting the surfaces of metals together by partial fusion, and the insertion of an alloy between the edges, which is called solder, it being more fusible than the metals which it unites. Solders are distinguished as hard and soft, according to their difficulty of fusion. Hard solders usually melt only at a red heat, but soft solders fuse at lower temperatures. In applying solder, it is of the utmost importance that the edges to be united should be chemically clean—free from oxide; and they should be protected from the air by some flux. The common fluxes used in soldering are borax, sal ammoniac, and resin. Hard silver solder is composed of four parts of fine silver and one of copper, made into an alloy, and rolled into sheets. It is quite difficult of fusion. Soft silver solder is composed of two parts of silver, one part of brass, and a little arsenic, which is added at the last moment in melting them. It will be understood that these alloys are commonly run into convenient bars, or strips, for use. Silver solders are used for soldering silver work, gold, steel, and gun-metal. A neater seam is produced with it than with soft solder. It is commonly fused with the blow-pipe. A strip of thin silver solder is laid on the joint to be closed, the blow-pipe is brought to bear upon it, when it melts and runs into the joint, filling it up completely. Button solder is employed to solder white metals, such as mixtures of copper and tin. It is composed of tin, ten parts; copper, six; brass, four. The copper and brass are first melted, then the tin is added. When the whole is melted, the mixture is stirred, then poured into cold water and granulated, then dried and pulverized, in a mortar, for use. This is called granulated solder. If two parts of zinc are added to this alloy, it makes a more fusible solder. Fine gold cut into shreds is employed as a solder for joining the parts of chemical apparatus made of platinum. Copper, cut into shreds, is used as a solder for iron. Hard silver solders are frequently reduced to powder, and used in that condition. Soft solder consists of two parts of tin and one of lead. An excellent solder is made of equal parts of Banca-tin and pure lead. It is used for soldering tin-plate, and, if well made, it never fails.

Starting Fires under Boilers.—A very mischievous practice exists in various parts of the country in reference to starting fires under steam-boilers preparatory to raising steam; this duty is intrusted to ignorant watchmen, who are too often the agents of disaster. These men are instructed to light the fire at a certain hour, and generally comply with their orders, without exercising the least judgment on the subject; they rarely try the gauges, to see that there is water in the boiler, before fulfilling their duty. We can call to mind several accidents, or injuries, that have occurred to boilers from this very cause. The Detroit Locomotive Works once had a boiler heated so hot, by the carelessness of a watchman, as to burn the felt lagging on the outside; and many other similar cases might also be cited. We have known instances where watchmen have started the fires under gangs of cylinder boilers, and raised steam in them to such an extent as to drive the water out of some into the others not in use, or not so full, thus running the risk of burning the boilers, and causing no end of delay and loss. The men in question ought not to be permitted to meddle in any way with a steam-boiler; and no persons, except those who are skilled in the management of them, and who are conversant with the properties of steam, should, under any circumstances, be intrusted with their control. Too many lives have been lost, and too much property scattered to the winds, by the ignorance of those who were temporarily left in charge of boilers.

New Chrome Green.—The London *Chemical News* gives the following receipt for manufacturing a beautiful new chrome green-color, adapted for painting and topical printing: Take ten ounces of boiling water, and dissolve in it one ounce of the bichromate of potash, and to this add six pints of the biphosphate of lime, and three ounces of brown sugar. When these substances are mixed, a disengagement of gas takes place, and the liquid fumes. It is allowed to stand until this action ceases; then it is decanted, and left to stand for about ten hours, when a beautiful green-color is deposited. It is washed with cold water, and dried in a warm room. The green-color thus obtained is stated to be fixed on cloth, in printing, by mixing it with albumen. It may be used both as a water-color and as an oil-paint.

Prevention of Decay in Timber.—The treatment of timber, to secure it from rapid decay, is a subject of great importance to ship-builders, railway engineers, bridge-builders, and all others who are interested in the preservation of wooden structures intended to be exposed to the winds, the waters, and the weather. Iron is, undoubtedly, taking the place of timber, with advantage, for many purposes; but the latter material is so convenient, and so capable of being shaped and combined in suitable forms, that it will always be used to a great extent. One of its chief defects is its liability to rapid decay, depending upon its condition, and the circumstances connected with its application. Every item of information, therefore, which will tend to promote its durability is of great value.

The sap of timber is composed of nitrogenous elements, which are called *unstable,* because, under certain circumstances, they are so liable to change, producing rot. When timber is treated so as to alter the nature of the sap, or to dry it completely, by what is called *seasoning,* it resists decay more effectually than if used without being dried. Moisture and confined air tend to procure decay in timber; and, on the other hand, timber, exposed to a free circulation of air, and shielded from moisture, will retain its strength, almost unimpaired, for centuries. The oak beams, rafters, and other timbers of old churches and houses which were built before the plastering of walls was introduced, have remained sound for six and seven hundred years. Of course, ships can not be kept dry, but if their timbers are well seasoned before they are exposed to the elements, it has been found, by experience at the French naval dock-yards, that they will endure five times longer than timbers not thoroughly seasoned.

It is well known that when timber is steeped for a certain period in water, then exposed to the air to dry, it seasons more rapidly. It has been customary, therefore, to immerse ship-timber in water prior to drying it. On this head, M. Lapparent states, that the practice of those ship-builders who steep their timber in sea-water is wrong, and that fresh water is the most suitable for this purpose. For oak planking, he states, it should be steeped one year in river water, two years in fresh water, not so frequently changed; while in brackish water, continually changing, it requires three years' immersion.

In drying timber to season it, exposure to the air is the most simple method, but this requires a very long period of time for large ship-timber. Another method consists in drying it in large rooms exposed to currents of hot air driven in by fans. By this system, the surface of the timber is liable to become dry, and crack before the interior is seasoned, and, for planking, it is, therefore, objectionable. Another method has lately been tried near Cherbourg, France, which consists in exposing it to the smoke, steam, and gas of wood and coal under combustion. The small amount of moisture in the smoke prevents the timber from cracking, and M. Lapparent looks upon this mode with favor. But his favorite method in treating timber, to prevent its decay, is the charring of its surface. He states that this plan was once tried, during the last century, in the British royal dock-yards; that the frigate "Royal William" was built of carbonized timber, and that it was one of the most remarkable cases of durability on record. This system has been revived in France, with improved apparatus, and it is about to be extended to all the dock-yards in the empire. The timber to be operated upon is secured upon an adjustable table, and its surface is slightly charred by a flame of gas mingled with a jet of air. The consumption of gas is 200 gallons for 10 square feet of carbonized surface, and one man can carbonize 440 square feet in ten hours. Some timber is improved by giving its surface a very thin coat of tar before it is charred. It is stated that the whole surface of timber is carbonized with great uniformity by this method; and M. Lapparent says: "It ought to be applied to every surface in contact with, or in general intended to be surrounded by, moist and stagnant air." It is also recommended for treating the beams and joints of house-timber intended to be imbedded in the walls, or surrounded with plaster. By carbonization, a practical and economical means is also offered to railway companies of preserving, almost forever, their sleepers, particularly those of oak. In France, the annual cost for vine-props amounts to no less than $24,000,000. By charring these, this cost will be reduced two-thirds, and a relative saving will also be effected in thus treating hop-poles. As the vine and the hop are extensively cultivated in America, this system also deserves the attention of our people who raise these agricultural products.

In building ships, M. Lapparent suggests that horizontal holes should be bored through the ribs, at certain distances apart, and there should be spaces between the outer and inner planking, to permit currents of air to be driven between the ribs; also that portion of the ribs should be smeared with a paint composed of flowers of sulphur, 200 parts; linseed oil, 135 parts; and manganese, 30 parts, to prevent the development of fungi. In conclusion, M. Lapparent says: "I have pointed out the means for preventing the rapid decay of timber; they are simple, logical, economical, easy of adoption, and perfectly innocuous. By employing them, we shall save that timber for building ships, which is, in my opinion, far superior to iron for the same purpose."

A correspondent of the London *Builder* states that the Belgian Government now require all the wood-sleepers used on the state railways to be creosoted, and the Government of Holland has adopted a similar resolution. The creosote used is simply what is called the "dead oil" of coal tar. M. Crepin, a Belgian engineer, has also made a series of experiments with creosoted timber, in harbors and docks; and in his report, lately published, he states that timber so treated was found successful in resisting the attacks of marine worms. Timber is used to a greater extent in America than in any country of an equal population in the world. If, by any mode of treatment, our ship, bridge, railway, house, fence, and other timber can be rendered twice or three times more durable, a saving to that extent may not only be effected in material, but in the labor required for preparing and applying it. All the processes, therefore, which have been set forth for preventing the rapid decay of timber deserve careful and general attenion, because they relate to interests which affect every class in the community.

Petroleum for Preserving Wood.—The oil-wells near Prome, in Burmah, have been in use from time immemorial. Wood, both for ship-building and house-building, is invariably saturated, or coated, with the products of those wells. The result is entire immunity from decay, and the ravages of the white ants that, in that country, are so generally destructive. M. Crepin, a Belgian Government engineer, who has tried experiments upon the relative advantages of creosote and sulphate of copper for the preservation of timber in marine constructions from the attacks of worms, &c., says that creosoting is the only process he has found to succeed for this purpose. He states that sulphate of copper affords no protection whatever against the action of salt-water and marine insects.

Another Method.—In order to prevent wooden posts and piles from rotting while in the ground, the following receipt will be found to answer every purpose: Fifty parts of resin; forty parts of finely-powdered chalk; about three hundred parts of fine hard sand; four parts of linseed oil; one part of red oxide of lead, and one part of sulphuric acid, are mixed together. The resin, chalk, sand, and linseed oil are heated together in an iron boiler; the red lead and the sulphuric acid are then added. They are carefully mixed, and the composition is applied while hot. If it be not found sufficiently fluid, it may be made thinner by adding some more linseed oil. This paint, when cold and dry, forms a varnish of the hardness of stone.

Testing Gilded and Silver Articles.—The following methods are employed in the German revenue-offices for testing the value of articles that are gilded or silvered, and described in the *Zeitschr. Deutsch. Ingenieure:*

Testing of Gold.—The ordinary method of testing gold is founded upon the insolubility of this metal in nitric acid. If a mark be made on the "touch-stone" with the article under examination, the gold is not dissolved by this acid, whereas golden-colored alloys of inferior value are dissolved and disappear immediately. When articles are very thinly gilded, the detection of the gold in this manner is uncertain, in which case the following method may be used with advantage. This process depends upon the fact that an aqueous solution of chloride of copper is without action on gold, whereas, on golden-colored alloys, as brass, pinchbeck, &c., it produces a black spot.

A little carbonate of copper is put into a test-tube, and to this is added, drop by drop, pure hydrochloric acid, till the blue powder has dissolved to a clear green fluid, occasionally warming it over a spirit-lamp. This concentrated solution of chloride of copper is diluted for use with from ten to eleven times its volume of distilled water. Before testing, the metallic surface must be well cleaned. This can be done effectually by brushing it for a minute or two with a little spirits of wine; or better, with absolute alcohol.

The surface having dried, a little of the testing fluid is dropped on, and allowed to remain in contact for about a minute. The fluid is then removed, by means of a small pipette, and the surface of the metal completely dried with bibulous paper; if no dark spot be then visible, the article is coated with pure gold. If the metallic surface is but lightly gilded, a very slight blackening is sometimes remarked, which may throw a doubt upon the result. In such a case, to make quite certain, a little of the surface may be scraped off, and then the testing fluid again applied. If a dark spot is then perceived, the article may be considered as very thinly gilded.

If a further and more direct proof of the presence of gold is required, the article to be examined, or a piece of it, may be put into a porcelain cup, and as much pure nitric acid poured over as will half cover it. The thin layer of gold covering the surface does not prevent the metal from being attacked by the acid, and the gold becoming separated, floats in thin films on the top of the liquid. The green metallic solution is now removed, and more nitric acid poured over the gold spangles: it is then somewhat warmed, and water finally added. The gold has now been fully tested by its insolubility in nitric acid, and it only remains to ascertain that it dissolves to a yellow solution in warm aqua regia.

Thin gilding of this description is often met with in the French mock jewelry; the coating is sometimes so thin that it not only deceives the eye, but it is difficult to test by the ordinary methods. Instead of putting the entire article into the acid, and thus risking its demolition, a portion of the surface may be scraped off with a knife, and tested with the nitric acid. When an article appears to be made of massive gold, the testing by means of the "touchstone" should be first resorted to.

Testing of Silver.—The ordinary and very accurate method of testing of silver is founded upon the insolubility of chloride of silver in dilute acids and in water. This otherwise satisfactory test is, however, difficult to carry out when an article is very thinly plated with silver; but in all these cases a simple and very accurate test can be used, which is based upon the reaction of chromic acid upon metallic silver. For this purpose testing fluid is prepared by adding pure nitric acid to powdered red chromate of potash, and mixing them in such a manner that a part of the latter remains in suspension, the whole being kept well stirred during the mixing. Equal parts by weight of each may be taken. The nitric must be quite free from hydrochloric acid, and have the proper degree of concentration, being neither too fuming nor too dilute; it should have a specific gravity between 1.20 and 1.25. When the mixture has been prepared for a few hours, and then stirred several times, the reddish-colored liquid is poured off from the residue and kept in a stoppered bottle. A drop of this liquid is then brought in contact with the metal to be tested, and immediately washed off again with water. If a visible blood-red spot remains, silver is present.

This method requires only the following precautions: First, the metallic surface must have been quite cleansed from grease, &c., with spirits of wine; secondly, water must be poured over the treated surface before judging of the color, as that of the testing fluid is altered by the metal, and the red precipitate is not distinctly visible until the colored liquid has been washed off. The red spot can afterward be very easily removed with the finger.

By this method the slightest trace of silver in an alloy may be ascertained. When an article is suspected to be only thinly plated, a very minute drop of the testing fluid should be used. With no other metal or alloy does this red spot, so characteristic of silver, appear. In some cases the testing fluid only corrodes the surface of the metal, while in others colored precipitates are formed, which, however, can not be confounded with those of silver. German-silver, brought into contact with the testing fluid, affords no red spot after being washed. The spot will, however, have been strongly corroded.

Britannia metal yields a black spot; zinc is strongly corroded; platinum is not attacked; lead gives a yellow precipitate; tin is strongly affected by the fluid; when the brownish-colored testing fluid is washed off, a yellow precipitate is perceived, which adheres tightly to the metal; copper is strongly attacked; a tarnished surface of this metal is brightened by the action of the acid. Bismuth yields a yellow precipitate; antimony does not; by this means, therefore, these two metals, somewhat similar in many respects, can easily be distinguished. Mercury, or an amalgamated surface, yields a reddish-brown precipitate, which, however, is entirely washed away by the water, and is not likely to be confounded with the silver reaction.

Destructive effects of Iron Rust.—The last published report of the Smithsonian Institution contains a translation from a German publication on the above subject, which affords considerable information of a useful and interesting character, some of which we shall present in a condensed form. It states that it has been frequently observed that, in the timber of old ships, the wood, in the proximity of iron-bolts, is entirely altered in its character. Around each bolt, for a space exceeding one inch, part of the wood is dissolved away, and the remainder is quite brittle, and easily broken. The appearance of such wood is such as if it were produced by driving in red-hot iron bolts. This injurious effect of iron-rust is one of the principal causes of the want of durability in iron-fastened ships. Rust not only originates where the iron is alternately exposed to water and the air, but also where the iron is permanently submerged under water. It is generally known that rust is an oxide of iron, but as soon as it comes into contact with wood, it gives off part of its oxygen, and becomes the protoxide. The latter takes up a new portion of oxygen, and transfers it to the wood, and, by the uninterrupted repetition of this process, a slow decay of the wood is effected. The protoxide of iron, in this case, plays a part similar to nitric oxide in the manufacture of sulphuric acid.

In order to demonstrate the fact that oxide of iron is reduced by mere contact with organic substances (such as wood) not yet in a state of putrefaction, M. Kuhlman, of Lille, has instituted different experiments, the results of which confirm the correctness of this assertion. When hydrated oxide of iron, for example, was mixed with cold solutions of logwood, cochineal, corcuma, and mahogany, they were decolorized, and the iron was found in a state of protoxide, the oxide having lost a portion of its oxygen by the action of the coloring matter. In every-day life, the destructive effects of the oxide of iron have been noticed. For example, linen or cotton cloth, containing ink-stains, becomes tender in its texture, in the stained spots, after repeated washings, and the spots ultimately fall out, leaving holes in the fabric. When cloth that is colored with copperas, to form a black, is submitted to an alkaline ley, the protoxide of iron is changed into an oxide, and the cloth becomes feeble in the texture; and the usual saying in such cases is, "It is burnt in dyeing." According to Kuhlman, the oxide of iron transfers oxygen directly to the cloth, producing slow combustion of the fiber. This is useful information for dyers, as it explains the cause of an evil connected with preparing cotton cloth, which has hitherto baffled much scrutiny and experiment to discover. It is also well known to bleachers, that when pieces of cotton cloth become stained with iron-rust they are liable to drop out, leaving holes, as if they had been sprinkled with sulphuric acid. Every spot of iron-rust should, therefore, be immediately discharged, when noticed, by the use of dilute hydrochloric acid and warm water, or oxalic acid and warm water.

In ship-building, iron nails and bolts should never be used. In all cases, copper or brass-fastenings should be employed where first cost is not an essential object. In cases where the expense will not warrant the use of copper-bolts, the iron-bolts should be galvanized. Recently we have noticed, with much satisfaction, the extended use of zinc-covered iron-bolts by our ship-builders. This is a step in the right direction; but, so far as we are informed, such bolts are confined to the construction of sea-going vessels. All our river-boats and schooners should be fastened with the same kind of bolts, because they are nearly as essential for vessels running on fresh water as those on salt.

To Put a Paper "Positive" into a Looking-glass.—Having cut out the picture, take a quarter plate-glass, well cleaned, lay a sheet of tin-foil on two or three thicknesses of cloth or paper, and spread some quicksilver with a piece of cotton-wool. Next, attach the portrait with varnish to the glass. All being ready, lay a sheet of clean paper on the top of the quicksilver, and place the glass, with portrait attached, on the sheet of paper. Now press hard, and draw out the sheet of paper gently. The quicksilver will run round the edge of the portrait, making a beautiful looking-glass, with a portrait in the center, giving an effect something like a daguerreotype.

Water-glass in Soap.—In the last number of *Silliman's Journal*, Mr. J. M. Ordway, who has devoted much attention to the composition and application of alkaline silicates, states that a mild silicate (water-glass) is now manufactured in Boston and New York, and has come into very general use among soap-makers. It is used as a substitute for resin, which had been largely employed in the manufacture of soap, before the blockade of the Southern ports. It materially reduces the cost of soap, and imparts neither color nor smell to it. About sixty per cent. of the fluid silicate, it is stated, may be mixed with the common materials that are employed for making bar-soap. Mr. Ordway says: "It is certainly quite safe to incorporate twenty-five or thirty pounds of liquid water-glass with one hundred pounds of pure oleostearate of soda. The compound thus produced has greater detersive power than common soap."

COUNSELORS IN PATENT CAUSES,

AND CONSULTING ENGINEERS.

☞ Daily Personal Attendance in U. S. Patent Office.

Search in U. S. Patent Office as to Novelty and Scope of Inventions, $5.00.

Questions of Infringement Examined, $25.00 to $300.00.

☞ Particular attention given to Rejected and Interfering Applications, Amendment of Defective Patents, Extension of Patents to 21 Years, and Questions of Infringement and Novelty.

FARMERS' DEPARTMENT.

To Make Cheese.—Skim-milk does not make good cheese. Take fresh milk, and heat it to ninety degrees before you put in the rennet. Three quarts of milk yield about a pound of cheese. Allow a quart of lukewarm water and a table-spoonful of salt to a piece of rennet about the size of your hand. The rennet must soak all night.

Put the milk into a large tub, warming a part until it is of a degree of heat quite equal to new; if too hot, the cheese will be tough. Put in as much rennet as will turn it, and cover it over. Let it stand until completely turned; then strike the curd down several times with the skimming-dish, and let it separate, still keeping it covered. There are two modes of breaking the curd; and there will be a difference in the taste of the cheese, according as either is observed; one is, to gather it with the hands very gently toward the side of the tub, letting the whey pass through the fingers till it is cleared, and lading it off as it collects; the other is, to get the whey from it, by breaking the curd. This last method deprives it of many of its oily particles, and is, therefore, less proper.

Put the vat on a ladder over the tub, and fill it with curd by the skimmer; press the curd close with your hand, and add more as it sinks; and it must be, finally, left two inches above the edge. Before the vat is filled, the cheese-cloth must be laid at the bottom; and, when full, drawn smooth over all round.

There are two modes of salting cheese; one, by mixing it in the curd while in the tub, after the whey is out; and the other, by putting it in the vat, and crumbling the curd all to pieces with it, after the first squeezing with the hands has dried it. Put a board under and over the vat, and place it in the press; in two hours turn it out, and put on a fresh cheese-cloth; press it again for eight or nine hours; then salt it all over, and turn it again in the vat, and let it stand in the press fourteen or sixteen hours, observing to put the cheese last made undermost. Before putting them the last time into the vat, pare the edges if they do not look smooth.

Management of Cream in Cold Weather.—For some reason not yet known, cream, skimmed from milk in cold weather, does not come to butter when churned so quickly as that from the same cow in warm weather. Perhaps the pelicles, which form the little sacs of butter in the cream, are thicker and tougher. There are two methods of obviating this trouble in a great degree. One is, to set the pan of milk on the stove, or in some warm place, as soon as strained and let it remain until quite warm—some say until a bubble or two rises, or until a skim of cream begins to form on the surface. Another mode recommended, is to add a table-spoonful of salt to a quart of cream; then it is skimmed. Cream, thus prepared, will generally come to butter in a few minutes, when churned. It is thought the salt acts upon the coating of the butter globules, and makes them tender, so that they break readily when beaten by churning.

We believe, upon good authority and practice, that the best temperature for churning milk is about 62 degrees Fahrenheit. It should never much exceed, or be allowed to fall, below this. If churned at a lower temperature, the butter will not separate freely; and if churned at a higher temperature, a considerable portion of the casen is always found combined with the butter. This gives it a lard-like appearance and taste. By the addition of hot or cold water, as may be required, and the use of the thermometer, to test the temperature, there is but little trouble experienced in churning it.

A New Method of Making Butter.—Put your sweet milk into tin pans, and simmer on the stove for fifteen or twenty minutes, being careful not to burn the milk; then churn in the usual manner. This will produce butter immediately, and of a far superior quality to that made in the ordinary way, and will keep sweet much longer. Besides, the milk being left sweet, is nearly as good for other purposes.

Packing Butter.—After laying down the first churning, make a strong brine, and cover it three or four inches deep. When you are ready to lay down the next one, turn off the brine, pack your butter firmly, and again cover it with the pickle, and so on till your firkin or jar is full, when it is to be headed or covered up with the brine on. In this way it will keep sweet two years.

Preserving Meat Under Ground.—Dig a hole in the earth, from four to six feet deep, and large enough for the amount of meat you have to cure; lay boards on the bottom, and on this pack your meat in salt—the usual quantity—and then cover the hole with boards and earth, keeping it in this condition till the meat is sufficiently salted. By this mode of preserving, no person need lose a pound of meat in the warmest climate.

Curing Bacon without Smoke.—Kill your hogs as early as the weather will allow, and salt as soon as the nominal heat is gone, with plenty of pure salt, and from one-half to one ounce of salpeter to each 100 pounds of pork. As soon as the meat is salted to the taste, which generally will be in about five weeks, take it out, and if any of it has been covered with brine, let it drain a little. Then take black pepper, finely ground, and dust on the hocks as much as will stick; then hang up in a good, clean, dry, airy place. If all this is done as it should be, you will have no further trouble with it, for by fly time in spring, your bacon will be so well cured on the outside that flies or bugs will not disturb it.

Curing Hams.—The following method of curing ham is given by R. M. Conklin, in the *Country Gentleman:* After cutting out the hams, they are looped by cutting through the skin so as to hang in the smoke-rooms hank downward; then take any clean cask, of proper dimensions, which is not necessary to be water-tight; cover the floor or bottom with coarse salt; rub the hams in fine salt, especially about the bony parts, and place them on the bottom of the cask with the rind down, covering the floor of the cask first; sprinkle dry fine salt evenly all over them wherever it will lie, so as to cover them perhaps half an inch; then lay others on them, letting the shank dip or incline considerably, placing salt in all cases between them where they come in close contact with each other or with the sides of the cask; small lumps of salt will be found very convenient for this purpose. Sprinkle fine salt over this as before directed, giving the thick part of the ham a good share, as the shank begins more and more to incline downward. Proceed in this way until the hams are all salted, always observing to place them skin down and flesh side up; and if they sometimes get standing too much on end, the difficulty may be obviated by using a small piece of pork as a *cheek.* Let them lie about five weeks, if of ordinary size; if larger, six weeks, and then smoke them.

I have constructed a smoke-room over my kitchen, in the garret—made dark—and so as to admit smoke from the chimney. Here I hang the hams and let in smoke until they are smoked enough, and this completes the entire operation; nothing more is done—no securing against flies, for they never enter this dark chamber, and when we want a ham we go to the smoke-chamber, and take it from the hook. During a period of twenty-five years, I have not lost a ham; but before adopting this mode, through careless smoking, injudicious salting, or from flies, I was continually suffering disappointment with my hams. Possibly hams may have a better flavor by using other ingredients with salt, yet where I have had opportunities of tasting such cured hams, I confess my inability to detect their superiority.

Sugar-cured Hams.—For one hundred pounds meat take seven pounds salt, five pounds sugar, two ounces saltpeter, and one half ounce saleratus, and dissolve in four gallons of water. Heat and skim it; then pour on your meat, sufficient to cover, and let it lay eight weeks; then take out and smoke, after which bag them and hang them up with the little end down.

Setting Sweet Potatoe Plants.—It is better to prepare your ground immediately before the planting, as the freshly-prepared ground is much looser, and is, therefore, more suitable to receive the plants. Having got the ground together with your plants all ready, no matter how dry the weather, commence about the middle of the afternoon, having tubs or barrels of water conveniently situated, and use about a tea-cupful of water to each plant. The ground being loose, the four fingers of the right hand are passed down about their length into the earth, and the dirt pulled up so as to make a hole large enough for a cup of water. With your left hand, carefully set your plant down as it should stand. Now let some person pour on the cup of water, which will cause the fibrous roots to swim and straighten out and stand in their natural position. Now quickly let the dirt in your right hand be conducted around your plant in as loose a manner as possible, leaving the top of the plant properly out of the ground. No packing is desirable in this case. By using this method we never have to wait for a suitable season, but get the plants ready as soon as possible. Thus set they commence growing right along, and live and do better than if planted in any other way, unless it is a very favorable season. Much time is saved, and we have a much larger and more abundant crop. If the water is slightly manured, it will still be better.

To Keep Sweet Potatoes.—To keep the sweet potato for use through the winter requires much care. One great requisite is, to have the potatoes gathered before they are injured by frost or by remaining in cold soil after the vines are killed. Another very important item is to have them carefully handled. If they are dry when brought from the field, they may be put up the following day; if moist, they should be allowed to dry 24 hours before putting up. If muddy and wet, a longer time is needed. Throw out all cut and bruised ones.

The potatoes may be placed in boxes or bins of any convenient size, only that they must not contain potatoes more than 16 inches in depth, and if placed one above another must have an air space of at least two inches between the bottom of one and the top of another. They should be raised from the floor four inches, and not nearer any wall than three inches. Sprinkle a little sand in the bottom of the box, then fill half full of potatoes, then shovel in sand until the crevices are well filled, then fill up with potatoes and finish with sand, having an inch of sand above the top of the potatoes. The sand should be dry, dusty and screened if possible, so that it will run well. The best time to secure the sand is in the months of August and September. Dry it on a platform of boards in the sun, and store it away in a dry place. It will require about one-third as much bulk of sand as there is of potatoes to be put up. To keep well, the sweet potato needs an even temperature.

How to Stow Potatoes and Preserve them from Rot.—Dust over the floor of the bin with lime, and put in about six or seven inches deep of potatoes, and dust with lime as before. Put in six or seven inches more of potatoes, and lime again; repeating the operation till all are stowed in that way. One bushel of lime will do for forty bushels of potatoes, though more will not hurt them—the lime rather improving the flavor than otherwise.

Another Method.—Fill a basket with potatoes and dip them into a kettle of boiling water, and let them remain two or three minutes. Repeat the operation till you have thus cured all you want for spring use. The boiling water kills the germ so they will not sprout and become soft. Dry them before packing away.

Cultivating Plants when the Dew is On.—The following interesting and practical information is from a correspondent of the *Country Gentleman*:

Fifteen years ago, I noticed a plot of cabbages, the large firm heads of which I could not account for from anything apparent in the soil. On asking the owner how he made from such soil so fine and uniform a crop, I found his only secret was that "he hoed them while the dew was on." He thought that in this way he *watered* them, but of course the good resulted more from the ammonia than the moisture of the dew.

I adopted the practice the following year, and with the result was so well satisfied, that I have since continued and recommended it to others. There will be a very great difference in the growth of two plots of cabbages, treated in other respects alike, one of which shall be hoed at sunrise, and the other at mid-day; the growth of the former will surprisingly exceed that of the latter.

A story in point sometime since went the rounds of the agricultural press of which the substance follows: A small plot of ground was divided equally between the hired lad of a farmer and his son, the proceeds of its culture to be their own. They planted it with corn, and a bet was made by them as to which should make the best crop. At harvest the son came out some quarts behind. He could not understand the reason, as he had hoed his twice a week until laid by, while he had not seen the hired lad cultivate his plot at all, and yet he had gained the wager. It turned out the winner's crop had been hoed quite as frequently, but before his rival was up in the morning. Providence, it seems, follows the hoe of the early riser, with a special and increased reward.

But there are exceptions. Cultivating while the dew is on, manifestly benefits such gross feeders as cabbage and corn, but there are plants very impatient of being disturbed while wet. The common garden snap and running beans are examples; and if worked while wet, even with dew, the pores of the leaves seem to become stopped, and the whole plant is apt to rust and become greatly injured. Whether the lima beans and other legumas are as impatient of being hoed in the dew, I have not ascertained. Experiments should, however, be tried the coming season on all hoed crops.

Planting and Cultivating Sorghum.—In the treatise on "Sorgho" of Isaac A. Hedges—who is said to have been the pioneer and practical experimenter with the Chinese sugar-cane in the West—he states that sufficient attention has not usually been given to the preparation of the soil and planting of the seed. The soil should be plowed very deep, as the roots sometimes penetrate three feet downward. A free use of lime and wood-ashes is advantageous to the crop. It has been recommended to plant the seed in rows running north and south, but as the westerly winds are most destructive in laying the standing crop, rows running east and west should be made, because they will stand up much better against such gales. The Chinese cane may be transplanted like cabbage plants, and early crops may be raised by starting hot-beds and transplanting in May or June. Or, when the seed is planted in the field, missing hills may be supplied with plants taken from a prepared bed. Every farmer who plants sorghum should pursue this method. If planted in hills, these should be about four feet apart; if in drills, the seeds should be about six inches apart. Careful planting is the first important step to secure an early and a paying crop.

Upon the subject of treating the seed of the imphee, Leonard Wray, who introduced it from South Africa, says: "I have sometimes soaked it for twenty-four hours in warm water previous to planting, in order to expedite its germination, as seeds so treated will, in warm, moist weather, be up in four days afterward; whereas, being planted (during showery weather) without this assistance, they usually take six or seven days for sprouting; and if dry weather sets in after planting, it will be ten or fourteen days before they appear above ground. The practice of soaking I hold to be a good one." An argument in favor of soaking the seed is also advanced by Mr. Hedges; he says: I would especially caution farmers against planting seed without first having tested its capability of germination; then having satisfied themselves on this point, let care be taken not to plant too thickly." Shallow planting is also recommended. In no case should the seed be set more than an inch in depth, and half an inch is sufficient. When set deep, the seed is liable to rot should rain occur immediately after planting. In all cases it should be planted in ridges—never in furrows, so that it may receive greater warmth from the sunshine, and not be so liable to be saturated with moisture during wet weather. About from eight to ten seeds are recommended for each hill.

After the plants of the cane are up, an occasional top-dressing of plaster and lime is suggested by Mr. Hedges. The best crop of sorghum we ever examined in New York was planted on loamy soil sloping to the south, and the plants had received a top-dressing of manure from the hen-house. A prize was awarded to this crop by one of the county agricultural societies. The custom of hilling around the rows, as in corn culture, is advantageous; and early cultivation between the rows, to keep down the weeds, is positively necessary to secure a good crop.

Cultivating Flax.—At a late meeting of the Munster (Ireland) Flax Improvement Society, a large cultivator of flax stated that the best seed to use was that of Riga, in Russia. Dutch seed was very good, but the American was very inferior, and sold for fifty per cent. less than Riga. More than one-half of the flax grown from American seed goes into tow when scutched, while three-fourths of that obtained from Riga seed was good long flax.

Flax-seed for sowing should be of the previous year's growth, and it should be plump, heavy, glossy, of a uniform size and a clear brown color. All seeds of a light drab color should be rejected.

Too much pains can not be taken to get seed which is fully matured and perfectly clean—free from all foul seed—both to secure a good ner chantable crop, and to preserve the land on which it is sown from troublesome weeds. Farmers often experience great difficulty in procuring such seed, as no ordinary funning mill will remove some of the worst eremies of the farmer and good flax. It was this fact, more than any other, that led to the system of "loaning seed and contracting the crop," which has been so long practiced in Ohio, Indiana and elsewhere. The lirseed-oil manufacturer who receives the crop of a large section of country is enabled to select choice lots of seed, and reserve them for sowing, and then, by machinery too expensive and crumbrous for ordinary use, to clean it so thoroughly that he can gin out each year an almost perfect article of sowing seed. Of the superiority of such seed over what can ordinarily be obtained in the market, and even in seed stores, we are convinced by examining a sample of that seed which E. W. Blatchford, Esq., proprietor of the "Chicago Lead and Oil Works," is preparing for his customers for sowing in the coming spring. Of course, when a manufacturer furnishes such seed year after year, requiring for it the return of only an equal amount of merchantable quality, he can not be expected to stipulate a price for the balance of the crop, beyond the ordinary average, taking a series of years into the account; and it is upon this basis that the business has been conducted hitherto, and it is still continued to the acceptance of a majority of the farmers in the largest flax-growing districts. In this connection we would add that, with good seed to sow, there is nothing like flax as a preparatory crop for wheat. The testimony of Ohio farmers, where flax has been extensively grown for over a quarter of a century, is explicit on this point, and to this fact we would call the especial attention of our Illinois and Wisconsin farmers, whose wheat-growing for some time has been so discouraging.— *Chicago Tribune.*

Cultivation of Tobacco.—The following is from the *California Farmer* by a contributor who has had an experience of several years in the cultivation of tobacco:

"In order to grow strong tobacco plants, the ground must be well prepared and worked very fine. In preparing the seed-bed I have found that the best way is to light a large fire on the ground; the soil is thus rendered loose and friable, and is easily reduced very fine. If it is not convenient to make a fire, mix the earth with a large dose of wood-ashes and small charred dust. By this means the ground becomes so loose that, when the plants are ready for transplanting, a good sprinkling from the garden-pot will make the ground so soft that each plant will bring with it a small ball of earth, which almost insures the plant's growing, and it must be borne in mind that young tobacco plants require very careful handling. It is better to have a large shallow basket or box to carry the plants in when transplanting, as by this means the plants do not lose the ball of earth or get bruised so much as if taken in the hand.

"The seed-bed being made fine with the rake, take the seed and mix it well with ten times (by bulk) as much fine earth and ashes. This enables you to sow the seed so thin that in drawing the larger plants you do not disturb the smaller ones.

"The ground being prepared and the seed well mixed as directed, proceed to sow, taking care to scatter the seed as equally as possible. Do not rake in the seed, but give the bed a slight beating with the back of the spade, and see that the earth does not rise with the spade. Let the seed-bed be in a sheltered situation. When the plants are about the size cabbage plants usually are at transplanting, operations may commence, making choice of a cloudy or even a rainy day for the business. The ground for the crop must be well worked and well manured with decayed manure; and it is better to have two shingles or other pieces of timber about six feet high, to stick on end in the ground, meeting over the plant so as to protect it from being scorched with the noon-day sun or nipped with the morning frost. A light, sandy soil suits the tobacco well, if well worked and manured. In another communication, I will explain the summer culture and gathering."

An old tobacconist of Sacramento informs the *Bee* that all the California tobacco he has seen has been spoiled in curing. It is cured in houses which are so hot that the leaf is burned and destroyed. The entire substance is taken out of it, and nothing but the coarse vegetable matter left, without any or scarcely any of the qualities of the plant. And this, he says, must ever be the result while the leaf is dried as it has been here. He proposes that it be dried under trees, through whose branches the sun does not penetrate, and through which the air can freely circulate, in order that the leaf may not be bleached of all its properties.

The best qualities of tobacco are said to be cultivated on new soil, on the southern sides of gently sloping hills.

Treating and Flavoring Tobacco.—A very common opinion prevailed for a long period, that tobacco was a tropical plant, and could not be cultivated in latitudes of moderate temperature. It is a fact, however, that it will grow, and may be cultivated, not only in all latitudes where corn or maize comes to maturity, but in regions much farther north. Large crops of tobacco are now raised in the valley of the Connecticut, and the leaf of the plant is smooth, and held to be well suited for the wrappers of cigars. It is also cultivated in some portions of Albany and Ontario counties in New York, thus proving that the plant may thrive in our most Northern States. And not only may it be cultivated in such latitudes, but it is well known that, soon after it was introduced from America into England, it was cultivated, for a period, with success in several sections of that country, and also in Ireland. In 1570, it was grown in Yorkshire, to a considerable extent; but its cultivation was prohibited by an act of government, for the purpose of deriving a large revenue from that which was imported. This occurred during the period of the Commonwealth, in 1652; and since then, not a leaf of tobacco, except as a curiosity, has been grown in England.

We have been told by those who are esteemed connoisseurs of tobacco, that, although this plant grows luxuriantly, when properly treated, in the Northern States, still it is not equal to the qualities which are cultivated in warmer latitudes. This is, perhaps, owing to the mode by which it is treated, after it has matured. In Virginia, the sun-dried tobacco is held to be the best for chewing, but most of it is finally cured by artificial heat. Tobacco, in leaf, is very sensitive to moisture in the atmosphere, because it contains so much potash, common salt, and lime. An analysis of this plant gave—potash, 8.7 per cent.; soda. 1.2; lime, 32.2; common salt, 3.8; magnesia, 2.8. In Richmond, which has been the head-quarters of the tobacco business, there are very extensive manufactories, where the leaf is cured, and afterward made into plugs for chewing. Great care and attention are necessary to the proper curing of it; and if the weather is moist during the operation it is very liable to mildew. In clear, dry weather, it is spread on the tops of sheds, and hung in every situation where it can be exposed to the dry air. The sky is watched with anxiety during such exposure, so that it may not receive a drop of rain. Very frequently it receives its final drying in warm apartments, and in many cases these are heated with open fires, dry corn cobs being about the best fuel that can be used. Pine and some other woods impart their resinous taste to the tobacco, if the smoke is permitted to permeate through the leaves.

After tobacco is perfectly cured, it is prepared for pressing. It is now a common practice to flavor it with some mixture of a sweet and aromatic character. A common preparation is that of the tonqua bean, which has a pleasant odor. Vanilla is also used, and different manufacturers have their special mixtures. The leaves are spread out and slightly sprinkled with the aromatic liquid until a sufficient quantity of the moisture is absorbed, to render them pliable. They are then rolled into cylindrical packages, and these are squeezed into flat plugs in powerful presses. A number of such plugs are subsequently placed together, and subjected to a second pressing operation, by which the plugs are converted into blocks, and thus fitted for transport and market. It was formerly the custom to place the pressed tobacco in a room called the sweat-house, where it remained for a considerable period exposed to a warm atmosphere. This treatment made the tobacco sweat; globules of juice appeared upon its surface, and dropped on the floor, and its taste was much improved thereby.

It is also common with some tobacco manufacturers to sweeten the dark and rank qualities for chewing, by dipping the leaves in bunches into sugar sirup, before pressing them. We have only referred to the treatment of chewing tobacco, the superior qualities being used for this purpose. The terms " honey-dew," "sweet leaf," &c., applied to different lots of tobacco, are of the " bunkum" order.

Melon-ground.—Look well to the linings of beds, and keep up a good heat; as they advance, keep the vines, both of melons and cucumbers, evenly trained over the surface. Add fresh mold, gradually, as required; remember that melons like a firm (we might almost say a hard) bed to grow in; therefore, the soil in which they grow should be quite firm. Take care, in planting out or earthening-up, not to cover the plants deeply at the collar, or bury the seed-leaves.

Maxims on Onion Culture.—Moisture at the base of the bulb for any length of time is most injurious to the onion; on the other hand, a dry heat at the surface is very beneficial, as it is the sun heat alone which renders the Spanish onions so superior to the English in flavor and beauty of the bulbs. The hotter the season or the climate, the sweeter is the flavor of onions; and the colder the season or the climate, the more pungent.

The hoe should never be used among onions. It does mischief; and if an onion is once loosened in the soil, it never makes much growth afterward. So, too, the bulbs should never be earthed up; they should stand wholly above ground, and have good depth of soil to root in.

To Sprout Onions.—Pour hot water on your seed, and let it remain two or three seconds, and they will immediately sprout, and come up much earlier.

Packing Fruits for Long Distances.—A correspondent of the *Cottage Garden* describes the following method for packing fresh fruits of various kinds. This system he has practiced with success for twenty years, and he has sent from distances varying from fifty to five hundred miles:

Take a box, soft paper and sweet bran. A box is chosen in size according to the quantity to be sent. A layer of bran is put on the bottom, then each bunch of grapes is held by the hand over a sheet of the paper; the four corners of the paper are brought up to the stalk and nicely secured; then laid on its side in the box, and so on until the first layer is finished. Then fill the whole over with bran, and give the box a gentle shake as you proceed. Begin the second layer as the first, and so on until the box is completed. Thus, with neat hands the bloom is preserved, and may be sent to any distance; but with clumsy hands, quite the contrary, and often an entire failure, as the putting and taking out of the box are the most important points to be observed. I have invariably packed sixty to eighty bunches of grapes, and fifty or sixty dozens of peaches or apricots in one box, and received letters from persons, who said they had arrived as safe as if they had been taken from the trees that morning.

Saved his Strawberries.—An exchange mentions an ingenious method by which a gentleman saved his strawberries from the daily attacks of an army of robins. He killed a worthless cat, skinned and stuffed her, and having fitted in glaring glass eyes, he mounted her in the center of a strawberry patch. Although the robins continued to congregate upon the fence and trees near by, and scolded incessantly, none of them ventured upon the patch again. Perhaps the same *scare robin* would save the cherries. It is worth a trial, particularly where cats abound as they do in some premises at night.

Washing Sheep.—*Eds. Prairie Farmer:* Most of the wool-growers whom I visited in Vermont are decidedly opposed to washing sheep. They think it often injures them, in which opinion I concur. When we see animals take the care sheep do to walk round or jump over the water, and struggle to get out when taken into it as sheep will, I think common sense teaches it is not good for them. I am confirmed in this opinion, from the fact that in this climate we have sudden changes of weather, and such changes often occur when we wash sheep, rendering it cold and uncomfortable for them. Before they are dry, they often take cold and sometimes die in consequence I think.

Another reason for not washing is we can shear earlier, and in cool weather the wool grows faster and protects the skin, and we get a better clip than when shearing is delayed for warm weather before washing. Often when sheep are shorn late in the season, the sun is so hot their skin is burnt, and sometimes blisters, and in consequence the wool grows very little for weeks. It may not be injurious as practiced by some in the central part of the State, viz.: make a dam on the little streams where the water becomes warm in the sun previous to washing. Still I think washing sheep a dirty job we might dispense with, and it would be better for all concerned, as the manufacturer has the wool to cleanse in any case. If all would shear without washing, our wool would, I think, find a market, and be bought on its merits as it should be, without any particular rule of deduction.—E. E. GORHAM.

Tanning Skins with the Wool or Hair on.—First wash the skin in strong soap-suds, to remove the grease and dirt from the wool, then rinse in clean cold water. The skin should now be tacked upon a board (with the flesh side out) and stretched, its edges trimmed, and the whole fleshy part scraped off with a blunt knife. It is now rubbed over hard with as much chalk as it will absorb, or until the chalk falls down in powder. Now take the skin down, fill it with finely-ground alum, wrap it closely together, and keep it in a dry place for two or three days; at the end of that time, unfold it, shake out the alum, and it will be ready for use, after being again stretched and dried in the air. This method is for white sheep-skins for door-mats. Another mode of treating them consists in applying a strong solution of alum, moderately warm, with a sponge, to the flesh side of the skin, when it is stretched, then allowing it to dry, before the chalk is rubbed in. It must always be dried in the

open air, or it will turn very hard. Another mode of tanning skins
with the hair on, after they are stretched on the frame and scraped, is
to apply a warm decoction of sumac, prepared by boiling one pound of
sumac in a gallon of water for about five minutes. The sumac liquor
is applied with a sponge to the whole fleshy surface, then the skin is
dried in the open air. Three applications of the sumac are given, and
when the skin is dried it is laid upon a smooth board or table, and rubbed down with pumice stone. Both alum and sumac combine with the
gelatine of the skin, and form leather.

Plant Strawberries.—As it is doubtful whether 1865 will bring a full
supply of fruit, it is recommended to plant the small fruits freely, especially the strawberry, that never fails. The spring is the best time to
plant this luxurious and healthful fruit; and March is the month. Soon
as the ground can be put in good order, plant Wilson's Albany Seedling
or Large Early Scarlet, in rows four feet apart and two feet in the row.
The summer cultivation can be chiefly performed with the cultivator, provided the weeds are not allowed to get the start of you. It is but a slight
job to dress out a considerable patch; and if frequently done, but little
work with the hoe will be necessary. As to keeping them in hills or letting them run at their pleasure, do as you please; though in September
or October the growing plants should be cut loose from the parent plant
of the Wilson's Seedling, or it may be exhausted and die. But if you
desire only a small garden patch, you had better plant two feet apart each
way, and let but few young plants grow, and such only as are set the
greatest distance from the hill. By this method, of course, hand culture
must be relied upon. If your daughters should attend to this as well as
other garden work, they will not be injured by the exercise. Let the girls
stir themselves out-doors, moderately, but regularly every day. Many
daughters of the country are becoming namby-pamby, like some of the
town—an evil that should be corrected by all parents who understand
the relations of out-door air and exercise to health. Those who have but
a limited tract of land, will do well to raise from one to ten acres of
strawberries, according as the market is more or less accessible. All farmers should have a family patch, as the cost is little, and the luxury very
great. We recommend Wilson's variety, because it has been tested, and
is a large bearer, as well as a good berry. The Large Early Scarlet is a
sweeter berry, the vine a vigorous grower, and can be allowed to run at
random. It is preferable as a berry for home use. If you have old patch-
es, thin them out thoroughly, and if grassy, turn them under and plant
a new patch. If the old patch is not too thick, the only labor required
in the spring is to spade under all the grass that may have made a start,
and the plants also in places where they are crowded. To get good
sized berries, the plants must have room. Plants set in March will produce nothing worth while; better pinch off the fruit stems as they appear, and let the plant have all the growth of the first season. The
writer of this has grown strawberries for market several seasons.

Cutting Timber.—The following information about cutting timber has
been forwarded to us from a correspondent, who states he found it among
the manuscripts of a deceased friend. It appears to be practical, and
deserving of general attention: Tradition says that the "old" of the moon
in February is the best time to cut timber; but from more than twenty
years of observation and actual experience, I am fully convinced that it
is about the worst time to cut most, if not all kinds of hard wood, timber.
Birch, ash, and most or all kinds of hard wood, will, invariably, *powder-
post*, if cut any time in the fall, after the tree is frozen, or before it is

thoroughly leaved out in the spring of the year. But if cut after the sap in the tree is used up in the growth of the tree, until freezing weather again comes, it will in no instance produce the powder-post worm. When the tree is frozen and cut in this condition, the worm first commences its ravages on the inside film of the bark, and then penetrates the wood until it destroys the sap part thereof. I have found the months of August, September, and October to be the three best in the year to cut hard-wood timber. If cut in these months, the timber is harder, more elastic, and durable than if cut in winter months. I have, by weighing timber, found that of equal quality got out for joiners' tools, is much heavier when cut and got out in the above-named months, than in the winter and spring months, and it is not so liable to crack. You may cut a tree in September, and another in the "old" of the moon in February following, and let them remain, and in one year from the cutting of the first tree you will find it sound and unhurt; while the one last cut is scarcely fit for firewood, from decay. This I know by experience. I know of several buildings, the frames of which were cut in the "old" of the moon in February, principally of beach timber, now literally eaten up by the powder-post worm; while other timber, cut before the frost came, remains perfectly sound, without the least mark of a worm. Chestnut timber for building will last longest, provided the bark be taken off. Hemlock and pine ought to be cut before being hard frozen, although they do not powder-post; yet if they are cut in the middle of winter, or in the spring of the year, and the bark is not taken off, the grub will immediately commence its ravages between the bark and the wood. I have walnut timber on hand which has been cut from one to ten years, with the bark on, which was designed for ax-helves and ox-bows, and not a worm is to be found therein; it was cut between the first of August and the first of November. I have other pieces of the same timber cut in the winter months, not two years old, and they are entirely destroyed, being full of powder-post and grub worms. Within the last ten or twelve years, I have stated the result of my observation on, and experience of, cutting timber in different seasons of the year, to many of my neighbors and others; and all who have made the trial are satisfied that the above statement is correct. Others, more incredulous, follow traditions. It is a fact which is beyond contradiction, that when there is the least sap in timber, it is the most durable and solid, and will, when seasoned, be the heaviest. And I am fully persuaded that nine cords of wood cut in those months above named, will go further than ten cut in the winter months. It will burn clearer, the coals will be more solid, and they will retain their heat double the length of time. Who does not know that wood cut in the winter, and suffered to remain in the log, or exposed to the weather, is of but little value? especially beach, birch, maple, &c.; being so far decayed, it rather molders away than burns, making no coals, and giving little heat. Hoop-poles ought to be cut before frost comes, and they will last three times as long as when cut in the winter, and will remain free from worms. The late Mr. Leonard Kennedy, of Hartford, Conn., stated to me some twelve years since, that he had lost more or less walnut timber yearly, which he was in the habit of purchasing for screws, printing-presses, vices, &c., by its powder-posting, although he had been particular to have it cut, as far as possible, in the "old" of the moon in February; and he inquired of me if I could inform him how to prevent it. I told him to order his timber cut in August and September, instead of February. He afterward told me that the advice was of much value to him, as he had lost none since, if cut in those months; and he thought the screws were better. Many others might be named who have followed the same advice, and none have failed of success. Most, if not all, persons are more or less interested in the above, either in building-timber or mechanical business; and, on a fair trial, they will find they have not been deceived by me.

Maple Sugar.—A correspondent of the *Country Gentleman* thus describes his method of making maple sugar: The sap, when gathered, should be boiled as rapidly as possible; for sometimes a very short time standing will injure the quality of the sugar, especially if the weather is warm. For the purpose of making a nice article, and for boiling fast, you should sirup down once a day, at least. The sirup should be boiled down so that it will drop from the edge of the dipper in broad drops, like honey; then it is ready to dip out and strain, through a wooden strainer, into a clean barrel kept on hand for the purpose. It should then be allowed to stand eight or ten hours, to settle. For sugaring-off, I use an iron kettle of about 14 gallons; fill it about two-thirds full; stir into it two eggs, well beaten; put it over the fire, and when it comes to the boiling point, the scum will rise, which should be carefully removed; then dip out until you can't boil it over; and as soon as it gets like soft wax return what you dipped out, in small quantities, until all is returned. Keep a good fire from the start; you can't boil too fast. There is no danger of burning until the water is all gone, then you should take it from the fire. To try it, drop it into water, and if it will snap like rosin, it is done.

The Potato Rot.—Thomas Carpenter, of Battle Creek, Mich., communicates the following as his mode of fighting off the potato rot: Now I will tell you how I manage, premising that I never yet had potatoes rot in the ground, and that I am 63 years old. I plant my potatoes in the latter part of April, or fore-part of May, and in the old of the moon. When they get up six inches high, I plaster and dress them out nicely. Now for the secret. When the sets show for blossoming, then is the time to take two parts plaster, and one part fine salt; mix well together, and put one large spoonful of this compound on each hill; drop it as nearly in the center of the hill as possible. Just as soon as the potatoes are ripe, take them out of the ground; have them perfectly dry when put in the cellar, and keep them in a dry, cool place. Some farmers let their potatoes remain in the ground, soaking through all the cold fall rains until the snow flies. The potatoes become diseased in this way more and more every year; hence the potato rot. With such management they should rot.

About Roses.—A correspondent of the *Culturist* writes to that journal concerning the care and treatment of roses. As the season of this beautiful nymph of Flora is rapidly approaching, our readers will doubtless find much advantage from perusing this letter, which we here append: Everybody loves the rose, and almost every one desires to possess information that will tend to give the greatest possible effect to this pet of the garden and conservatory. It is not as well known, perhaps, as it might be, that to have roses in full perfection of size and color, proper planting and exposure are absolutely essential. The rose requires abundance of air and light, and, to look their very best, I think that judicious grouping is indispensable. I know no way of accomplishing this more effectually than by pyramidal grouping—that is, forming a rose pyramid, rising, gradually, in highth, from the minutest dwarf at the base, to the tallest standard at the apex. As the varieties are almost endless, it would be impossible to enumerate them. Almost every florist's catalogue will supply the list, and the taste of the operator direct the arrangement. A proper discrimination should, of course, be manifested in regard to the time and continuance of blooming, so as to secure the finest possible effect. I once read of a very simple method of imparting a stronger and more agreeable odor to the rose. It is done by planting one or two large onions close to the root. It is said that water distilled from roses grown, under such circumstances, is decidedly superior to that prepared from ordinary rose-leaves. It is a French idea, and, as it will cost little to try it, perhaps some persons may feel disposed to experiment on it.

Charcoal for Turkeys.—A correspondent of the *Germantown* (*Pa.*) *Telegraph* states that he has made successful experiments in feeding turkeys with charcoal. He took eight of these fowls, and put four in each of two separate pens, and fed them alike with meal, boiled potatoes and oats, with the exception that one set had a pint of pulverized charcoal daily, while the others had none. They were killed on the same day, when it was found that those which received the charcoal averaged each one, and a half pounds more than the others, and their flesh was more tender and pleasant.

Feeding Oats to Horses.—A correspondent of the *Rural Register* gives his experience as follows, on feeding horses. He says:

The same quantity of oats given to a horse produces different effects according to the time they are administered. There is, decidedly, a great advantage in giving horses water before corn, and an injury in giving water after corn. There is a bad habit prevalent, namely, that of giving corn and hay on their return to the stable after hard work. Being very hungry, they devour it eagerly and do not masticate; the consequence is, it is not so well digested. When a horse returns from work perspiring and out of breath, he should be allowed to rest for a time, then give a little hay, a half an hour afterward water, then oats. By this plan, water may be given without risk of cold. This correspondent states that he has made many experiments with his own horses, and the foregoing are conclusions based on his experience.

Blanketing Horses.—Most persons who have the care of horses in winter, make a serious mistake in throwing a blanket on the animal as soon as he is stopped after becoming heated by hard labor or long traveling. The vapor that steams up from the hot sides of the horse condenses and wets the blanket, and as he continues to cool, the cold and wet covering chills, instead of warming him. The better plan is to allow the horse to stand uncovered until cooled down to about the ordinary temperature, which, of course, will depend on and must be regulated by circumstances, and then throw on a dry blanket.

Let Animals have Daily Exercise.—Horses require daily exercise in the open air, and can no more be expected to exist without it than their owners. Exercise is an essential feature in stable management, and, like well-opportuned food, tends alike to preserve the health of horses. Daily exercise is necessary for all horses unless they are sick; it assists and promotes a free circulation of the blood, determines morbific matter to the surface, developes the muscular stricture, creates an appetite, improves the wind, and finally invigorates the whole system. We can not expect much of a horse that has not been habituated to sufficient daily exercise; while such as have been daily exercised and well managed, are capable, not only of great exertion and fatigue, but are ready and willing to do our bidding at any season. When an animal is overworked, it renders the system very susceptible to whatever morbid influences may be present, and imparts to the disease they may labor under, an unusual degree of severity. The exhaustion produced by want of rest is equally dangerous;

such horses are always among the first victims of diseases, and when attacked their treatment is embarassing and unsatisfactory.

Salt for Animals.—Animals that are permitted to roam in the salt marshes are generally the most healthy, as they consume a large amount of saline material. The antiseptic property of salt is too well known and appreciated by most husbandmen, and the farmer might as well think of entirely dispensing with food as to fail in seasoning food with salt. No animal can long exist without salt; in the stomach it operates favorably, and has a healthy action on the liver. It also prevents the food from running into fermentation, and is death on intestinal parasites.

Chloride of Lime as an Insecticide.—In scattering chloride of lime on a plank in a stable, all kinds of flies, but more especially biting flies, were quickly got rid of. Sprinkling beds of vegetables with even a weak solution of this salt, effectually preserves them from caterpillars, butterflies, mordella, slugs, &c. It has the same effect when sprinkled on the foliage of fruit-trees. A paste of one part of powdered chloride of lime, and one-half part of some fatty matter, placed in a narrow band round the trunk of the tree, prevents insects from creeping up it. It has ever been noticed that rats and mice quit places in which a certain quantity of chloride of lime has been spread. This salt, dried and finely powdered, can, no doubt, be employed for the same purposes as flour of sulphur; and be spread by the same means.

To Prevent Fence-posts from Decaying.—Char about two feet of the ends which you put in the ground, by burning them, and they will last ten times as long.

Hot-Houses.—Use blue glass for hot-houses, and your seeds will germinate much sooner, and plants will thrive much better.

To Protect Animals from Flies and Insects.—Walnut leaves, four ounces; lobelia leaves, four ounces; boiling water, one gallon. Let the mixture stand until it cools; then press the fluid through a cotton cloth, and add four ounces of the tincture of aloes. Apply a small quantity of this compound, daily, to the surface of the body, by means of a sponge, and the flies will not trouble them.

To Make Hens Lay in Winter.—Raise a sufficient quantity of sunflowers for the hens to feed upon the seeds all the winter, and you will have plenty of eggs. The best way to raise them is to plant with potatoes; then you can also plant butter or lima-beans, which will run up the stalks, and save the expense of polling. The sunflowers will shade the potatoes, and make them grow better and be much sweeter, so that three crops can be raised off one piece of ground. Cut your sunflowers up, when ripe, at the bottom of the stalk, and set them up on the ends, with their heads close together near your fowl-yard, where the hens can run under between the stalks, and pick up the seeds as they fall down.

CONTENTS.

CULINARY DEPARTMENT.

MEDICAL DEPARTMENT.

MECHANICS' DEPARTMENT.

FARMERS' DEPARTMENT.

PORTRAITS & BIOGRAPHIES

OF THE LEADING

Military and Naval Officers

OF THE

UNITED STATES,

INCLUDING THOSE OF

PRESIDENTS LINCOLN AND JOHNSON.

———————

——— ———

CINCINNATI, OHIO:

WRIGHTSON & COMPANY, PRINTERS, No. 167 WALNUT STREET.

1867.

GEORGE WASHINGTON,

The Father of his Country.

Entered according to Act of Congress, in the year 1865,

In the District Court of the United States for the Southern District of Ohio.

ABRAHAM LINCOLN,

THE SAVIOR OF HIS COUNTRY.

ABRAHAM LINCOLN, sixteenth President of the United States, was born in Hardin County, Ky., on the 12th day of February, 1809, of obscure and humble parents. His father, Thomas Lincoln, and his grandfather, Abraham Lincoln, after whom he was named, were natives of Rockingham County, Virginia, their ancesters having emigrated from Burks County, Pennsylvania. Further back than this but little is known pertaining to the genealogy of the Lincoln family.

Abraham Lincoln, the grandfather of our present subject, removed to Kentucky in the year 1780, and settled on a small tract of land in the deep and almost impenetrable recesses of the forest, surrounded only by the stealthy savage, and the wild beasts which roamed at will, unmolested by the hand of the white man, over a large area of the western country at that early period. Here in the gloomy depths of the forest, far remote from the nearest white settlements, and isolated from all society, except now and then a visit from a straggling "red-skin," eager, perhaps, for a favorable opportunity to get a crack at some "pale-face,' our hardy pioneer commenced the erection of a hewed log cabin, for the shelter of his family, preparatory to clearing up his farm for its support. In this perilous and unprotected situation he was permitted to pursue, uninterruptedly, his usual avocation of hunting and tilling his scanty acres in corn and potatoes for a period of four years, when, on a certain occasion he was hewing timber, about four miles from home, a bullet from the gun of treacherous savage put an end to his earthly career; and, thus, in the same manner as his illustrious grandson, he was snatched from the bosom of his family without a moment's warning, by the ruthless hand of an assassin. Failing to return to his home as usual in the evening, the most painful apprehensions for his safety were entertained by the family during the lonely night, when on making search in the morning, his scalped remains, mutilated by the tomahawk of the redskin, were discovered by the side of the tree on which he had been at work the preceding day. The widow, thus bereft of her natural support, with no provision for the maintenance of herself and family but the scanty yield of a few acres of cultivated ground, still surrounded by a primeval forest, was compelled through sheer poverty to a separation of her family, composed of three sons and two daughters, and a removal to more hospitable and less dangerous quarters, retaining only Thomas, her youngest son and the father of our martyred president. Owing to the straitened circumstances of his mother, Thomas was compelled to be a wandering farm boy, and thus grew up without the advantage of an education. In 1806, in the 28th year of his age, he married a Miss Nancy Hanks, also a native of Virginia, who became the mother of our present subject. Both were equally uneducated, being barely able to read, while Thomas could bunglingly manage his own signature, which was the extent of his acquirements in the art of chirography. They subsequently removed to that portion of Hardin County which has since been formed into the county of Lareu, where Abraham, the youngest of three children, two sons and a daughter, was born, as we have before said, in the year 1809. His brother died in infancy, and although his sister lived to arrive at adult age and marry, she has long since been dead, so that Mr. LINCOLN, at the time of his death, had neither brother nor sister living.

In the autumn of 1816, Mr. Thomas Lincoln having become thoroughly disgusted with the institution of slavery, for which he seems to have had an inherent dislike, and which had begun to assume considerable proportions in his neighborhood, determined to leave the State and seek a home in another clime uncontaminated by the effects of the peculiar institution on his own class, north of the Ohio river. Having disposed of his Kentucky farm for ten barrels of whisky and twenty dollars in money he proceeded to construct a rude flat-boat, on which he placed his cargo of whisky and such other effects as could be immediately dispensed with by the family, and embarked down the Rolling Fork to the broad current of the Ohio, in quest of a market for his whisky, and with the intention of investing the proceeds in a new home in a free state. He swiftly glided down the rapid stream uninterruptedly till he reached the Ohio, where an accident happened to his frail craft which came near costing him his life, with the loss of all his effects, except three barrels of whisky and a few tools. A sudden gust of wind capsized his boat and spilled her captain, whisky and all, into the Ohio river, from which perilous condition he was rescued by some woodmen near by in a skiff, who were attracted thither by his lusty cries for help. Having righted his boat, with the assistance of his rescuers he placed the three barrels of whisky, together with his axe and some other tools fished from the water, aboard once more and proceeded on his voyage down the Ohio, no further mishap occurring to interrupt his progress.

His point of debarkation was at Thompson's ferry, on the north bank of the Ohio, in the State of Indiana, where he sold his boat and the remaining three barrels of whisky, and set out in company with a man by the name of Posey, with whom he had fallen in at the landing, for Spencer county, distant about twenty miles through an unbroken forest, where he had some relations residing. Here he selected a site for his future home, and returned on foot to his family in Kentucky, and commenced making preparations for their journey. Being able to muster three ponies, Mrs. L. and the daughter were placed upon one, little Abe on another, and the head of the family on the third, when they proceeded, Indian style, on theirway for their new home in the Hoosier State. Their route lay in an almost wholly uninhabited wilderness country through which they were obliged to travel, and after a wearisome journey of seven days, camping out by night, they arrived at their destination in their adopted State, north of the Ohio. The father at once commenced clearing a site for a homestead, and with the assistance of a neighbor erected a log cabin, 18 feet square, with only one room, into which the family moved and resided for many years. Two years after their removal to this place Abraham had the misfortune to loose his mother, but as his father was soon after married to an other very excellent woman, the void which had been created in the family circle was partially filled. This lady, to whom young Lincoln became strongly attached, on account of her kind and motherly treatment, is still living in the southern part of Illinois, and she continued to be the recipient of his favors down to the time of his death. Mr. Thomas Lincoln, with his family, continued to reside in his Indiana home for a space of 14 years—master Abraham during this time devoting himself to the employment common to back woodsmen, of hunting, of felling trees, splitting rails, etc., during the day, and devoting all his leisure hours during the evening to the improvement of his mind, by the perusal of such meager reading matter as a new and sparsely populated country afforded. Although he learned the rudiments of common arithmetic, together with reading and writing, from an itinerent school master who set up in his neighborhood for a short time, he declared that the aggregate of his schooling would not exceed twelve months; but like all great men in whom a thirst for knowledge is inher-

ent, he improved every opportunity, from the imperfect and scanty means
at his command, for the cultivation and developement of his intellectual
powers.   A story illustrating this desire for knowledge and his prover-
bial honesty is told as follows: "A Mr. Crawford had lent him a copy of
Ramsey's Life of Washington.   During a severe storm Abraham improved
his leisure by reading this book; at night he laid it down carefully, as
he thought, and the next morning he found it soaked through with water.
The wind had changed, the rain had beaten in through a crack in the
logs and the book was ruined.   How could he face the owner under such
circumstances?   He had no money to offer as a return, but he took the
book, went directly to Mr. Crawford, showed him the irreparable injury
and frankly and honestly offered to work for him until he should be
satisfied.   Mr. Crawford accepted the offer, and gave Abraham the book
for his own, in return for three day's steady labor in pulling fodder."
His manliness and straight-forwardness won the esteem of the Crawfords,
and indeed of all the neighborhood."   During the last two years of his
father's residence in Indiana, Abraham was employed as a flatboatman
on the Ohio and Mississippi rivers, at ten dollars a month; his employer
being principally engaged in trading stores along the Mississippi and
Louisiana plantations.   It was during one of these voyages that our
youthful hero and his only shipmate, the son of his employer, met with a
fearful rencounter, by being attacked at the dead hour of night by a
gang of half a dozen or more of black river pirates, who sought to capture their boat, with the view, no doubt, of first murdering them and
then robbing them of their stores.   They were approaching the Cresent
City, and had disposed of a portion of their cargo, when this noticeable
incident in their voyage occurred.   "Their boat was made fast to a lone-
some shore, when some where near the middle of the night, young Lincoln was startled from his slumber by a noise which aroused his apprehensions.   Awaking his comrade he called out through the darkness, in
order to learn if any one was approaching the boat.   A ferocious shout
from several throats, in concert, was his answer, and the boat was immediately attacked by a party of seven desperate negroes from some of
the neighboring plantations, who, doubtless, suspecting that there was
money on board, had thought it an easy undertaking to overpower and
murder the sleeping boatmen and possess themselves of the property
they guarded.   There was no time for parley.   The robbers upon finding
their stealthy approach discovered made a bold push for the coveted
prize.   Hardly had young Lincoln's call of inquiry passed from his lips
before one of the ruffians sprung upon the edge of the boat, but no
sooner did he touch the deck with his feet than he was knocked sprawl-
ing into the water by a blow from our backwoodsman's terrible fist.
Nothing daunted by their comrades fall several more of the black river
pirates leaped upon the boat with brandishing billets.   But by this time
the courageous boatmen had armed themselves with huge cudgels, to the
serious detriment of the dark assailants   Heavy and rapid blows fell
upon either side, until the fighting-quarters became so close that the
clubs were partially relinquished for a hand to hand fight.   After a
desperate struggle of several moments duration three more of the ruffians
were tumbled into the river, and those who still remained on the boat took
counsel of prudence and beat a sore-headed retreat shoreward, as best
they might   But, young Lincoln nothing disposed to rest satisfied with
an indecisive victory was after them in an instant.   Before the last three
who had been plunged into the river had succeeded in crawling up the

bank, Abraham had pounded two of them on the shore almost to death
with a ponderous cudgel. The first negro who had been knocked into
the water fled from the avenging boatman in utter dismay, in fact, all
of the "land-forces" of the enemy were speedily scattered in panic-
stricken rout, when the victors paid their respects to the marine reinforcements, dealing heavy blows upon the luckless darkies before they
were well out of the water. Feeling that it was a case of life and death,
doubting not that the negroes meant to murder them, the young boatmen fought with desperation; while the negroes driven at bay were
scarcely less determined; Abraham's strength is said to have been almost
superhuman on this occasion; but both he and his comrade were badly
bruised by the negroes' cudgels before the latter were compelled to beat
a final retreat. Though aching from the blows which they had received,
the next immediate care of the victors was to unfasten their craft and
push her far out in the stream, as a precaution against further attacks,
but none other were made."

How little did those benighted black men think that the man whose
life they sought would become the future liberator of their race! A
similar circumstance occuring to most of youths, of his age, would have
so prejudiced their minds against the negro that the lapse of no time
would have been sufficient to eradicate the antipathy. Not so, however,
with the broad and comprehensive intellect of Abraham Lincoln. He
knew that there were good and bad among all classes, races and colors,
and that, perhaps, the very institution which a narrower and less comprehensive mind would have justified from so trival an occasion, if from
no other motives, was the cause of rendering them brutal and ferocious.
About the time that Abraham arrived at age, news of the wonderful
fertility of the western prairies began to spread throughout Indiana and
Ohio, and many settlers were attracted thither. The movement became
contagious, and Mr. Thomas Lincoln not being exempt from it sinfluence
determined to sell his Indiana homestead and remove to the broad and
rolling prairies of Illinois. Accordingly, in the month of March, 1830,
all arrangements having been completed, he set out with his family in
quest of a new home in the Sucker State. The journey, this time, was
performed by means of ox-teams, and fifteen days were consumed in the
transit. Their point of destination was Macon county, in which they
halted, on the north bank of the Sangamon river, about ten miles from
Decatur, in a westerly direction. Here they erected another log-cabin,
into which the family removed and resided. The next improvement was
to split the rails and fence and break ten acres of ground, in which
master Abraham assisted, these being the identical rails which subsequently became so famous in history. On this small patch of ground
they raised a large crop of sod-corn the first year, which, with the game
procured by Abraham's rifle was their only sustenance through a long
and rigorous winter, which was the most severe of any that had ever
been known in that climate.

In the following spring Abraham hired himself out to a man by the
name of Offult, to assist in building a flat-boat, on the Sangamon river,
about seven miles northwest of Springfield, on which he made another
voyage to the Cresent City. Being much liked and highly respected by
his new employer, he was engaged by him, after his return from New
Orleans, as a clerk in a store and mill at New Salem, Ill., where he
remained till the breaking out of the Black-Hawk war in 1832, when he
joined a volunteer company, of which he was duly elected captain. His

company was immediately marched to the expected scene of conflict in the northern part of the state, but as its time of enlistment (30 days) expired before any engagement ensued, it was disbanded and the men sent home without the honor of participating in a battle with the "pesky red-skins." A new levy, however, was soon called for, and Capt. Lincoln not being content with his first campaign, and being anxious to serve his country in some capacity, re-enlisted as a private. Time passed on without any noticeable incident till the term of their enlistment again expired, and they were disbanded before the termination of the war. Still determined to serve his country till the end of the war, and being desirous of participating in a battle, young Lincoln enlisted a third time with the same results so far as a battle was concerned.

The war being over, he returned to his home and began to look about for something to do, when, greatly to his surprise, he found himself nominated, by his friends, as a candidate for the State Legislature He accepted the nomination, and notwithstanding the issue was averse to him, he had the gratifying compliment of receiving two hundred and seventy-seven votes out of the two hundred and eighty-four cast in his own town, New Salem. This is said to be the only instance wherein he was ever beaten in a direct issue before the people; but, taking into consideration the fact that he had been a resident of the county only nine months, and that there were eight aspirants for the same office, the result was not to be wondered at. The large vote polled for him in his own town, where he was best known, shows his extreme popularity, and had he been as well known throughout the county the result of the election would doubtless have been in his favor by an overwhelming majority. We next find him officiating as post-master of the town, and the joint proprietor of a small stock of goods which he and his partner had purchased on credit. This proving a profitless speculation, he soon retired from the mercantile business, and commenced the study of law, in the practice of which he afterwards became very proficient.

He continued his study, by borrowing books, about one year, at the end of which time he formed the acquaintance of one John Calhoun, (afterward the president of the notorious Lecompton-Kansas Constitutional Convention,)by whom he was persuaded to take up the study and practice of surveying. He soon found plenty of business in his new profession, which he continued to prosecute profitably for upwards a year, when he was again nominated for the Legislature of Illinois. Having become well known throughout the surrounding country, by means of his profession, as surveyor, and now being very popular, he was this time elected by a large majority over his competitor. This was his first political preferment, and his rise from this time was rapid and uninterrupted. In this, as in all former positions, he must have been a faithful and industrious servant; for he was three times re-elected to the same office, in which he served from 1834 to 1842—a period of eight years—during which time he devoted himself dilligently to the study of the law. Having obtained a license to practice in the courts in 1836, he removed to Springfield in April, 1837, and commenced practice as a partner of the Hon. John T. Stuart.

During the exciting presidential campaing of 1844, Mr. Lincoln, being an old-line Whig, "stumped" the State of Illinois for Henry Clay. His name headed the Whig electoral ticket, in opposition to that of John Calhoun, which headed the *Democratic* electoral ticket. Calhoun was regarded as the ablest debater of his party in that State and he and Mr. Lincoln stumped the State together. It was in these debates that Mr. Lincoln first demonstrated his ability as a clear-headed, augmentative debator, and he came out of this canvass the acknowledged champion of the Whig party in that State. During this campaign, at a convention held at *Vandalia*, the old capital of the State, an old man carried a banner with this device :

"ABRAHAM LINCOLN, PRESIDENT IN 1860."

"This is a well attested fact," says the writer, "but what was the prophet's name we have not been able to learn."

If this be true, as we have no reason to doubt, it was remarkably prophetic, as it was some sixteen years before Mr. Lincoln's name was ever thought of by any one else in connection with the Presidency.

In 1846 Mr. Lincoln was elected a Representative to Congress from the central district of Illinois. He was the first Whig who had ever been elected to represent the State in Congress—his six colleagues all having been elected under Democratic reign. Although Mr. Lincoln's Congressional career was brief, he always took an active part in all measures which came before the house for its deliberation—voting either *pro* or *con* upon all questions. In 1849 he was a candidate before the Illinois Legislature for U. S. Senator, but that body being strongly Democratic, elected Mr. Shields in his stead. For four or five years succeeding this period Mr. Lincoln devoted himself almost exclusively to the study and practice of his profession, being but little engaged in public affairs. But the desperate political struggle which ensued in 1854, on the repeal of the Missouri Compromise, again brought him into the political arena in defense of freedom and the right; and it was mainly through his influence and labors that Illinois elected her first Republican Legislature, which gave her in return Lyman Trumbull, a lawyer and statesman of no ordinary ability, for United States Senator. Mr. Lincoln was a candidate for the same office, the Republicans invariably casting their votes for him on every ballot, while the anti-Nebraska Democrats united on Mr. Trumbull. Mr. Lincoln fearing that the latter would withdraw from Trumbull and unite upon some one else of less ability, and whose anti-slavery record was not so clear as that of Mr. T., begged of his friends to desert him and cast a solid vote for Mr. Trumbull. Although the sacrifice was a dear one to them, they finally, through Mr. Lincoln's personal appeals yielded, and thus elected Mr. Trumbull. It was in this year that the anti-Nebraska (afterwards the Republican) party offered Mr. Lincoln the nomination for governor, but he declined, saying, "No, I am not the man ; Bissell will make a better governor than I, and you can elect him on account of his Democratic antecedents." Bissell was accordingly put in nomination and elected.

The next important event in the history of Mr. Lincoln, which contributed very materially to his growing celebrity, and which was the cause of bringing him out more prominently before the American people as a representative man, was his canvassing the State of Illinois, in the campaign of 1858, in connection with Stephen A. Douglass ; though this was not the first time that he had measured his strength with the *Little Giant*. Their first meeting in debate took place in Springfield, Ill., in October, during the campaign of 1854, in which it is said that Mr. Lincoln came out gloriously triumphant. A similar passage was tried at Peoria, but

Mr. Douglas came out of this so badly worsted, that he afterwards "failed to come to time," by keeping out of the way during the remainder of the campaign.

But it remained for the great senatorial contest of 1858 to engage the herculean strength of these two representative men in deadly conflict for the mastery of a principle.

Judge Douglas was the universally acknowledged champion of Democracy, and was considered by far the ablest man of the party; while the position which Mr. Lincoln held in the Republican ranks, was but little inferior.

It, therefore, was not at all surprising that the eyes of an entire continent of people, who were then standing upon the brink of a mighty revolution, which might at any time launch them upon an unknown political sea, without either chart or compass, were turned to the scene of conflict, to await the result with breathless anxiety.

The day of election finally arrived, and although Mr. Lincoln received the popular vote, indirectly, the direct vote, which was cast by the Legislature, was in favor of Mr. Douglas who was thereby returned to the Senate by a majority of eight. The contest, however, was not merely to decide who should represent the State of Illinois in the National Councils, but it was for the ascendency of a principle, and *that* principle involving the stability, nay, the very existence of our republican institutions. For the able manner in which Mr. Lincoln disposed of his antagonist, and his popular dogma of "Squatter Sovereignty," we must refer the reader to the published reports of those debates, as the limits which we have set for this work will not admit of even a summary of the powerful arguments by which he carried his points on those memorable occasions. As an instance, however, of his eloquence and patriotism, we will here subjoin the following tribute which he paid to the Declaration of Independence, during that campaign:

"Now, my countrymen, if you have been taught doctrines conflicting with the great land-marks of the Declaration of Independence; if you have listened to suggestions which would take away its grandeur and mutilate the fair symmetry of its proportions, if you have been inclined to believe that all men are not created equal in those inalienable rights enumerated by our chart of liberty, let me entreat you to come back — return to the fountain whose waters spring close to the blood of the revolution. You may do anything with me you choose, if you only heed these sacred principles, You may not only defeat me for the Senate, but you may take me and put me to death. While pretending no indifference to earthly honors, I do claim to be actuated in this contest by something higher than an anxiety for office. I charge you to drop every paltry and insignificant thought for any man's success. It is nothing; I am nothing; Judge Douglas is nothing. *But do not destroy that immortal emblem of humanity—the Declaration of American Independence"*

After the close of this senatorial contest, and before the opening of the Presidential campaign of 1860, Mr. Lincoln visited several other States, where he made a large number of speeches, which were received with great enthusiasm; but the crowning effort of his life was made at the Cooper Institute, in New York, in February, 1860 With this speech he ended his labors in that direction, and remained quietly at home till after his nomination and election to the Presidency, when, on the 4th of March, 1861, he entered upon the eventful life of the past four years, with the history of which all are familiar. Never did a President of the United

States come into power under such perplexing and embarrassing circumstances as those which surrounded the Government at the advent of Mr. Lincoln's Administration. Six of the Southern States had already passed ordinances of secession, while several others were on the eve of doing the same. Fort Sumter was completely beseiged by a gordian line of batteries, nearly surrounding it on all sides, and cutting off its garrison from all reenforcements and supplies, while several other forts, arsenals, navy yards, &c., had already fallen into the hands of the enemy. The United States Treasury had been robbed and plundered of the last dollar and copper coin by the sneak-thieves of Mr. Buchanan's Cabinet. John B. Floyd, Mr. Buchanan's Secretary of War, had completely dismantled and stripped all the Northern forts and arsenals of all ordnance, arms, ammunition, &c., and had them shipped to the South to be used in the destruction of the Government. The small standing army had been dispersed along the frontier of Texas and to other remote territories beyond the immediate control of the in-coming Executive, while the few ships belonging to the Navy were scattered to the remotest quarters of the globe. United States Senators and Representatives had sat in mid-night conclave in the Legislative Halls of the Nation, concocting treason for the overthrow and subversion of the Constitution which each had solemnly sworn to uphold and support. The Cabinet of the preceding administration, with two or three honorable exceptions, was reeking with damnable treason of the foulest dye, while nearly every branch of the Government was administered by the hands of its enemies instead of those of its friends, and even the Chief Executive himself, either paralyzed with fear, or purposely conniving with the treason-mongers of his own creation, looked quietly on and saw the noblest work of man — a republican government—disappear, as *he* supposed, beneath the dark waters of oblivion, over which the mighty waves of rebellion and despotism, for aught that he cared, might roll for ages unborn. Bold, defiant treason, disrobed of all habiliments of pretended loyalty, stalked abroad in mid-day through the highways as well as the byways of the National Capital, hissing fiery intonations of hatred to the Union through a thousand serpent tongues, and breathing bitter imprecations upon the heads of its supporters. An impenetrable gloom, like a funeral pall, hung over the future of the Nation, and the stoutest hearts quailed with fear before the impending storm which none, save a providential hand, could then avert. Such were the circumstances under which the administration of Abraham Lincoln came into power and assumed control of the Government.

The events of the first term of his administration —his re-election to the same office in 1864, and the dreadful tragedy of the 14th of April, 1865, which terminated his life on the succeeding day, must here be omitted, as they belong to a more detailed history of himself and the war to which the student is respectfully referred.

The only fault, if any, that can be found with the Administration of Mr. Lincoln, was that he was too mild and lenient with traitors, and not sufficiently vigorous in the prosecution of the war. True, his enemies—the Copperheads of the North—charged him with being a tyrant, and with wielding the military power of the Government with despotic sway, for the advantage of himself and party, and to the disadvantage and oppression of his political opponents; but the very fact of their having been allowed to go about the country spouting treason from every rostrum, and abusing the Administration in the most unmeasured terms, was a sufficient refutation of these charges, and gave the lie to the foul mouths and hypocritical hearts of those who uttered them. Many of his friends, with more impulsive temperaments than that which Mr. LINCOLN possessed, were impatient at the dilatory manner in which the war was conducted during the first two years of its progress, and judging from a *material* stand-point, they were correct in their estimates; but when the whole situation is viewed from a more *interior* perception of the nature and causes of the difficulty and the results necessary to be brought about, it will readily be acknowledged that all has been for the best; or in other words, that the hand of a *special* PROVIDENCE, whose purposes were far above the comprehension of all human wisdom, has guided the Nation through the perilous storm of the past four years, and shaped its destinies in accordance with the great fundamental principles of HUMAN RIGHTS, inherent in *all* men, of *all* colors, and of *all* nationalities.

The curse of human slavery was not only a foul blot upon the otherwise bright escutcheon of the Nation, and a libel upon the Declaration of Rights, which preceded American Independence, but it was a canker of immense proportions, gnawing at the very heart of the Nation, and destined, sooner or later, to absorb its vitality, but the question of how to dispose of four millions of human beings, held in abject servitude to the will of the master, who was bound to the institution by all the selfish ties of his nature, without disrupting the Union, was one which baffled the skill of the wisest statesmen. To have made war directly upon the institution, with the avowed purpose of exterminating it, would have thrown the responsibility of all the blood-shed, crime and unutterable horrors growing out of it, upon us of the North, from which all, but the most reckless of hot-headed abolitionists, would have shrunk appalled; yet nothing short of a hostile collision between the two antagonistic sections and conditions of society, would accomplish the result. It therefore became necessary to verify the old adage of "Whom the Gods would destroy they first make mad." That the friends of the Government might be in the right and clearly acting on the defensive, it was necessary that its enemies should be *instigated* to strike the first blow. That such was the case the writer of this not only believes, but he also believes that "Old Crazy John Brown," so-called, was merely an instrument in the hands of a Higher Power to probe this purulent sore, and bring the morbific matter to the surface before it should strike in so deep as to destroy the vital organism of the patient. The Government had become so corrupt under so called Democratic rule, that had things been allowed to proceed uninterruptedly for a few years longer, it would have fallen to pieces of its own inherent rottenness, and consequently been past all cure.

The war, ostensibly commenced in the interest of slavery, was one, nevertheless, on the part of a Higer Power, for the destruction of the institution and the purgation of the Government. Now had Mr. LINCOLN been possessed of a military genius and the strong iron will and individuality of an ANDREW JACKSON, he would have brought the entire strength of the Government down upon the rebellion at once, and wiped it out, in which event the status of slavery would not have been disturbed, as the public opinion of the North would not have sustained the President, in case of any attempted interference in that direction, in so radical a measure. Under this adjustment of the National difficulties, the doughfaces of the North, in order to placate the slave-drivers of the South, lest they might be instigated to a renewal of hostilities, would not only have yielded their liberties, but even their manhoods to the behests of their Southern masters, who would have become more imperious and domineering than ever before. The only effectual plan which supernal wisdom could devise, was to prolong the war under the most cruel and barbarous practices of the rebels, till the people of the North should be educated, as it were, into the idea of exterminating slavery, root and branch, and till the haughty and overbearing spirit which it engendered, should be completely cowed and whipped into submission; and nothing short of great tribulation to the people of the North, and complete physical prostration of the people of the South would accomplish this result, and how well it has been done, let the proceedings of the recent conventions of Mississippi and South Carolina, two of the most rabid of the late Confederate States, attest

A greater reformation of the political, social and moral status of the United States has taken place within the last four years, under the scourge of cruel war, than could have been accomplished in centuries without it, so that what at first appeared to be a great National calamity, has proven to be a great National "blessing in disguise." True, the iron heel of relentless war has left its foot-prints in deep scars all over the land, and nearly every family has been called upon to mourn the loss of a victim to its remorseless hand; but war, with all its horrors, is not the greatest calamity which can befall a nation. It is better to suffer the amputation of a limb, than that the entire body should perish with it.

So far, then, as the general results of the war are concerned, they could not have been bettered. Not that Mr. LINCOLN, or any other *living* man, foresaw the results and shaped the course of the Old Ship of State accordingly; but, as has been intimated, a HIGHER POWER was at the helm, and no fitter instrument than ABRAHAM LINCOLN could be found as an agent in the *hands* of that Power to carry out its general designs.

Again: had Mr LINCOLN adopted the rigorous policy pursued by Mr. Davis in *his* dominions, respecting the free expression of opinion, and put a padlock upon every man's lips, the consequence would have been that as soon as the fortunes of war were decided in our favor, every copperhead of the North would have sworn that he was just as good a union man as his neighbor, and had *always* been in favor of *coercion;* but every man having been allowed to freely express his opinions, the enemies of the Government—the Vallandighams, the Woods, the Seymours, the Voorhees, etc—unwittingly committed themselves, and are now—they and their posterity—indelibly stamped with the "Seal of traitor on their brows," and, consequently, under the ban of all respectable society, and forever excluded from holding any office of profit or trust under the Government, with decently civilized people for constituents. *One* of the objects of the war, as we have already stated, was to purge the Government of all corrupt and dirty politicians of the North, as well as to break down the slave aristocracy of the South, and nothing could have contributed so effectually to this end as the mild course pursued by the Administration with respect to its enemies in the North, so that in this arrangement, also, we clearly perceive the wisdom manifested in selecting a man of ABRAHAM LINCOLN's kind and genial nature for such an occasion. THAT THE ASSASSINATION OF ABRAHAM LINCOLN was also Providential, is the humble opinion of the writer Not that a kind PROVIDENCE instigated the minions of slavery to the fiendish and cowardly act, but it was in their wicked and rebellious hearts to do so from the beginning, and the same guardian hand which had protected him so far, might, as on former occasions, have interfered so as to have averted the calamity. Why then, it may be asked, was not this power brought into requisition,

that his life might have been spared to the nation, and he permitted to
reap the reward of his labors? The war was virtually ended, and the
angel of Peace was about to smile again upon the Nation, and oh! how
cruel that he, who was about to extend the olive branch of peace and
fraternal love to his bitterest enemies, should thus be stricken down and
snatched in such a manner from the field of his labors. Where, oh,
where was that protecting hand which had guided his every step
through the fiery ordeal from which the Nation was just emerging?
Had the Gods abdicated their Thrones and abandoned the control of the
Universe to blind Fate that anarchy and misrule might reign Supreme?
Why permit the enactment of this dreadful tragedy which plunged an
entire Nation into the profoundest grief, and sent a reverberating echo
of thrilling horror to the remotest parts of the civilized world? We
answer, for wise and benevolent purposes, that good might come out of,
or through evil.

ABRAHAM LINCOLN *had finished his work*, and when the hour came wherein he could serve his country better in death than in life, then, and not
till then, was the enemy permitted to carry out a long cherished design.
The military power of the rebellion was broken, and in the work of
reconstruction, a hand of sterner justice was needed to hold the reins of
government, lest the fruits of victory, so dearly won, might, in a great
measure, be lost through mistaken kindness. But this was not all·
Another victim, still, was required as a sacrifice upon the altar of Freedom. There was no crime, however revolting, which the rebels had not
been guilty of during the progress of the war; but the murdering in cold
blood of the good, the noble, the kind-hearted President of the people was
demanded as the *last crowning act of* INFAMY to place the institution of
slavery, in whose interest the deed was committed, under the ban of the
whole civilized world, *for all time to come.* The sentence has been passed,
and nearly every man in the South, identified with the interests of slavery, *now* feels that the blood of that great and good man is upon his own
head, and this, in no inconsiderable degree, tends to humble his pride
and render him obedient to the powers that be. It was for these, and
perhaps other kindred reasons, that the lamented President was permitted
to be removed from earth's scenes to a brighter and more exalted sphere
of existence, where his pure spirit now commingles, in council, with
those of Washington, Jefferson, Franklin, etc., who are *not* dead to the
interests of their country.

Should the reader differ with us in opinion, theologically as well as
politically, we would ask if he believes in an OVERRULING POWER, which,
acting either directly or through *intermediate agents*, shapes and controls
the destinies of nations? If so, we would suggest that *that* POWER has
neither looked quietly on, maintaining a position of "armed neutrality,"
and let things take their *own* course during the mighty events of the
past four years, *nor left its work half done.*

ANDREW JOHNSON.

'ANDREW JOHNSON, the seventeenth President of the United States, was born in Raleigh, North Carolina, December 29, 1808. His father died while he was yet scarcely advanced beyond infancy, and the family was thus left in extreme poverty. At ten years of age ANDREW was apprenticed to a tailor. Here a casual circumstance gave direction to his whole after life. Among his master's customers was an eccentric gentleman who habitually visited the shop and read aloud from books or newspapers to the journeymen. The boy soon learned to read from this gentleman, and after the long day's work was over he regularly devoted two or three hours to study. Upon the expiration of his apprenticeship he was seventeen. He then left Raleigh, and pursued his trade for two years at Laurens Court House, South Carolina. Thence he returned to Raleigh, and very soon afterward moved westward with his mother to Tennessee, and at Greenville again appears as a tailor. Here he married, and a choice of a partner proved exceedingly fortunate for his future prospects. He knew now how to read. But his wife taught him writing and arithmetic.

It was in 1829 that Mr. JOHNSON held his first office—that of Alderman. He was elected Mayor in 1830, and served in that capacity three years. In 1835 he was sent to the State Legislature. His politics were those of the party then known as Democratic. His first speech was against a measure for internal improvement In 1841 he was elected to the State Senate, and two years afterward representative in Congress. In regard to the admission of Texas into the Union, the Mexican war, the Tariff of 1846, and the Homestead Bill, Mr. Johnson took very strong Democratic ground. In 1851 he was chosen Governor of Tennessee, to which office he was re-elected in 1855. In 1857 he was elected to the United States Senate for the full term, which ended in 1863.

Mr. Johnson's record during the revolutionary period, out of which we are now passing, at first may be said to have fluctuated in certain respects, but it was never for a moment doubtful as to the necessity of the Union. In a speech of his delivered December 19, 1860, while he was defiant against the threat of Southern States to force the Border States into the Confederacy, he also gave some ambiguous utterances as to the insult which would be offered to any State by the threat of coercion from the North. But in that speech his argument against secession was very strong as affecting Southern interests. He predicted that disunion must destroy slavery; that a hostile or even alien government upon the border of the slaveholding States would be the natural haven of rest to the hunted slave. He said that if one division was allowed another would follow, "and," said he, "rather than see this Union divided into thirty-three petty governments, with a little prince in one, a potentate in another, a little aristocracy in another, a little democracy in a fourth and a republic somewhere else—a citizen not being permitted to pass from one State to another without a passport or a commission from his government—with quarreling and warring among the petty powers, which would result in anarchy—I would rather see this government to day—I proclaim it here in my place—converted into a consolidated government."

In a speech made March 2, 1861, he said : "Show me those who make war on the Government and fire on its vessels, and I will show you a traitor. If I were President of the United States I would have all such arrested, and, if convicted, by the Eternal God I would have them hung !"

On the 4th of March, 1862, after the capture of Nashville by the National forces, Mr. Johnson was appointed by the President Military Governor of Tennessee, with the rank of Brigadier General. The acceptance of this position necessitated, of course, the resignation of his situation in the Senate. As Military Governor Mr. Johnson was both just and firm. If he exacted a very rigorous test-oath from the disloyal, it was because he was convinced that, in justice, all government must be in the interest of loyal men. If he exacted from rich secessionists large sums of money for the support of the poor citizens who had been impoverished by the rebellion, it was because those men were responsible for the poverty which was thus alleviated.

As to Mr. Johnson's future policy, his explicit statements leave us no room for doubt. Except in the abolition of slavery, the States are to retain the character which belonged to them before the war. We are pledged, according to the requirements of the Constitution, to secure to these States a republican form of government. In reply to the question, What constitutes a State? Mr. Johnson answers, "Its loyal citizens." It is into the hands of these that the work of reconstruction will be committed.

Mr. Johnson comes into power through a most melancholy occurrence, but he has entered upon the duties of his office with a dignity and firmness that elicits at the same time the confidence of the American people May God spare his life and guide his steps !'

U. S. GRANT.

LIEUTENANT GENERAL ULYSSES S. GRANT, Commander-in-Chief of the United States forces, was born at Point Pleasant, Clermont County, Ohio, on the 27th day of April, 1822, and is consequently forty-three years of age. He entered West Point in 1839, and graduated in 1843, with Franklin, Reynolds, Steel, etc. Having entered the fourth Infantry, he obtained his full commission at Corpus Christe, in 1845, and served at all the battles under Taylor. His regiment subsequently joined General Scott, and young Grant figured conspicuously at all the battles of the old hero's campaign. For Molino del Rio he got a brevet of First Lieutenant, and for Chaupultepec one of Captain. He subsequently obtained his full rank as Captain, and accompanied his regiment to Oregon. In 1854 he resigned his commission, and took up his residence at Galena, Illinois.

On the outbreak of the rebellion he tendered his services to Governor Yates, and was shortly afterward appointed Colonel of the Twenty-first Ill. regiment. On May 17th, 1861, he was commissioned Brigadier General, and filled various commands in Missouri and vicinity. After the capture of Fort Henry, February 6, 1862, a new district was created, under the denomination of the District of West Tennessee, and General Grant was assigned by General Halleck to the command of it on the 14th of that month. He was in command of the Union forces at Fort Donelson from February 13 to the 16, 1862, and his noted correspondence with General Buckner gave him the *sobriquet* of Unconditional Surrender Grant. For the success of that action he was created Major-General of Volunteers, dating from February 16, 1862. After the attack and failure of General Sherman at Vicksburg, December 27, 1862, a regular plan of operations had to be worked out, and many schemes were planned and attempted, to get into the rear of the rebel strong-hold, either from above or below, among which may be particularized the Yazoo Pass expedition, the Big Sunflower expedition, the Vicksburg Canal, the Lake Providence Canal and Great Union River, and several others; but the one that has most successfully contributed to the grand result was the moving down of Grant's troops overland by way of the Louisiana shore, running transports and gun-boats past the Vicksburg batteries, and so carrying the men across the Mississippi to Bruinsburg and landing them under cover of the gun-boats.

These maneuvers took up time, but with the exception of the last, were mere feints to draw off the attention of the rebels from his main movement. With three out of his four corps of troops, he advanced into the heart of the rebel State, took possession of its capital, and beat the rebels in four pitched battles. Having captured the place, and leaving the brigade of General Mower to destroy the property of the Rebel Government, General Grant, on the morning of the 14th of May, 1863, took up his march for Vicksburg. On his way thither, he fought the battles of "Champion's Hill," and "Black River Bridge," capturing nearly two thousand prisoners and thirteen guns in the former action, and seventeen guns and over two thousand prisoners in the latter. On the 18th of this month he pitched his camp near Vicksburg, and laid siege to the town, which he continued, pressing the rebels closer each succeeding day, till finally, on the fourth day of July, over six weeks from the time he arrived in front, he had the satisfaction of seeing the place fall into his hands, with its entire garrison of over thirty thousand prisoners.

For his heroic conduct on this occasion, President Lincoln made him a Major-General in the regular army, and he subsequently received " a vote of thanks" and a gold medal from Congress for meritorious conduct on various occasions. The same Congress, on the nomination of the President, made him Lieutenant-General, and having received his commission on March 9, 1864, as Commander-in-Chief of the United States forces, he immediately transferred his own head-quarters to the Army of the Potomac, leaving General Sherman as his vicegerent to carry on the Western Campaign. No sooner was he in command than he set to work to re-organize and re-enforce Meade's Army in the most effective manner, for the most momentous and decisive campaign of the war. His Corps Commanders, as well as all subordinate officers, were carefully selected and judiciously distributed, and all things being in readiness, the grand Army of the Potomac once more received the word of command: "Forward to Richmond." But this time there was to be no "child's play," for Grant drove Lee, step by step, within the fortifications of Richmond, where he held him with a tenacious grip, till he was obliged to evacuate that strong-hold, and finally compelled to capitulate for the surrender of his entire army.

WILLIAM T. SHERMAN.

Major-General William T. Sherman was born in Ohio in 1818, and is consequently forty-seven years old. He graduated at West Point in 1840, in the same class with General Thomas, and was promoted to a first lieutenancy in 1840. He served in California during the Mexican war, and was brevetted captain for meritorious conduct. At the commencement of hostilities with the South, he offered his services to the Government, and was appointed Colonel of the Thirteenth Infantry, which regiment he commanded in Bull Run. Afterward appointed a Brigadier General he succeeded General Anderson in command of the Department of Ohio, from which he was subsequently removed because he said that 200,000 men would be needed to fight the rebels successfully in Kentucky. This statement—afterward found to be true—was at that time suggestive of insanity. At the battle of Shiloh, he took so prominent a part that Halleck reported to the War Department that the final success of the battle was mainly due to him. Having been promoted to a Major-Generalship, he was placed in command of the Fifth Division of General Grant's Army, and took an important part in the seige of Vicksburg.

In February, 1864, General Sherman left Vicksburg on a big raiding expedition through the State of Mississippi and into the interior of Alabama. General Smith, with a large cavalry expedition, left Memphis, Tennessee, at the same time with the view of co-operating with Sherman and ultimately forming a junction with his forces, but being overpowered by the concentrated cavalry forces of the enemy, he was compelled to return to Memphis, and this necessitated also the retreat of General Sherman before the object of his expedition was fully accomplished.

Although General Sherman's expedition failed to reach Selma, Alabama—its objective point at the time of leaving Vicksburg—it was by no means one barren of results, for it turned out to be the most destructive to the enemy of any which had occurred during the progress of the war. The army marched 400 miles in 24 days, penetrating to Meridian, Mississippi, where it destroyed the rebel arsenal, stockade with valuable machinery for the manufacture of small arms and all sorts of ordnance stores, and burned twelve extensive government sheds, a large number of warehouses filled with military stores and ammunition, several great mills with 20,000 bushels of corn, and nearly every building in any way occupied for war purposes. The towns of Enterprise, Marion, Quitman, Hillsboro, Lake Station, Decatur, Briton, and others, devastated; while depots, flour-mills, cotton, bridges, &c., at all points along the route, were either destroyed or rendered useless to the enemy. Nearly one hundred miles of railroad were completely destroyed or damaged beyond immediate repair, together with locomotives, cars, &c. Besides all this, nearly ten thousand slaves were liberated, nearly six thousand of whom accompanied the expedition back to Vicksburg. The entire loss of the expedition did not exceed fifty men in killed and wounded.

On the 5th of May, 1864, General SHERMAN, with an able corps of commanders, commenced his great campaign in the State of Georgia, which culminated in his unparalleled raid through that State and the Carolinas, and the final capitulation of the rebel forces in North Carolina under General Johnston, which gave the finishing blow to the Rebellion. Nearly a whole year was consumed in consummating the objects of this raid through the heart of the Southern States, but it probably done more towards crushing out the rebellion than the same army could have accomplished in *three* years in any other position. True, GRANT had already administered a mortal wound to the enemy in the capture of Richmond and Lee's Army, but his ability to accomplish this result in the time and manner in which it was done, was, undoubtedly, owing to Sherman having greatly weakened the Confederacy by cutting it twain, and to the fact that Johnson drew heavily from Lee's army to check the onward march of SHERMAN in the direction of the doomed Capitol.

Had the combined forces of GRANT and SHERMAN been concentrated in front of the enemy before Richmond, its evacuation by the rebels would probably have been necessitated months before, but in that event, Lee would have fallen back a short distance and again fortified, thereby necessitating another assult by our forces upon a second stronghold, which would have been defended with the same tenacity by the enemy, and thus he would have contested every inch of ground from Virginia to the Gulf of Mexico. It, therefore, is not saying too much for General SHERMAN, nor detracting from the well earned reputation of his illustrious Superior, when we assert that to his genius more than to that of any other general, is the country indebted for the overthrow of the military power of the rebellion. *Indeed he is, without exception, the greatest military genius of the age,* but of this, more anon in a future work, embracing phrenological characters as well as biographics of all the leading generals.

PHILIP HENRY SHERIDAN.

MAJOR-GENERAL PHILIP HENRY SHERIDAN was born of Irish parentage in Perry County, Ohio, in 1831. He was appointed to a cadetship at West Point in 1848, and graduated there in June, 1853. In the same year he was appointed Brevet Second-Lieutenant in the First United States Infantry, and ordered to duty at Fort Duncan, Texas, where he remained about two years. Early in 1855, he was promoted to a Second-Lieutenancy in the Fourth United States Infantry. In July of that year, he went to California in charge of a body of recruits, and was appointed to the command of the escort of Lieutenant WILLIAMS, engaged in surveying a route for a proposed branch of the Pacific Railroad from San Francisco to the Columbia River, Oregon.

Detached at Vancouver's Island, in September, 1855, he was assigned a command of a body of dragoons which accompanied Major Raine's expedition against the Yakima Indians. In an engagement with them, April 28, 1856, Lieutenant SHERIDAN acquitted himself so gallantly as to be mentioned in general orders.

On the 14th of March, 1861, he was promoted to a Captaincy in the Thirteenth Infantry, and from that position he gradually advanced until June, 1862, when he became commander of the Second Brigade of the Cavalry Division, Army of the Mississippi, having served with great gallantry in some of the heaviest engagements in the Southwest. In July, 1862, he defeated the rebel General CHALMERS before Corinth, and was at once promoted to the grade of Brigadier-General. He participated in the battles of Perryville, where he held the key of the Federal position, and repulsed two desperate charges of the rebels. General SHERIDAN was in command of a division at the battle of Stone River, and distinguished himself in a most remarkable manner, for which, on the special recommendation of General ROSECRANS, he was made a Major-General. In April, 1864, General SHERIDAN was transferred to the Army of the Potomac, and on the 29th of the same month he was installed as Chief of Cavalry. On the 9th of May following, he commenced his great cavalry raids in Virginia, his first expedition being the capture of Ashland, Va., where he destroyed two trains of cars, several locomotives, engine-houses, Confederate store-houses, and six miles of railroad. At Yellow Tavern, on the Fredericksburg and Richmond Railroad, he was intercepted by the rebel Chief, J. E. B. Stuart, who started from Richmond with a large force of fresh troopers, boastful and confident of success; but after a fight of great severity, in which the enemy suffered severely, SHERIDAN completely scattered the rebels in every direction, and killed their notorious leader.

On the 6th of August, 1864, General SHERIDAN was assigned to command of the armies of West Virginia. He immediately commenced a vigorous campaign against the rebel General EARLY, who had been having things all his own way in the Shanandoah Valley. His first skirmish with the enemy was on the 8th, ten miles from Winchester, and on the 11th, a part of his cavalry met a body of rebels near Martinsburg, which, after a short engagement, was put to rout. On the 12th, SHERIDAN's advance came upon Early's army, at Cedar Creek, which retreated toward Strasburg, but SHERIDAN vigorously pursued, and compelled him to retreat still further westward. On the 19th of September, near Winchester, General SHERIDAN attacked Early, who had recently been largely re-enforced, and captured 2,500 prisoners, 5 guns, 9 battle-flags, and completely routed the enemy, who fled in dismay. On the 22nd, he again met the enemy at Fisher's Hill, and carried his works by gallant charges, taking 16 guns, 3,000 prisoners, and thoroughly routing him.

In a subsequent raid through the Shanandoah Valley, he destroyed 200 well-filled barns, 70 mills filled with grain, killed over 30,000 sheep for his army, and herded several thousand head of cattle. On the 17th of October, during a temporary absence of SHERIDAN, his army was surprised early in the morning by Early, and driven back four miles with the loss of 20 guns. The General being at Winchester, heard the roar of battle, mounted his horse and started full speed for the scene of conflict. He met his army retreating in great disorder, but he quickly united his corps, changed position of his forces, and at 3 P. M. attacked the enemy, capturing 43 guns, a large number of prisoners, wagons, ambulances, &c. The enemy fled in great tumult, and SHERIDAN, pursuing, came up the next day with his retreating forces, and scattered them in every direction; Early's whole losses exceeding 10,000 men and over 300 wagons. Having completely cleaned the rebels out of the Shanandoah, General SHERIDAN rejoined the Army of the Potomac, and rendered valuable assistance in the siege and capture of Richmond and the subsequent capture of Lee, whom he headed off by several days' forced marches. General SHERIDAN is a thorough soldier and ranks among the ablest generals of the army.

JOSEPH HOOKER.

Major-General Joseph Hooker was born in Massachusetts in 1817, and is consequently 48 years of age. At the outbreak of the war with Mexico he accompanied Brigadier-General Hamer as Aid-de-camp, and was brevetted Captain for gallant conduct in several conflicts at Monterey. In March, 1847, he was appointed Assistant Adjutant-General, with the rank of Captain At the National Bridge he distinguished himself, and was brevetted Major; and at Chaupultepec he again attracted attention by his gallant and meritorious conduct, and was brevetted Lieutenant-Colonel.

At the close of the war with Mexico he withdrew from the service, and soon afterward emigrated to California. The outbreak of the rebellion found him there, and he was one of the first of the old West Pointers who offered his services to the Government. He was one of the first batch of Brigadier-Generals of Volunteers, appointed by President Lincoln on the 17th of May, 1861; and was, on his arrival, placed in command of a brigade of the Army of the Potomac, and subsequently of a division.

When the Army of the Potomac moved to the Peninsula, General Hooker accompanied it in charge of a division. In the contest at Williamsburg his division bravely stood the brunt of the battle, the rank of the Excelsior Brigade actually being mowed down as they stood up in line At Fair Oaks the men again showed their valor, and the General his fighting qualities. In the various minor contests Hooker took his

part, and bravely went through with his share of the seven days' fights.
When M'Clellan's army was placed under the command of General Pope,
we find the names of "Fighting Joe Hooker" and General Kearney
mentioned together in the thickest of the struggle; and again at South
Mountain and Sharpsburg he seems to have been second to no one. At
the latter fight he was shot through the foot and obliged to leave the
field; but for this accident, he thinks he would have driven the rebels
into the Potomac. On the 25th day of January, 1863, General Hooker
superseded Major-General Burnside in command of the Army of the
Potomac. His first engagement with the rebels after assuming command
of the army, was with Lee's forces at the battle of Chancellorsville, on
the Rappahannock, on May 2d, 1863. The battle raged furiously on both
sides from the 2d to the 4th, and Hooker being overpowered and driven
back by the forces of Lee, was compelled to return with a loss of ten
thousand in killed and wounded.

On the 27th day of June, following, General Hooker was relieved of
the command of the Army of the Potomac, and subsequently transferred
to the Army of the Cumberland, where he commanded a division in its
advance into the State of Georgia, greatly distinguishing himself at the
battles of Mission Ridge, Lookout Mountain, etc.

In the spring of 1864, General Hooker was assigned to the command
of the Department of Ohio, with headquarters at Cincinnati, where he
remained till the summer of 1865, when he was transferred to command
in New York in place of General Dix, whom he superseded, the latter
having resigned his commission as Major-General.

At the present writing (Oct. 4, 1865) we see by announcement in the
Cincinnati Commercial, that he has just been married to a Miss Olivia
Groesbeck, of Cincinnati, O., which, says the *Commercial*, is the first time
he has ever surrendered.

In person, General Hooker is very tall, erect, compactly, but not
stoutly built, extremely muscular, and of great physical endurance, of a
bright complexion, a fresh, ruddy countenance, full, clear, mild eyes,
intellectual head, brown hair, slightly tinged with gray—and altogether
one of the most commanding officers in bearing and appearance in the
army.

In social intercourse, he is frank, unpretending, and courteous. removing embarrassment from even the humblest personage that approaches
him. It is only when at the head of his command and in the storm of
battle that he arrays himself in the stern and lofty aspect of a commanding military chieftain   Perhaps it may not be uninteresting to know
how he obtained the historic name of "Fighting Joe Hooker "   On one
occasion, after a battle in which Hooker's men had distinguished themselves for their fighting qualities, thus adding to the favor of their commander, a dispatch to the New York Associated Press was received at
the office of one of the principal agencies announcing the fact. One of
the copyists, wishing to show in an emphatic manner that this commander was really a fighting man, placed over the head of the manifold
copies of the dispatch the words "Fighting Joe Hooker." Of course the
heading went to nearly every newspaper office of the country, through
the various agencies, and was readily adopted by the editors and printed
in their journals. The *sobriquet* was also adopted by the army, and he is
now universally known by it. Thus, an unpretending, innocent copyist,
unaware that he was making history, prefixed to this General's name, a
title that will live forever in the annals of the country!

GEORGE H. THOMAS.

MAJOR-GENERAL GEORGE H. THOMAS was born in Southampton county, Virginia, in July, 1816, and is consequently forty-nine years old. He was appointed from that State to West Point in 1836, graduated on July 1st, 1840, and was appointed to the Third Artillery. In the following year he distinguished himself in the war against the Florida Indians, and was brevetted First Lieutenant for his gallantry. He accompanied General Taylor to Mexico, and at Monterey won the rank of brevet Captain. At Buena Vista, again, he distinguished himself nobly, and was brevetted Major. On the close of the war he returned home, and in 1850 assumed the responsible post of Instructor of Artillery and Cavalry at West Point.

At the outbreak of the war, Major THOMAS was one of the five Virginians whose honor would not suffer him to rebel against his country's flag, and in May, 1861, he was appointed Colonel of the Fifth Cavalry—the Colonel, Robert E. Lee, and the Lieutenant-Colonel, having joined the rebels. In August, of the same year, he received the appointment of Brigadier-General of Volunteers and proceeded to the west. where for some time he had an independent command. It was he who, when all around seemed black and hopeless, restored joy to the hearts of loyal people by the victory of Spring Mill, in Kentucky, the first of the brilliant series of victories which ended with the seven days' fights before Richmond. He was subsequently appointed to the command of a corps in Buell's army. When General Buell was superseded by General Rosecrans, General Thomas assumed command of a corps in the Army of the Cumberland, and on the removal of General Rosecrans, he was appointed to the command of the army.

At the Battle of Chicamauga, his skill and the unfaltering courage of his troops, saved us from an irreparable disaster, and he is justly entitled to be considered the hero of those bloody days. When General Sherman cut loose from Atlanta, he left General Thomas with a large force in the rear to take care of Hood, who had flanked Sherman's army at Atlanta, and was making a detour in the direction of Nashville.

While Sherman was creating great havoc with the rebels in the interior of Georgia, they consoled themselves with the idea that Hood at the same time was "thundering away at the gates of Nashville." This, however, turned out to be poor consolation to them, for the superior generalship of Thomas drew Hood into a snare from which it cost him nearly one-half his entire army to extricate himself. Thomas fell back before Hood from Pulaski, Tenn., in the direction of Franklin, and Hood, taking this as an indication of Thomas' inability to cope with him, vigorously pursued and gave fight at the latter place on the 30th of November, which resulted in his being repulsed with a loss of 5,000 killed and 1,000 prisoners. Thomas immediately fell back again to Nashville with the view of drawing Hood on, and commenced to fortify, and Hood, not being satisfied with the results of the last battle, pursued and invested the city. Thomas waited till every thing was in complete readiness, when, on the morning of December 15th, the whole force under his command, was formed ready for action by 6 A. M., according to orders of the day previous. The different corps commanders made a simultaneous attack on the enemy's whole line, drove him from his position, capturing 1,200 prisoners, 16 pieces of artillery, several thousand small arms, and 40 wagons, with comparatively small less on our side.

On the morning of the 16th, Thomas' forces continued in pursuit of the enemy toward Franklin to his lines formed, during the night at Overton's Hill, about five miles from Nashville; and at 3 o'clock P. M., the enemy's forces were again assaulted with the same disastrous results to Hood as on the day previous. The enemy fled precipitately, leaving his dead and wounded on the field. Our captures this time amounted to 3,500 prisoners, 40 pieces of artillery, and several thousand small arms. The next morning, Thomas still pursued Hood to Franklin, driving him beyond and capturing 1,800 of the enemy's wounded and 200 of our own at the Hospital there, and a large number of prisoners, guns, &c. The enemy fled toward Columbia, where he tried to rally, but was forced again to retreat, leaving his artillery, a full battery, wagons, arms and ammunition, &c, his forces being thoroughly routed and scattered in every direction. Hood continued his flight, hotly pursued by Thomas' forces, till the 28th, when he finally succeeded in making his escape across the Tennessee River, his losses having amounted to over 15,000 men, including seven generals, and nearly 1000 officers of all grades, 72 cannon and 32 battle-flags. This was one of the most complete and overwhelming victories of the war.

AMBROSE EVERITT BURNSIDE.

Major-General Ambrose Everitt Burnside was born of Scotch parents, at Liberty, Union county, Indiana, on the 23d of May, 1824, and is consequently in his forty-second year. He entered West Point in 1842, graduated in 1847, and was appointed to the artillery. He accompanied Bragg's Battery throughout the Mexican war, and with it entered the city of Mexico. At the close of the Mexican war Lieutenant Burnside was detailed for duty against the Apaches in New Mexico, and served some two years in frontier warfare. In 1852 he was appointed to the command of Fort Adams, Newport, Rhode Island, and while there he married Miss Bishop, of Providence. In 1853 he resigned his rank in the army, and devoted his time and energy to the manufacture of the famous rifle which bears his name. When Buchanan was elected to the Presidency, his Secretary of War, Floyd, agreed with Burnside to arm a large portion of the army with his rifle, and induced him to establish extensive factories for its manufacture. The works were no sooner complete than another gun-maker offered Floyd pecuniary inducements to break his contract with Burnside, who was ruined in consequence. Assigning all his property to his creditors, Burnside went to New York without a dollar, sold his sword and uniform in Chatham street, and went West in search of employment. He found it in the office of the

Illinois Central, where, as soon as his energies and capacity became known, he received a salary of $2000 a year. Of this sum he paid one-half regularly to his creditors, until, by the help of a timely legacy, he was enabled to liquidate his debts in full.

The outbreak of the rebellion found him at work in the office of the Illinois Central, at New York. His oppinions on the state and prospects of the country had been frankly expressed, not only to his friends here, but to the leading citizens of New Orleans, which city he visited in February, 1861. He told the Southerners that they were going to plunge the country into a terrible war, in which they would be crushed, and, like Banks, he constantly strove to impress upon the minds of his Northern friends his belief that the war was no such child's play as Mr. Seward and others wished us to believe. When the call for troops was issued on 15th April, he tendered his services to the Governor of his adopted State—Rhode Island—and was appointed Colonel of the 1st Rhode Island Regiment. At the head of this and other regiments, with the rank of Brigadier-General, he fought, and fought well, at Bull Run. He wept bitter tears that night at the result, which, in his opinion, might have been avoided by better management. On the appointment of General M'Clellan to the Supreme Command, BURNSIDE was appointed Brigadier-General, and was charged with the duty of brigading the new levies as they arrived at Washington. In November, 1861, General BURNSIDE set sail with his expedition for North Carolina. His brilliant triumphs at Roanoke, Newbern, and Fort Macon are matters of history; they proved him to be not only an able and skillful but a lucky General. His administration of affairs in North Carolina was characterized by judgment and sagacity.

After the six days' battles before Richmond, BURNSIDE was summoned to the aid of the Army of the Potomac, and arrived at Newport News with the bulk of his army. He was soon after dispatched to Fredericksburg, and, subsequently to the defeats at Centreville and Bull Run, was given the command of a corps in the Army of the Potomac. He led the advance in the march of that army through Maryland, and at the battle of Antietam commanded at the post of danger—the Bridge. The final charge which carried the Bridge was led by the General in person.

On the 5th of November, 1862, General BURNSIDE succeeded General M'Clellan in command of the Army of the Potomac, and on the 12th of December, following, having transferred his Army to the Rappahannock, he made preparations to advance on the rebel works south of Fredericksburg. He succeeded in laying his pontoons, on which he crossed to the south bank of the river and took possession. On the morning of the 14th, BURNSIDE advanced upon the rebel fortifications to the south of the city. The ground here is in the form of a plateau, from a quarter to half a mile wide, on the first of which stands the city; on the third or upper one was the rebel position, fortified with great skill and strength, and commanding every approach. The middle one was the principal battle-ground. Several charges were made by the Union troops, but they failed to make any impression on the works of the enemy, and night found the two armies in the same position as in the morning. Both armies maintained their respective positions with continual skirmishing along the lines till the night of the 15th, when General BURNSIDE withdrew his forces and recrossed to the North bank of the river.

The Union losses in this battle amounted 1,512 killed, about 6,000 wounded, and nearly 1,000 prisoners.

QUINCY A. GILMORE.

MAJOR-GENERAL QUINCY A. GILMORE was born in Ohio about thirty-eight years ago. He entered the Military Academy at West Point in 1845, and graduated in 1849, at the head of a class of forty-three members. He was appointed to the Engineers, and was promoted to a First Lieutenancy in 1856, and to a Captaincy in 1861. From 1849 to 1852 he was engaged on the fortifications at Hampton Roads; from 1852 to 1856 he was instructor of Practical Military Engineering at West Point, and during this time he designed the new Riding School on the crest of the Hill. He served from 1856 to 1861 as purchasing agent for the department in New York, where he made many friends. In 1861 he was assigned to the staff of General Sherman, and accompanied him to Port Royal. General Sherman appointed him Brigadier-General of Volunteers—a rank which the President made haste to confirm. General GILMORE had entire charge of the siege operations against Fort Pulaski, and it was to his skill that the success of the bombardment was due. It was very truly said of him: "The results of the efforts to breach a fort of such strength and at such a distance confers high honor on the engineering skill and self-reliant capacity of General GILMORE. Failure in attempt made in opposition to the opinion of the ablest engineers of the

(27)

army would have destroyed him. Success, which in this case is wholly attributable to his talent, energy and independence, deserves a corresponding reward." That reward he won.

On the failure of Admiral Dupont's first naval attack on Charleston, he was superseded by Admiral Dahlgren, and General Hunter, who was in command of the land forces, was superseded by General GILMORE. The latter at once commenced his attack on Charleston, proceeding to land on Morris Island and advance on Fort Wagner with his customary energy and caution.

Having planted his guns in the most advantageous positions, he completely battered down the walls of Fort Sumter, and continued to rain down fire and shell upon the doomed city up to the time of its final evacuation, which was necessitated by Sherman's approach in the rear.

The following extracts show the mad and fanatical delusion which possessed the minds of those who first raised a parricidal hand against the Government, and the awful retribution which followed: From the *Charleston Mercury,* Jan. 10, 1861.—"The expulsion of the steamer, *Star of the West,* from the Charleston harbor yesterday morning was the opening of the ball of the revolution   *   *   * We would not recall that blow for millions.   *   *   * The haughty echo of her cannon has ere this reverberated from Maine to Texas, through every hamlet of the North, and down along the great waters of the Southwest. And, though greasy and treacherous ruffains may cry on the dogs of war, and traitorous politicians may lend their aid in deceptions, South Carolina will stand under her own palmetto-tree, unterrified by the snarling growls or assaults of the one, undeceived or deterred by the wily machinations of the other. And if that red sea of blood be still lacking to the parchment of our liberties, and blood they want, blood they shall have, and blood enough to stamp it all in red. For by the God of our fathers, the soil of South Carolina shall be free."

From a letter to the New York Tribune, Feb. 20, 1865.—"The wharves looked as if they had been deserted for half a century—broken-down, dilapidated, grass and moss peeping up between the pavements, where once the busy feet of commerce trode incessantly. The warehouses near the river; the streets as we enter them; the houses, and the stores, and the public buildings – we look at these and hold our breaths in utter amazement. Every step we take increases our astonishment. No pen, no pencil, no tongue can do justice to the scene. No imagination can conceive of the utter wreck, the universal ruin, the stupendous desolation. Ruin! ruin! ruin! above and below; on the right hand and the left; ruin! ruin! ruin! everywhere and always—staring at us from every paneless window; looking out at us from every shell-torn wall; glaring at us from every battered door and pillar and veranda; crouching beneath our feet on every sidewalk. Not Pompeii, nor Herculaneum, nor Thebes, nor the Nile, have ruins so complete, so saddening, so plaintively eloquent, for they speak to us of an age not ours, and long ago dead, with whose people and life and ideas we have no sympathy whatever. But here, on these shattered wrecks of houses—built in our own style, many of them doing credit to the architecture of our epoch—we read names familiar to us all; telling us of trades and professions and commercial institutions, which every modern city reckons up by the hundred; yet dead! dead! dead! as silent as the graves of the Pharaohs, as deserted as the bazaars of the merchant princes of Old Tyre."

JOHN A. LOGAN.

MAJOR-GENERAL JOHN A. LOGAN was originally known to the public as a member of Congress from Illinois, and in that capacity was associated with the DOUGLAS school of politicians. He was originally a strong proslavery man, and cast his influence in favor of all Southern measures up to the time of the breaking out of the rebellion; but when the time arrived at that point where it became necessary to choose sides for or against his country, he did not hesitate as to which side his duty called him. Like STEPHEN A. DOUGLAS, who had also been guilty of catering to the interests of slavery, he said, when the naked issue of disunion was forced upon us, that there was but one course for all loyal men to pursue, and that was to meet the issue manfully and fight it out to the bitter end. When secession was first broached, with the threat to blockade the great highway of the Mississippi, Mr. LOGAN said that "the men of the North-west in that case would cleave their way with their swords down the Mississippi Valley to the Gulf of Mexico." It happened to be Mr. LOGAN's privilege not only to witness but also to participate in the execution of this threat. He resigned his seat in Congress at the outbreak of the war, and having raised the Thirty-first Illinois Regiment, became its Colonel. He behaved with great gallantry at Fort Douelson, where he was quite severely wounded in the thigh, but yet retained his post on the field; on the surgeon's advising him to leave the field, he simply ordered that his wound be attended to secretly, and then addressed himself again to duty, arguing that he had fired twenty two rounds since his hurt, and that he could fire at least as many more now that the wound had been dressed. The next month he was made a Brigadier-General; and in the autumn, when the army of the Tennessee was reorganized, he was appointed to the command of a division with a Major-General's commission. Afterward, in all Grant's campaigns in the West, he was one of the ablest of that General's division commanders. He did not accompany General Sherman in his raid through Georgia, but rejoined the army and resumed his command at Savannah.

General LOGAN has rendered double service to the country since the war, by fighting its enemies in the rear as well as those in the front. Before the last Presidential election, when the Copperheads were rampant all through the Southern part of Illinois, he left the front for a time, and returned home to do battle for the cause of freedom in the political arena. He made several stump-speeches in which he completely flayed the "Butternut Democracy," and being himself an old Jacksonian Democrat, his speeches told with powerful effect at the approaching election. Generel LOGAN, notwithstanding his former proslavery antecedents, has shown himself a thorough patriot, a good soldier and an able officer, but we are tempted to narrate, at his expense, a good anecdote illustrating his former prejudices against the negro, which was told of him while a member of the Illinois Legislature with Senator Trumbull. The latter, in course of certain remarks, in which the "inevitable negro" stood out prominently, was interrupted by Mr LOGAN who inquired if the speaker was in favor of a law allowing intermarriage between the races? to which Mr. Trumbell replied that that was a mere matter of taste, and should be left entirely to the option of the parties. Mr. LOGAN thought this answer was evasive, and got up again demanding a direct and explicit answer. Mr. Trumbull looked for a moment at his interrogator (who was then a young man of a dark and swarthy complexion,) and then turning to the immense audience which filled the house and galleries, deeply interested in the proceedings, and said: "Well, if my friend," (referring to Mr. LOGAN) "should be so fortunate as to secure the affections of some respectable *white* girl, I should be very sorry, indeed, if we had a law on our statute books preventing his marrying her." This, of course, "brought the house down," and put a "quietus" on Mr. LOGAN during the balance of the session.

JOHN McALLISTER SCHOFIELD.

MAJOR-GENERAL JOHN McALLISTER SCHOFIELD was born in Chautauqua County, New York, in 1831. He graduated at West Point in 1853, and his present rank in the regular army is Captain of Artillery. He was at an early period of the war connected with the operations in Missouri, and was with General LYON at the battle of Wilson's Creek, where the latter was killed. He was temporarily in command of the Department of Missouri when General Halleck took the field in person in the Corinth campaign in the spring of 1862, and during the summer of the same year he commanded the Army of the Frontier, and fought the battle against Hindman and other rebel leaders near Boston Mountains, in Arkansas, and subsequently, upon the removal of General Curtis, was placed in full command of the Department of Missouri. His administration of affairs was not, in all respects, satisfactory to a large body of the people of the department of which he commanded, so early in 1864, to allay this dissatisfaction, he was relieved of his command in Missouri and transferred to East Tennessee. He took a prominent part in General Sherman's summer campaign; and when the latter started upon his grand march through the State of Georgia, he was left with General Thomas to assist in the campaign against the rebel General Hood. General SCHOFIELD, in his conduct of the retreat of our forces upon Nashville, gave fresh evidence of his distinguished ability as a soldier and commander. The battle at Franklin was forced upon him by a pressure on his rear of a rebel force greatly outnumbering his own command, and but little time was afforded him for defensive preparations. But he succeeded in gaining a signal victory, and so severely punished the enemy that his retreat was conducted without further molestation. He also took an important part in the battle at Nashville, which resulted so disastrously to the entire rebel forces under Hood.

After this battle and the thorough rout of Hood's forces from the State of Tennessee, Major-General SCHOFIELD was transferred to the Department of North Carolina, where he is still in command. His first military exploit, after his arrival, was to drive the rebels from Kinston, which he occupied on the 13th of February, 1865, after heavy fighting in which the enemy was driven with considerable loss.

General SCHOFIELD is a good soldier, a fine officer, and highly esteemed as an amiable gentlemen of social qualities.

FRANCIS J. HERRON.

MAJOR-GENERAL FRANCIS J. HERRON is a native of Pittsburg, Pennsylvania. Some nine years ago he removed to Dubuque, Iowa, where he entered into business. Here he took an active part in the organization of the "Governor's Grays," which became one of the noted companies of the Northwest. This company, of which he was Captain, tendered its services to the Government in December, 1861. When the President's Proclamation, calling for volunteers, was issued, the "Grays" became a part of the first Iowa regiment, entering service in May, 1861. Captain HERRON distinguished himself at the battle of Wilson's Creek, August 10th, where the gallant and lamented General Lyon fell. He then returned home and raised a three years' regiment, of which he was appointed Lieutenant-Colonel. This regiment was attached to General Curtis' forces, and took part in the battles of Pea Ridge, March 7 and 8, 1862, where HERRON commanded the regiment, its Colonel having command of a brigade. During the second day's fight HERRON was wounded, his ankle being broken by a cannon-shot, which killed his horse. Yet he led his men for an hour, until the enemy's batteries were reached. Here he was surrounded and taken prisoner, but was soon after exchanged for the rebel Colonel Hebert. In July, 1862, he was promoted to the rank of Brigadier-General of Volunteers, and at the battle of Prairie Grove, December 7, he commanded two divisions, and, though fighting against overwhelming odds, won the battle before reinforcements came up. Twenty days after he captured Van Buren, Arkansas. For his gallantry on those occasions, he was promoted to the rank of Major-General, his commission dating from November 29, 1862. Early in 1863, HERRON's divisions were sent to Vicksburg, and during the latter part of the siege, they formed the left wing of Grant's army. After the fall of Vicksburg they were sent to New Orleans, where they operated in the Atchafalaya and other districts of Louisiana. HERRON's health failing in October, 1863, he was relieved by General Dana.

ALFRED H. TERRY.

Major-General Alfred H. Terry, the Hero of Fort Fisher, is a native of Connecticut, born about the year 1830. He was a lawyer by profession, but devoted considerable attention to military matters. He commanded one of the best militia regiments at Hartford. He answered the first call for men in the war, and his regiment, the Second Connecticut, was among the first in the field. He took part in the first battle of Bull Run, under Kings and Taylor's Division. The Second Connecticut was enlisted for three months, and at the expiration of its term of service, Terry took command of the Seventh Connecticut, which belonged to the command of General T. W. Sherman, in the expedition against Port Royal. Terry was prominent in the siege operations on Tybee Island, which resulted in the capture of Fort Pulaski. For distinguished services on this occasion, he received the appointment of Brigadier-General, to date from April 25th, 1862. He led a brigade of the Tenth Corps in the battle of Pocotaligo, South Carolina, in October, 1862, and, subsequently, under General Gilmore, served in the capture of Morris Island, at the siege of Charleston. The Tenth Corps, in which he commanded the First Division, was subsequently transferred to the James; and when General Gilmore was relieved of command Terry succeeded him, though he afterward yielded to the more pressing claims to the late General Birney. His conduct in the rebel assault on the Darby town road in the summer of 1864, saved the corps from a serious reverse. After Birney's death the Tenth and Eighteenth Corps were consolidated, forming the Twenty-fourth, and the command of the First Division was assigned to General TERRY. The first expedition against Fort Fisher, the land forces of which were commanded by General Butler, having failed, General TERRY was selected by Grant to command in the second attack, which proved a glorious success, and hermetrically sealed the only remaining port of the Confederates against the ingress of the English blockade runners, which, up to this time, had been doing a thriving business, in the way of importing contraband articles and exporting cotton.

The attack was made on the 15th of January, 1865 by Rear Admiral Porter, in command of the naval forces, and General TERRY in command of the land forces, which numbered about 8,000 men, being some 1,500 more than were under the command of General Butler when he abandoned the idea of taking the fort by assault, and pronounced it impregnable except by seige. In justice, however, to General Butler, who made no pretensions to engineering knowledge, it should be mentioned that he acted upon the advice of General Weitzell, who was a professional engineer. The Fort was manned by 2,300 men, and in just seven hours from the time the assault was commenced in good earnest, it was ours, and its entire garrison made prisoners—not a man escaping to tell the tale. The loss of the Confederates in killed and wounded amounted to about 400, while the Union losses have been estimated at about 900, which shows the terrible and desperate struggle in which they were engaged.

With regard to the strength of the fort, Admiral Porter in his report said: "I have since visited Fort Fisher and its adjoining works, and find their strength greatly beyond what I had conceived. An engineer might be excusable in saying they could not be captured except by regular seige. I wonder even now how it was done. The work, as I said before, is really stronger than the Malakoff Tower, which defied so long the combined powers of France and England."

ALBERT AMES.

BRIGADIER-GENERAL ALBERT AMES, who commanded a division in the attack on Fort Fisher, is a native of Maine. He entered the Academy at West Point in 1858 and was commissioned May. 1861, Second-Lieutenant in the Second United States Artillery. He was soon afterward commissioned First-Lieutenant of the Fifth Artillery. He participated in the seige of Yorktown in the Peninsula campaign, and for distinguished services rendered on that occasion was brevetted Captain in the Regular Army. For other meritorious services in the battles of Malvern Hill and Garnett's Farm, he was brevetted Major, July 1st, 1862.

In August he was commissioned Colonel of the 20th Maine, and in the subsequent campaign of the Army of the Potomac won considerable reputation as an officer. He was commissioned Brigadier-General, May 20, 1843. During General Grant's Virginia Campaign, General AMES commanded first the Third Division of the Tenth Corps and afterward the Second. When the Tenth and Eighteenth Corps were reorganized he was placed in command of the Third Division of the Twenty-fourth. His division took a prominent part in the capture of Fort Fisher.

WINFIELD SCOTT HANCOCK.

MAJOR-GENERAL WINFIELD SCOTT HANCOCK is a native of Pennsylvania, from which State he was appointed a cadet to West Point Military Academy in the year 1840. He graduated on the 30th of June, 1844, standing number eighteen in his class, in which was Simon Bolivar Buckner, the notorious rebel General of Fort Donelson fame. He was promoted to a brevet Second-Lieutenancy in the Fourth United States Infantry on the 1st of July, 1844; and on the 18th of June, 1846, received his commission as full Second-Lieutenant in the same regiment. He served gallantly in the Mexican war; and in August, 1848, was brevetted First-Lieutenant for gallant and meritorious conduct in the battles of Contreras and Churubusco, his brevet dating from August 20, 1847. During the years 1848 and 1849 he filled the position of regimental quarter-master, after which he became regimental adjutant of the Sixth United States Infantry. In January, 1853, he was promoted to a full First-Lieutenancy; and on 7th of November, 1855, was appointed an assistant quarter-master in the Quarter-master General's Department, with the rank of Captain. This position he held at the breaking out of the rebellion in 1861, and still

(35)

holds that position in the army of the United States. On the 23d of September, 1861, he was appointed a Brigadier-General of Volunteers, and ordered to report to General McClellan. He was assigned to the command of a brigade in the Army of the Potomac, which was a part of the force that occupied Lewinsville on the 9th of October, 1861. He was also engaged in several grand reconnoissances which were generally attended with success. The manner in which he advanced, attacked, and captured the redoubts of the rebels, at Williamsburg, merited and obtained from General McClellan special mention and praise. He was subsequently a Major-General of Volunteers, and has since that time been one of the principal corps commanders of the Army of the Potomac. He was one of Grant's 'right-hand' men in the grand campaign of 1864, and rendered valuable assistance, as a corps commander, in the seige and capture of Richmond. General HANCOCK is much liked by his command, and his acquaintances speak of him as being a perfect gentleman in his deportment and a pleasant and agreeable companion.

AUGUSTUS L. CHITLAIN.

BRIGADIER-GENERAL AUGUSTUS L. CHITLAIN was born in St. Louis, Missouri, December 26, 1824, of French-Swiss parents who emigrated to America in the year 1823. He received his education at Galena, Illinois, where he afterward embarked in mercantile pursuits. In 1859 he visited Europe and spent a year on the continent, visiting the battlefields of Magenta and Solferino, and interesting himself in military matters. On returning to this country he took an active part in the political campaign of 1860, and on the bombardment of Fort Sumter enlisted as a private, being the first man in North-western Illinois to respond to the nation's call. Five days after the bombardment he was joined by one hundred of his fellow-citizens of Galena, who elected him Captain of the company. He immediately marched his company to Springfield, the Capital of the State, (being assisted and accompanied by Captain Grant, now the Lieutenant-General Commanding the United States Armies,) where he reported for further orders. Captain Chitlain's company joined the Twelfth Illinois Infantry, he receiving the Lieutenant-Colonelcy on the consolidation. At the battle of Donelson he was in command of the regiment, and received a promotion from General Yates (Governor of Illinois) for gallantry in the field. Colonel CHITLAIN led the Twelfth Illinois in the subsequent battles of Shiloh, the seige of Corinth, at Iuka, and at Corinth. After the battle of Corinth, he was assigned to command at the Corinth post, and then, in the month of December, 1862, raised the first colored troops of the present war. His efforts were successful beyond hope; and after organizing and equipping two regiments of blacks, he was, at the solicitation of General Grant, appointed, by the President, Brigadier-General of colored troops, and ordered, by the Secretary of War, to the command of all the colored troops of the State of Tennessee, with head-quarters at Memphis. He persevered in the work which he had commenced till, at one time, he had no less than fifteen thousand colored troops under his command, thoroughly organized and equipped for active service.

GEORGE STONEMAN.

MAJOR GENERAL GEORGE STONEMAN was born in the State of New York about the year 1825. * He graduated at West Point in July, 1846, and entered the dragoons as Second-Lieutenant. He rose steadily in his profession, and when the war broke out was Captain. The resignation of Southern traitors facilitated his advancement, and in May, 1861, he became Major of the Fourth Cavalry. General McClellan realized his merit, and in September, 1861, he was appointed Brigadier-General of Volunteers, and given the command of all the cavalry of the Army of the Potomac. In the advance of the army upon Richmond, from Yorktown he commanded the vanguard, and conducted his column with judgment and vigor. His services during the campaign were conspicuous, and

---

* Some of these biographies are indefinite and not wholly reliable as to dates and facts, but they are as nearly so as can be made from the present imperfect sources of information pertaining to them. In the forthcoming work, to which we have alluded, this will be remedied by obtaining, as nearly as possible, all the data direct from the subjects of the sketches themselves, which will make them perfectly reliable in this particular. Each sketch will then be enlarged to eight or ten pages, including phrenological descriptions of characters, as indicated in the outlines of the portraits.

raised him high in public esteem. We believe he went nearer to Richmond than any other man in the army. In the campaign in Maryland, and that under Burnside, he commanded a corps, giving continued satisfaction to the President and the people. In the spring of 1863, he performed a feat which cast all the famous raids of the rebel Stuart completely in the shade. He made a complete circuit around Lee's army, destroying his communications with Richmond, and creating general consternation in the rebel Capital, which his men approached within two miles. A dispute between General Hooker and General STONEMAN for a time, kept the latter in the back-ground; but he was subsequently appointed to the management of the new Cavalry Bureau, at Washington, and has continued to enjoy the favor and confidence of the Government. He was subsequently made a Major-General and transferred to the command of the Cavalry Department in the West.

On the 27th of July, 1864, General STONEMAN started out, with 5,000 men, to cut the rebel communications on the Macon Railroad. He succeeded in burning a large number of cars and locomotives, and in tearing up some 18 miles of the track, causing only a temporary damage, however. On his return he was surrounded and captured, with a portion of his command, 700 in number, by General Iverson, heading a force of 1,600 Confederates. He lost 2 guns, and had to yield up 1,000 captured horses. Seeing the desperate state of affairs, STONEMAN permitted two-thirds of his force to escape back to the main army, while he held the enemy in check for a short time. Some of the regiments cut their way through, while one escaped intact; but the most of those who escaped found their way back to camp unarmed and afoot, losing everything in their hasty flight. This casualty occurred in consequence of the failure of STONEMAN to form a junction with M'Cook (who was sent on the same mission with 4,000 men) at Lovejoy's Station, on the Macon road. M'Cook, through some mismanagement on the part of one or the other of the commands, having failed to unite his forces with those of STONEMAN, according to instructions, was, on his return, surrounded by Ransom, and also badly cut to pieces, but made good his escape with 1,200 of his men, without falling into the hands of the rebels, as did the less fortunate STONEMAN with 700 of his command.

General STONEMAN was taken a prisoner to Macon, Georgia, but being shortly afterward released or exchanged, he was reinstated in his old command, and, when Sherman left Atlanta for his Southern tour, was sent out on the railroad leading from East Tennessee into Virginia, for the purpose of destroying the road and depots, so as to cut off the retreat of the rebels from Richmond in that direction. The first we hear of him is at Bristol, which place he captured, with a train of over 200 hogs for Lee's army, 5 locomotives and a railroad train of stores. Abingdon next fell into his hands, then Saltville, where he destroyed property, including buildings and salt, to the amount of $2,000,000. These salt works were the largest in the world, turning out over 5,000 bushels a day. This was one of the most successful raids of the war; 11 foundries, 90 flouring and saw mills, 30 bridges, 10 locomotives and 100 cars were destroyed; 20 pieces of artillery, several thousand head of stock, 900 prisoners, and several hundred negroes were captured. The army marched 460 miles in 18 days.

JUDSON KILPATRICK.

MAJOR-GENERAL JUDSON KILPATRICK, the great Cavalry Raider, was born near Deckertown, Sussex County, New Jersey, on January 14, 1836, and is therefore only twenty-nine years of age. He was admitted to West Point, where he graduated in 1861, and entered the United States army as a Second-Lieutenant of Artillery on May 6, just after the war broke out. A week after, he received a commission as First-Lieutenant. He entered the war as Captain of a company in Duryea's regiment (the Fifth New York,) and was severely wounded in the battle of Big Bethel, June 10, 1861. As soon as he recovered he was made Lieutenant-Colonel, and afterward Colonel of the Harris Light Cavalry. In Pope's Virginia campaign his regiment formed part of the late General Buford's brigade. He took part in the Maryland campaign under General Pleasanton, and in Burnside's campaign he particularly distinguished himself at Falmouth. He participated in Stoneman's raid, commanding a brigade, and traversing two hundred miles in five days, capturing over three hundred prisoners. For this success he was made Brigadier-General of Volunteers, his commission dating from June 13, 1863. At Aldie, Middleburg, and

Hanover, KILPATRICK distinguished himself in the movements preceding the battle of Gettysburg: he also commanded a division in that battle, and was engaged in the pursuit of the rebels to the Potomac. Afterward he went to New York City, where he commanded the Cavalry forces during the riots of the summer of 1863. In Sherman's grand "march down to the sea," General KILPATRICK was in command of the cavalry forces, and rendered valuable assistance to the success of the undertaking by his bold dashes, hither and thither, which kept the enemy completely foiled as to the whereabouts and objective point of the main army. He continued to render valuable service to the country down to the close of the war, and is ranked among the ablest cavalry commanders of the army.

ALFRED PLEASANTON.

GENERAL ALFRED PLEASANTON, one of the most gallant Cavalry officers of the army, was born in the District of Columbia about the year 1821, and is consequently forty-four years of age. He graduated at West Point on July 1, 1844, and entered the First Dragoons. In November, 1855, he was transferred to the Second Dragoons, and accompanied General Taylor on the expedition to Mexico. At Palo Alto and Resaca de la Palma he distinguished himself and was brevetted in consequence. He obtained his First-Lieutenancy in 1849, and in his company (in the Second Cavalry) in 1855. At the outbreak of the rebellion he received a Major's commission, and on July 16, 1862, he was commissioned Brigadier-General of Volunteers. He was appointed to the Army of the Potomac, and served throughout the Peninsula campaign with distinction. When General Stoneman took command of a division, before the battle of Antietam, General PLEASANTON succeeded him in command of all the cavalry of the army, and discharged the duty of pressing on Lee's rear on his retreat. He has since filled various cavalry commands in that army with gallantry and success.

JOHN BUFORD.

GENERAL JOHN BUFORD, another familiar name associated with the cavalry department, was born in Kentucky about the year 1827, but removed with his family to Illinois at a very early age. He was appointed from that State to West Point, and graduated in 1848, entering the Second Dragoons as Second-Lieutenant. He served in his regiment until the outbreak of the rebellion, when he was transferred to the Inspector General's Department, with the rank of Assistant Inspector-General. In 1862, he obtained permission to go on active service, and got a cavalry command in the army of the Potomac, at the head of which he gallantly distinguished himself.

The names of STONEMAN, KILPATRICK, PLEASANTON, BUFORD and CUSTER will stand out prominently in the history of the war as able and gallant Cavalry Commanders.

DAVID GLASGOW FARRAGUT.

REAR ADMIRAL DAVID GLASGOW FARRAGUT, the Naval Hero of the war, was born near Knoxville, Tenn., about the year 1803, and is now sixty-two years of age. His father was an officer in the army, well known to General Jackson by whom he was much esteemed. When only nine years of age, little David determined to be a sailor, and was taken by Commodore Porter on board the Essex as midshipman. He shared the fortunes of that famous craft in her memorable cruise in the Pacific, and took part in the battle off Valparaiso. A person who was familiar with the facts tells the following story of the boy's behavior on that occasion:

He was ordered by the Commodore, while the contest was at its height, to go below and bring up some friction-tubes that were needed for the guns. While descending the ward-room ladder the Captain of the gun, directly opposite, was struck full upon the face by an 18-pounder shot. He fell back against young FARRAGUT and they both tumbled down the hatchway. The man was a stout, heavy fellow, and it was fortunate for the young midshipman that his full weight did not fall upon him as they reached the deck. Commodore Porter seeing him covered with blood

(41)

inquired, "Are you wounded?" "I believe not," was the reply. "Then where are the tubes?" asked the Commodore. The words brought him to his senses, and he immediately went below and got them.

When at last it was determined to surrender the brave little brig, the Commodore sent Master FARRAGUT to throw overboard the signal-book, in order that the enemy should not come into the possession of our code, it being reported that the signal-master could not be found. After a protracted search the lad discovered the book upon the sill of one of the ports, and at once threw it overboard. A few minutes afterward the recusant signal-master appeared, and excused himself for being absent from his post, by stating that he had been over the side to extricate the book from the wreck, where it had been lodged; but the falsehood cost him dearly.

During all this time young FARRAGUT bore himself like a man, never shedding a tear till he saw the American colors hauled down, and *then* he sobbed like a child. From this heavy grief he was soon aroused, however, by hearing an English middy (a young midshipman, like himself,) exultingly shout to his men, "Prize-oh, boys! here's a fine grunter, by Jove!" He knew the young reefer alluded to a young porker that had been petted by himself and all the sailors, and had helped to beguile away many a weary hour; therefore he energetically laid claim to the animal. "But," said the young Englishman, "you're a prisoner and your pig, too." "We always respect private property," said FARRAGUT, and he seized the squealing bone of contention, and asserted that he should retain possession until compelled to yield to superior force. Here was sport for the older officers, who called out, "Go in, little Yankee; and if you can thrash 'shorty' (a *soubriquet* for English middies) you shall have your pig." "Agreed," said FARRAGUT, and the lads went at it in pugilistic style. "Shorty" soon failed to come to time, and the victor walked off with the pig under his arm. He afterward said that he felt, in mastering the young Englishman, that he had wiped out the disgrace of being captured.

On another occasion he was placed in command of a prize-vessel, when only thirteen years of age. The original captain of the prize became very turbulent, and threatened to interfere with the navigation of the ship. FARRAGUT reported him accordingly to the Essex, upon which the man excused himself by saying that he only meant to "frighten the boy." "Ask him, Sir," replied FARRAGUT to his Captain, "how he succeeded." The boy resumed command of the prize and took her safely into port.

At the close of the war young FARRAGUT was sent to school, and thence into the navy. His life, for the next forty years, was the usual routine of a sailor's in peace-time, with its alternations of sea and shore duty, furlough and foreign station. He spent some time in South America, and, it is believed, took part in some of the revolutionary contests which are indigenous to that country. He married his wife in the South, and settled at Norfolk, Virginia, where he purchased some little property. The rebellion found him living there, surrounded by Southerners, whose sympathies were all with the rebels. How he left Norfolk, the following extract from the New York *Times* tells:

"On the 18th of April he left Norfolk, just the night before the navy-yard was burned, and no better proof of his loyalty can be given than the fact of the premeditated attack upon the navy yard at Norfolk being kept a secret from him. The morning before leaving Norfolk he was expressing very decidedly his opposition to the course of the Southern people, when he was told by some of the leading men and naval officers, residents of the place, that he could not remain there with such sentiments. "Then I will go where I can live with just such sentiments," was his reply; and he accordingly went home and notified his family that they must get ready to leave for New York in a few hours. He arrived in Baltimore to learn that the railroad track had been torn up the day before, and had great difficulty in getting a passage for himself and family in a canal-boat. This was accomplished, however, after a few hours delay, and they managed to arrive safely at New York. He immediately sought a house at Hastings, upon the Hudson, in which to place his family, removed from the excitement of the times, so that he could be assured of their safety when he was called upon to go forth and battle for his country. With that same freshness of feeling and devotion that he possessed when a midshipman on board the Essex, he obeyed the call. Had Admiral FARRAGUT remained in Norfolk *one* day longer, he would have been imprisoned, as was the fate of one Union officer, to whose disgrace, be it said, that, after remaining a few hours in prison, he yielded to the Southern coercionists and joined their navy. The Admiral says he does not deserve so much credit for his prompt action in this matter, as, having had some experience in the revolutionary countries of South America, he was well posted as to what might be expected from revolutionary times.

For some months after the outbreak of the war, Captain FARRAGUT was without a command, partly because the Department had no vessels. At length, when the expedition against New Orleans was resolved upon, he was selected to lead it. He entered the Mississippi River early in March, 1862. On the 17th of April, Porter's mortar-fleet began the bombardment of Forts Philip and Jackson, and on the 24th, Commodore FARRAGUT, with his entire fleet, ran past the forts, encountering a fire almost unparalleled in severity, a fleet of gun-boats, including several iron-clads, fire-rafts, obstructions and torpedoes innumerable. An idea of the brilliancy of the exploit may be formed from the fact that some French and English officers, who had been to New Orleans, laughed outright at the bare notion of running the batteries, and indulged in characteristic sneers at the insanity, as they pleased to term it, of the project. It was done, however, as every one knows; and at a late hour on the 25th of April, 1862, the Commodore anchored off the city of New Orleans, and sent word ashore that all rebel flags must come down.

The rebel Commodore Barron, who was captured at Hatteras Inlet, was a prisoner at Fort Warren, and heard the recital, from a newspaper, of FARRAGUT's victorious entry at New Orleans. Profoundly interested, and forgetting his treason, and remembering only the glory of the service with which his own name had been honorably associated, Barron exclaimed vehemently, "Yes, yes; I tell you nothing can stand against our navy."

FARRAGUT's performances at Mobile Bay, in August, 1864, were no less brilliant than those of Forts Philip and Jackson notority of 1862. At sunrise, on the morning of the 5th, he moved up Mobile Bay, past Fort Morgan, with his whole fleet, his vessels lashed two abreast, each acting consort to the other. The Monitor *Tecumseh*, proceeding to the left of the fleet, struck a torpedo and went down. The infernal machine exploded almost directly under the Monitor, whose side was lifted six feet above the water, when she settled down so rapidly that only five of her crew, who tumbled out through her port-holes, escaped. She sank at the very commencement of the action, carrying down with her one hundred of her crew, including her gallant commander, Craven.

After this result, it was not to be wondered at that Commodore FARRAGUT had previously expressed his dislike to "fighting in an iron kettle," as he termed it, for in a casualty of this nature, there appears to be no chance of escape from the Monitors except through the port-holes.

The rebel gun-boat *Selma* soon struck her colors to the *Metacomet*, but the most spirited naval engagement of the war, was the conflict with the *Tennessee*, which was only rivaled in interest by the fight between the *Monitor* and the *Merrimac*, early in 1862. After the *Selma* had surrendered, and the *Morgan* and *Gaines* had been driven under the guns of Fort Morgan, FARRAGUT ordered the whole Federal fleet to engage the *Tennessee*, and to close in upon her as rapidly as possible. The order was none too quickly given, as the ram was uninjured by our fire, and in the rear of our fleet, threatening seriously to interrupt our progress.

FARRAGUT was lashed to the maintop of the *Hartford*, and gave his orders through a speaking trumpet. At the time of the engagement he was passing the water batteries under Fort Morgan. The fire of all the vessels seemed to have no effect on the ram. When the order was given to run her down, the *Monongahela*, *Lackawanna* and *Brooklyn*, all butted against her. Although the Monitors appear to have made but little impression in butting the *Tennessee*, further than to make the splinters fly inside the heavy iron and wooden armor of the vessel, they, finally, forced her to surrender. The *Manhattan* sent a solid 15-inch shell through her side at a distance of twenty-five yards. The *Chickasaw*, also, did splendidly with her 11-inch guns. The *Winnebago* was less rapid in her movements. Probably the chief causes of the surrender of the ram were the wounding of Admiral Buchanan (her commander, and probably a relation to the ex-President,) and the injury done to her rudder chains. The vessel was otherwise uninjured, and she was the most powerful ram then in existence. Her length was 200 feet, her breadth 48, and her draught 14 feet 8 inches.

From the time of the brilliant exploit at New Orleans, Admiral FARRAGUT (for he was immediately promoted to that rank) was actively engaged down to the close of the war. He run almost every battery on the Mississippi River, silenced a number, and only left the river when there were no more to silence. The part he took in the reduction of Port Hudson, as well as that at Mobile Bay, was most important; and had he been placed in command of the naval forces which were first sent to attack Charleston, he would doubtless have fought his way past all the forts and batteries, and steamed defiantly up to the gates of the haughty city.

Of all our Naval Commanders he ranks, without question, as the first— the naval hero of the war. One who knows him well writes of him thus :

"From his childhood, Admiral FARRAGUT has been remarkably self-rant and determined, and although of very amiable disposition, never would consent that others should do for him what he could do for himself. Industry is a decided trait in his character. When not on active duty he has always been a student, and while in foreign ports never neglected to acquire the language of the people. At one time he spoke the Spanish, French, Italian and Arabic with great fluency—the latter language he acquired when he was 18 years of age, during a residence of 9 months in Tunis. In connection with his Arabic, the following anecdote is related. On approaching some islands in the Mediterranean, the captain of the ship remarked on deck that he did not know how they were to converse with the people, as they had no interpreter. At that moment a boat came along side with some of the natives, and an officer replied, "Captain, we have an officer on board who seems to speak all languages intuitively; he is doubtless in league with the 'old boy;' but suppose you send for him, and see if he can not communicate with these people." So Lieutenant FARRAGUT was called for, and told in a peculiar manner that he must show if what he was accused of was true. He looked into the boat, and seeing an old Arabian woman, immediately commenced conversing, and transacted for the ship all the trading. Imagine the surprise of all on board, as FARRAGUT did not tell them that it was Arabic he was speaking, and so he kept up the joke for some time, amused to hear them often repeat 'that he was indebted to the devil for such a gift.'"

JOHN A. WINSLOW.

CAPTAIN JOHN A. WINSLOW, the hero of the *Kearsage*, was born in Wilmington, North Carolina, in 1811, and is consequently 54 years of age. His father was a Northerner, descended from the old Plymouth stock of WINSLOWS; his mother was a Southerner. He was educated at Dedham, Massachusetts, and entered the Navy as midshipman at the age of fourteen. DANIEL WEBSTER secured for him his position. His family reside at Roxbury, near Boston. He was placed in command of the *Kearsage* as soon as that vessel arrived off the European coast. Before his conflict with the *Alabama* he had some apprehensions, and repeatedly advised the Naval Department to increase the force off Cherbourg, but said he would do the best he could. We believe he has since been made a Commodore. The following account of the destruction of the *Alabama*, alias "290," which had so long been the scourge of our commerce and the terror of the seas to all American craft, on June 19th, 1864, off the coast of France, is given :

"The *Alabama*, Captain SEMMES, arrived at Cherbourg on the 14th, from a cruise in the Indian Ocean. In accordance with the French law of neutrality, she was warned to leave that port. On the morning of the 19th she steamed out of the harbor, having previously sent a challenge to Captain WINSLOW. The *Kearsage* stood off for about three leagues, so as to be sure that the action should take place clear of French maritime jurisdiction; she then turned to meet the enemy. The force of the two vessels was, as nearly as possible, equal. The *Alabama* opened fire at 11 o'clock, at long range, the *Kearsage* reserving her fire until they came closer. During the action both vessels moved in a series of circles, gradually diminishing, and having a common center, so that each kept her starboard battery bearing upon her opponent. The fire of the *Alabama* was more rapid, that of the *Kearsage* more accurate. The commander of the *Kearsage* had taken the precaution to protect, in a measure, some vital points of his vessel, by suspending the iron anchor-chains over the side of the ship. In less than an hour, the *Alabama* was in almost sinking condition, and the commander attempted to run toward the shore, in order to reach French water; the *Kearsage* crowded all steam to cut her off, and, coming within 400 yards, delivered a broadside, which reduced the enemy to a helpless condition. Captain Semmes finding his vessel going down, struck her flag, ordered his crew to jump overboard, and sent a boat, with an officer, to surrender his vessel, and ask assistance to save his crew. Meanwhile an English yacht, the *Deerhound*, owned by a Mr. Lancaster, had come out of Cherbourg to see the fight. He was hailed from the *Kearsage*, and requested to assist in saving the crew of the *Alabama*. His boats picked up about forty, including Captain Semmes and most of his officers; the boats of the *Kearsage* saved sixty. The *Alabama* lost seven killed on board, seventeen drowned, and twelve wounded. The loss of the *Kearsage* was three wounded - only one mortally. The vessel was scarcely harmed. Meanwhile, the commander of the *Deerhound* put off for the English coast, with the men whom he had picked up. Captain Semmes was landed in ENGLAND, and received with much warmth."

The *Alabama* was built in England, and sailed from Liverpool for the Azores, July 29, 1862, where she took her armament on board. Captain Ralph Semmes assumed command August 24, 1862 This pirate vessel captured and destroyed about eighty ships and barks belonging to merchants of the United States, including the U. S. gun-boat *Hatteras*.

Captain WINSLOW, on his arrival in Boston, after this exploit with the *Alabama*, was honored with a public reception, and was presented with a silver service by the citizens.

MAJOR-GENERAL WEITZELL.

www.ingramcontent.com/pod-product-compliance
Lightning Source LLC
Chambersburg PA
CBHW021132020726
47500CB00003B/1036